DEVOURERS *from* SURYAKSH

RACE TO THE LAST EVENTUALITY

VARUN SAYAL

ISBN: 978-93-5382-745-8

ABOUT THE AUTHOR

Varun Sayal is a science fiction author who has built considerable repute in the writing world within a short span of time. His science fiction works such as 'Time Crawlers' and 'Demons of Time' have been phenomenal hits on Amazon. Testimony to that fact are over five hundred positive reviews on, Amazon and other platforms, within just months of publishing these books.

DEDICATED TO MY PARENTS;
I AM WHAT I AM TODAY,
BECAUSE OF THEM.
AND TO MY LOVELY WIFE,
WHO IS THE SOURCE
OF ALL MY STRENGTH
AND HAPPINESS.

TABLE OF CONTENTS

1
WITCH
WITH A SCAR

Year 3057 BC | Rigu's Ashram, India

In the chamber of time travel, Rigasur's body lay on the same kind of cement block as the bodies of Kumbh and Vetri. Like them, he was also bound in heavy metal chains. One week had passed since Tej imprisoned him. Tej had since left for his village, Sarp-Nagar.

After the news of Rigu's deceit spread, several kings who used to support the ashram had withdrawn their support. As a result, the security cover was spread thin.

It was an hour past midnight, and a light mist had engulfed the ashram. Two guards were stationed outside the chamber where the time-demons' bodies were kept.

Both the guards were half-asleep when three women attacked them. The assailants wore long, dark robes, their faces covered with hollow-eyed demonic masks. They pressed anesthetic-dipped cloths over the noses of the guards and subdued them within seconds.

After hiding the bodies of those guards in bushes nearby, the attackers opened the lock on chamber's door. They slipped into the room without making much noise.

One woman walked in the front like a leader, and the other two followed her. They strode to the center of the room, surrounded Rigasur's body, and stood there for a few seconds. Rigasur had been tranquilized and showed no movement at all. His breathing was feeble, his pulse was low as if his body was frozen.

The leader bowed down and whispered in Rigasur's left ear, "I kept my promise, my friend. I came here in person to commend you for getting rid of Kumbh. You executed the hardest part of the plan with finesse. It saddens me that you underestimated the kid, and in the process, martyred yourself. We will miss you in the refurbished seventies. But don't worry, we'll get what we want—with or without you. Happy sleeping, mate!" The leader smirked and sauntered out of the room, followed by the other two women.

Rigasur lay there, unconscious, unaware of the surroundings. For a moment, the index finger of his right hand flickered a little.

The leader came out, removed her mask, and threw it away. She was a woman in her early thirties. With a pale complexion, wide eyebrows, and a thin jaw, she wore black lipstick. Beneath the thick eyeliner smudged around her eyes, a thin scar ran from the corner of her eye, stopping in the middle of her cheek. When she spoke, the small gray pearl of a piercing was visible on her tongue.

She was Nefe, the lead Wiccan of the Maagitra coven. The other two were her next-in-command priestesses, Jarna and Miran. They looked at her as she took off her mask.

"What? It's so humid here, and this mask is suffocating me. In fact, this whole robe getup was a bad idea. Why did we come here in stealth mode?"

Jarna and Miran kept quiet.

"Was it your idea?"

Jarna and Miran shook their heads in negation.

Nefe removed her robe and let her hair loose. Beneath the robe, she wore traditional Wiccan attire: a bright red backless blouse and a long black skirt, tightened by a shining silver chain belt. Her neck and back were girded with several demonic tattoos and several silver bangles on both of her arms.

"Let's wake everyone up and have a party." She smiled.

A few minutes later, a huge bonfire had been lit at the ashram's central clearing area. It was a rarity to have a bonfire in the ashram at night. A small army of men and women, Nefe's armed guards, woke all the disciples. They forcefully pushed them to the central area at knifepoint. As a few disciples protested and engaged with the assailants, the situation grew chaotic. Some were brutally beaten, and some had to be dragged by their hair. The chaos ensued for a few more minutes, after which almost all inhabitants of the ashram finally stood around the bonfire.

Nefe, Jarna, and Miran stood next to the blaze. Nefe stood with her arms crossed and a delightful smile on her face. Disciples stood around them, forming a circle—their clothes torn, bodies bruised, and fearful expressions on their faces. Armed guards surrounded them from every side.

"Who are you, and why have you brought us here?" one disciple screamed. Everyone started shouting questions and abuse at Nefe.

Nefe smiled even more and pressed her palms to her ears. When the wailing and shouting didn't stop, she screamed on top of her voice, "Shut up, all of you!"

There was pin-drop silence. Her voice not only struck their ears but resounded inside their brains. Their throats were jammed.

Nefe wore an angry expression on her face for a few moments but finally smiled. "No need to panic, my friends. I came here for a party. I was told this place is too gloomy. People here just wake up, pray, eat, study, and sleep. That sort of life is monotonous and boring. I wanted to inject some color in your pathetic lives."

All the disciples stood frozen.

"Oh, I did not offer a proper introduction. I am Nefe, the lead Wiccan of Maagitra. All praises to the Lord of Blood, the giver of life."

The crowd gasped with fear. Nefe was a well-known evil entity of the Dandak forest and the adjoining river basin area. Nefe's clan worshipped an ancient tribal god, Maagitra, known as the Lord of Blood. Their activities included human sacrifice and other gory rituals. Although she was known to seclude herself in the mountains, she visited the river on the night of the full moon.

"Now that we have gotten acquainted, shall we all dance together?"

The crowd kept quiet, not even offering a murmur of dissent. Each disciple was now praying for his or her own life.

"No? You don't want to relax? I am disappointed. But in that case, let me get to the point. I want to know which one of you is Kuntala? ... Kuntala? Does that name ring a bell? She's a disciple of your ashram."

Everyone looked around, trying to identify Kuntala, but she was not there. Nefe brought her lips near to Jarna's ear and whispered, "Have we searched the entire ashram?"

"Yes, Nefe. Everyone present in the ashram is here. There is no one else left in the sheds and huts."

"Hmm. I cannot detect her energy signature in this crowd." Nefe addressed them all. "So, Kuntala is not here, but one of you must know where she is. And until you tell me, we will all stay here."

The crowd remained silent.

"But that is no excuse to stay boring. Until we find Kuntala, we will keep ourselves entertained." Nefe curled the index finger of her right hand and signaled to one young man. "You, come here."

The man looked sideways to make sure he was the one she'd called. Then slowly walked towards her.

"What's your name?"

"H-Hari."

"Hari. Good. Why don't you dance and entertain us?"

"I—I don't—"

"Dance!" Nefe shouted.

Hari's whole body shook, convulsing in a weird dance.

Nefe started to clap. "Everybody clap, come on. Your friend Hari is entertaining us. Come on, everyone."

Slowly, some in the crowd started to clap, and others caught up with light claps. They were all afraid—and had no choice but to comply. Every passing moment made them certain of whether they would live or die.

The crowd kept clapping, but Nefe stopped and took Hari's hands in hers. She started dancing with him. "Faster!" Nefe shouted. The crowd's clapping intensified.

At first, Hari was petrified of her touch but then went

with the flow. They both were now dancing to the tunes of the claps. The clapping grew faster, and Nefe's dance moves got swifter. Hari was dancing happily now.

Suddenly Nefe pushed him, drew out a knife and slashed his throat, making a deep cut. The clapping stopped. Hari dropped to his knees, his eyes full of surprise as blood spurted out of his jugular vein. He fell flat onto the ground, dead.

There was now pin drop silence. Nefe eyed everyone. "There is no reason to be sad, my friends. He left this world in a happy state. Dancing and rejoicing. Lord Maagitra loves these blood sacrifices. The one offering his soul did so in a state of happiness. Now, who's next? Who wants to now dance with me. You?" Nefe pointed the bloodstained knife towards a girl from the crowd. The girl gulped and shook her head.

"Come on, little girl. Join me. And let's not stop the clapping. We were getting a good beat going."

There was a sudden commotion on one corner. Everyone saw one of the Nefe's guards flying from above the crowd and crashing in the bonfire. Despite the distance, someone had thrown him right into the fire. Two guards rushed to his help, pulled him out of the blaze, and tried to douse his flames.

Nefe took a piece of cloth, wiped her knife, and holstered it in her belt, apparently unconcerned.

Everyone looked in the direction where the guard came from, and the crowd parted. A muscular man around seven feet tall was walking towards the center of the circle with big strides. He held one guard each in his both hands, clasping them by their necks. Two other guards were grasping his legs but were being dragged on the ground with the force of his momentum. This giant was Gajendra.

Many in the crowd sighed in relief. Gajendra was the only one who could handle these aggressors.

Gajendra came near the center and dropped the two guards. He came very close to Nefe and looked her in the eyes. Several guards came running to attack Gajendra, but Nefe signaled for them to stay put.

"Who the hell are you?" he addressed Nefe.

"I introduced myself sometime back. You missed it. I am Nefe, the lead Wiccan of the Maag …"

"I don't care," Gajendra cut her off. "Whoever you are, you take your puny guards and leave this ashram right now. These are sacred grounds."

"Sacred? I thought you all were serving a time-demon here. Demons and sacrosanct areas rarely go together. I was, in fact, also looking forward to meeting this time-demon Rigasur, the master manipulator. But looks like he is sleeping tight."

Gajendra immediately looked in the direction of the chamber of time travel.

"No, don't worry. I have not touched those bodies." Nefe smiled. "The world is better off without these time-demons. Anyhow, my visit is not just a social call. Someone from the time-reading world visited me in the future, which is very rare because time-readers cannot usually read us. I only got her name, which was Kuntala. I want to meet her and ask her, how did she break our barrier?"

The lines on Gajendra's forehead deepened as he clenched his teeth in anger. "Listen to me, you Wiccan. All disciples here have stopped their time-readings. We only meditate and pray. And we have no one by the name Kuntala here. Now get lost!" he thundered. He knew very well who Kuntala was, but he was not going to give her up that easily.

"You're an angry beast, a real hot hunk. I'm already in love with you." Nefe licked her lower lips. She tried touching Gajendra's cheek with her hand, but he shrugged her off.

"I said, there's no Kuntala in this ashram. Leave now."

"I don't believe you, handsome. Everybody leaves a cosmic signature, a unique radiation. And I sense her radiation here. She may not be here right now, but she was. And one of you knows her whereabouts. So, until you tell me what I need to know, I'm not leaving."

"I may have to explain it to you in a different way." Gajendra reared back to attack Nefe, but all the guards present there pounced on him.

Nefe walked a few steps away, watching Gajendra and the guards getting enmeshed in a chaotic fistfight.

The Guards were flummoxed. Even knives and daggers could not penetrate Gajendra's skin. He flung some guards backward with his muscular shoves. Others had their jaws smashed by his meaty punches. A few other disciples tried to intervene and aid Gajendra, but guards subdued them.

After a few minutes of a messy brawl, fifteen bruised men managed to subjugate Gajendra. They shackled his hands at the back using thick metal handcuffs.

"Wow, one of the brawniest men I've ever seen. You not only have super strength, but your skin also is impenetrable. Interesting. But let me show you a piece of magic."

Nefe came close to Gajendra. She took a sharp dagger and ran it against Gajendra's stomach. His shirt was torn, but his skin was unaffected. "Nothing happened?

Now you will see what a witch's saliva can do. This knife will tear through your skin."

Gajendra smirked. This was not the first time he'd been threatened with a blood-bath. But his skin had withstood sharpest of the blades.

Nefe then licked the knife and ran it against his skin. This time, the knife slashed through the skin, and blood oozed out. Gajendra winced in pain, and his eyes couldn't hide his surprise. This was the first time he had experienced any object cutting across his skin.

"Now you know I *can* hurt you. Will you tell me where can I find this Kuntala?"

Gajendra's lips were sealed shut.

Nefe closed her eyes. "I suppose this torture would mean nothing to you. You are a man with an iron will and a powerful resistance to pain. I don't want to waste time attempting to break you. But I know what matters to you. I know what will crush your resolve."

Nefe turned around, eyed the disciples and laughed. "You are going to enjoy this."

She stretched her arms on the side and clasped her fists. As she did that, all the disciples present there felt a tight grasp on their necks, as if an invisible noose was tightened around the neck of each man and woman present there. All of them were being strangled by the Nefe's telekinetic force.

Her guards smiled at the sight.

Nefe slowly raised her arms, and the disciples' bodies rose with her. Their feet no longer touched the ground. Asphyxiating, they vigorously shook their bodies, struggling. The higher she raised her arms, the higher they rose.

"Stop this!" Gajendra murmured. His hands were still

cuffed in the titanium-shackles. The slash wound on his stomach dripped blood.

"You said something?" Nefe was interested.

"I said, stop this. I will tell you where Kuntala is."

"I will stop, but only after you tell me."

"Stop this now, please!" Gajendra pleaded.

"You're wasting time, Gajendra. See how these people are gasping for their lives? A few more seconds and some of them will begin their travel to the afterlife."

Gajendra had no choice to give up one disciple to save the lives of a hundred others. "I don't know where Kuntala is, but another disciple of the ashram was always around her. Manika. Find her. She can tell you where Kuntala is."

"We didn't find Manika either. Where would she be?" Nefe looked Gajendra in the eye, her arms still stretched out.

"I don't know! She might have fled."

"Anyone else who knows her?" Nefe waited.

Gajendra couldn't think clearly. All his friends hung in the air struggling for their lives. "Tej! Manika is good friends with Tej!" Gajendra blurted out. "Please release these people now!"

"Okay? And where the hell can I find this Tej?"

"Tej stays in a village called Sarp-Nagar. I can take you there."

"Got it. See? That was easy." Nefe smiled.

"Now please, stop this!"

Nefe brought her arms down in slow motion. All the disciples hanging in the air, struggling for their lives, came down. Nefe unclasped her fists, and the invisible nooses around their necks were loosened. All of them took a fresh breath of air. Most of them fell to their knees, supporting each other. A few vigorously coughed, while some others fainted. Their necks all bore red strangulation marks.

Nefe clasped her hands into fists again. All the disciples again started struggling.

"I gave you what you wanted!" Gajendra shouted.

"You did. But I didn't enjoy that enough." Nefe jerked her wrists with force and snapped the necks of all the disciples. Their lifeless bodies crashed to the ground.

"NO!" Gajendra screamed in agony. He pulled on his shackles with all his might and broke them. He freed himself of the fifteen guards holding him and ran towards Nefe. All her guards came running after him, but Nefe signaled for them to stay out.

Gajendra clasped her throat and lifted her three feet above the ground as if she was a rag doll. He was trying to strangle her with his muscly hands, but she kept smiling. He realized his hands were not touching her throat. There was an invisible force between his grasp and her neck.

Gajendra felt his grasp loosening, and his hands left Nefe's throat. He brought her down and released his grasp. His arms were stretched around behind his back, and the invisible force pushed him down to his knees. He tried very hard to resist, but his muscle strength was no match for Nefe's telekinetic powers.

"Wow. You have remarkable strength. I am impressed. These shackles were built from ultra-pure titanium. I have never seen a human break them." Nefe brought her lips close to Gajendra's lips. "I have a proposal for you. Why don't you join me? Be my bodyguard. I promise you, I'll make you my right hand." Nefe licked Gajendra's left cheek as if tasting it.

"You just killed all my fellow disciples—my brothers and sisters! You are filth. You disgust me." Gajendra spat on her face.

Nefe took offense but kept her calm. She took a red handkerchief out of her robe pocket and wiped her face. "I would have given you such a painful death for what you just did. But you are fortunate, because I'm short on time, and I've wasted enough of it here, already."

She raised her left hand, then slowly brought her thumb and middle finger together.

"You spat on my face. That irked me. But I am glad we shared bodily fluids—though not in the way I was hoping." She snapped her thumb against her middle finger, and Gajendra's chest collapsed on the inside. His rib-cage was crushed, and internal organs ruptured. He dropped to the ground, dead.

Nefe called Jarna. "Find out the location of this Sarp-Nagar. And let's leave for that village as soon as possible."

The Wiccan bowed a little and replied, 'But Nefe, this Tej...'

"What about him?"

"He was the one who brought down Kumbh."

"Interesting. Then he is our ally. Our paths have finally crossed. Go, find out."

"But isn't he a dangerous—"

"Right now!" Nefe screamed. Jarna rushed away. "And what are you all doing?" Nefe addressed the guards, "Burn this whole place to ashes and get ready to move. Meanwhile, I need to pay a visit to someone special."

The guards dispersed. Nefe sat on the ground in a meditative pose and closed her eyes.

2
INITIATION
OF DAMNATION

12ᵗʰ July 2057 AD | Haryek Hall of Commerce, 152ⁿᵈ Floor, Global Trade Building, New York

anhattan Entrepreneurship Society—MANESO—was conducting a conclave. Vedika Sharma and her wife and co-founder Rubina Vance were guest speakers. They were representing their seed-funded artificial intelligence start-up, Vedvance Technologies. Vedika had a dual Ph.D. in Mathematics and Artificial Intelligence, and Rubina held dual PhDs in specialized Human Anatomy and Computer Science.

"I still think your start is too negative, Ved. It may be repulsive to many in the audience," Rubina whispered in Vedika's ear. They sat in the first row.

Vedika was next in line to speak at the conclave. "Fuck it. Let it be repulsive. What's a speech if it doesn't rile up a few people?" Vedika was not going to tone down her words. "And you, don't come so close to me. I may end up kissing you in public."

Rubina chuckled. Twelve years of marriage and Vedika still made her laugh.

"Yeah, that camera-drone up there belongs to NBWC. It will capture snaps of us in a lip-lock. We will be on the first page of Manhattan Masala for wrong reasons," Rubina mocked. She hated the paparazzi, who'd been chasing them since Vedvance had secured three billion dollar seed-funding two years ago.

"As if I fucking care. Let them publish what they want." Vedika did care for her media image, but she didn't give two hoots about trashy tabloid publications.

The lead anchor for the conclave, Pearl Jenkins, came onto the stage and made an announcement. "And next, I would like to call upon a speaker who is another very successful rising star. She is the founder of a dazzling technology startup which aims to change the way we think and act. Through her venture, she wants to boost the intelligence of the masses. Bravo, I say, because a lot of people today need exactly that." The crowd burst into laughter.

"Without wasting any further time, Please welcome Mrs. Vedika Sharma of Vedvance Technologies!"

"Easy with the f-words, Missy. Swearing will only get us in the news," Rubina whispered as Vedika got up from her seat.

"Isn't that what we want?" Vedika winked to her and briskly walked to the dais. She climbed the seven-step staircase, where Pearl met her. They shook hands, and Pearl directed her onto the podium in the middle. A standing desk and a tiny drone-microphone waited for her. The microphone was designed to float in tandem with speaker movements to get the best audio.

Vedika was thirty-four years old, with a sleek build. She wore a full business suit, with a charcoal gray coat and matching trousers. She wore her favorite pristine white formal-shirt neatly tucked in, adding an off-white pearl necklace and a small golden brooch on her left pocket. Her stylists had advised against the unfashionable brooch, but she ignored them. The brooch was a lucky charm for her, and she wore it to key speeches and meetings.

She tapped on the mic and started to speak. "Damn, this feels like an Academy Awards speech." The crowd let out a light laugh.

She took a pause, a deep breath, and started.

"Technology is the villain, right? That's the resounding thought among the rebels of our generation. But that sounds foolish to me, and I will tell you why. Let's skim over the morning of a sixteen-year-old girl today. She comes out of her shower. While a maid-robot is drying her hair, she taps the chip inserted in her wrist to open her social media app, Gramophonic. The interface is a 3D holographic projection. She logs in into Gramophonic using her voice-enabled password. Then she records a video for her two million followers saying, 'I hate technology. It has made us its slave. We don't go out anymore. There are no real relationships. Blah, blah, blah.'

"She goes on with her whining, cursing technology with each word slipping off her tongue. And it doesn't stop here. Within five minutes of her Grammacast, she has thousands of text, audio, and video comments on her timeline, all validating her concerns. Everyone is just cussing about science and tech. Do you see the irony of it all? Using every piece of revolutionary technology available to them, these so-called rebels curse the same.

If this is not asinine, then what is?"

The light over the crowd was dim but Vedika could see that many in the crowd were nodding in affirmation. She looked at the silhouette of Rubina and saw her smiling, too. For a moment, she thought she saw a shadow sitting next to Rubina on her own seat, smiling. But when she blinked, the seat was empty. She continued.

"Let's look at us today. We have what, five thousand people here in the audience here?" She looked at Pearl who nodded. "Five thousand people here, and I thank you all for coming in person. And I am told that twelve million people are attending this conclave from their homes. And out of these, two million are attending using the Immersive Reality Experience, the I.R.E. tech. Which means these two million people are experiencing this event as if they were here. Right here. Some of you remote viewers may be sitting on your beds, on your sofas—heck, you may even be sitting on your toilet seats." Several in the crowd chuckled.

"But you are all here, all thanks to technology. And I must thank the inventors of I.R.E., Paul and Norine. They are good friends. They have changed the landscape of how movies, TV programming, and every kind of viewing experience is consumed. We owe gratitude to many such inventors, who have quietly revolutionized the way we live our lives. They inspire us.

"Vedvance is still taking baby steps. But we are aiming for nothing short of the moon. We are, as many of you know, working on integrating the human brain with machine intelligence—what we call a human-machine singularity. Providing each human with an exceptional level of mental acuity is our vision for the future.

"Some say that we are trying to play God. I get a ton

of hate mail every day; people spew venom on my social media every hour. But my question here is very simple, and I want to leave you all here tonight with that question. When we get unwell with deadly diseases, and we treat ourselves with modern medicine, is that not us playing God? When nanobots enter our bodies and fight deadly viruses alongside our antibodies, is that not us playing God? If not, then why is the integration of human intelligence with machines being derided? It's another effort to enhance ourselves, another attempt to take our civilization to a whole new level. That's what it is. Not an atom more, not an atom less. Thank you."

The crowd remained silent for a second, then burst into applause. Many stood up and continued clapping until Vedika walked out from the dais and sat at her seat.

"How did I do?" Vedika murmured.

"You were a spitfire, as usual. I am monitoring our Y-Fac ratings on BlueTech App, let's see."

"You should have accompanied me to the dais, Ruby."

"Nah, you're the face of Vedvance. You were enough up there."

"If I am the face, what are you? The buttocks?"

Rubina tried hard to control her laughter. "No, missy, I'm the vagina. I take all the pounding."

"Be ready for a pounding tonight."

"Shut up, Ved!" Rubina clenched her teeth. "The camera drone may be fitted with lip-detection software."

"Come on, that's not permitted under MERRPA."

MERRPA, the Media Regulatory and Restricted Practices Act, had been passed by the US Senate in the year 2045 and had put severe restrictions on media abuse of celebrities.

"Yeah, but since when have paparazzi played by the

rules?"

Vedika recalled a moment during her speech. "Hey, did somebody come and sit here while I was gone?"

Rubina thought her wife was joking again. "No, no one did. I saved the seat for you."

"Okay."

"You all right, Ved?"

"Yeah, just want to get outta here."

A few hours later, Vedika and Rubina were back at their apartment, a plush seven-bedroom suite on the 223rd floor of a Los Angeles skyscraper. In a loose shirt and underpants, Rubina sat on her bed, going through Vedvance's financial statements. Her eyes had been fitted with a common surgically added, flexible metamorphic lens. This lens adjusted her vision on the go, but she preferred to turn it off and read using old-style spectacles.

Vedika was in the bathroom, immersed in her tub, relaxing and listening in to podcasts. After a few minutes, she got up, dried herself off, and put on a soft bathrobe. Wiping her face with wet tissues, she looked at the mirror as she wiped the area around her nose and upper cheeks. The shadow under her eyes was visible. She sighed and closed her eyes.

When she opened her eyes, she saw that the mirror had turned slightly hazy because of the mist. She wiped the mirror with her palm and saw another face. Nefe stood inside, smiling back with her pale skin, blackened lips, and blood-stained teeth.

Vedika stiffened. *Am I hallucinating? This can't be real.*

But it was. Those terrifying eyes were gazing right

into hers. Sweat beaded on her forehead, and she gulped in fear. Another blink and the image in the mirror was gone. She was now staring at her own self. She rushed out of the bathroom, unable to think.

Rubina eyed her wife wrapped in the short bathing gown, adjusted her thick specks, and smiled. "Don't you try to seduce me, babe. Not now. We have an important meeting tomorrow."

Vedika was stunned and still covered in goosebumps.

Rubina realized something was wrong. She immediately got up. "Are you all right?"

Vedika nodded. "I'm fine. I—I just …"

"What?"

"Don't know. I'm seeing things. Maybe it's the Protzicone."

"Did you take it today?"

"Yeah, one pill in the morning."

"Did you do the legalized-cocaine shit? Be honest with me, Ved."

"No!" Vedika looked at Rubina with anger. "I would never do that."

"Is it tomorrow's meeting? We can always move it and apologize."

"Are you kidding me? Fourteen investors from China and India have confirmed. We've got to make it."

"These kinds of things never got under your skin."

Vedika was trying to relax but still shaken. "And they never would. This is something different."

There was a knock on the door. "Mommy, please open the door." It was the voice of their six-year-old daughter, Jess.

"Are you good?" Rubina whispered, her eyes full of concern and worry.

"I'm fine. But you should put on some pants."

"Oops." Rubina laughed and rushed to her wardrobe.

"Mommy, open the door, please, please." There was another soft knock.

They both dressed up in haste and opened the door.

Jess came running inside, followed by her nanny Naaz.

Mommy, what were you two doing inside? Were you two kissing?"

"Yeah, big girl, we were kissing." Rubina picked up Jess. "And now we are gonna kiss you." She planted a few soft kisses on Jess's cheeks, and she giggled.

"My apologies ma'am. Jess was adamant about saying goodnight." Naaz was a little flustered. Being a new venture, Vedvance was picking up speed. As a result, Vedika and Rubina were out more often than before, and Naaz felt completely responsible for the child.

"Yeah, it's way past your bedtime, girlie. Why aren't you tucked in your bed?" Vedika took Jess in her lap.

"You two are going out again tomorrow, and you're not taking me with you."

"Mommies are going for office work. We'll be busy. You'll be bored all day long."

They chatted for a while. After a promise of the hefty bribe of a new automated doll and ten different types of chocolates, Jess went to sleep.

Rubina cuddled and slept in Vedika's arms, but Vedika, restless, kept looking at the bathroom door.

The next day, at 5:15 AM, Vedika, Rubina and their executive assistant Nguyen stood at a private airstrip. Vedika was in her usual business attire of a gray business suit and a white formal shirt. Rubina wore a cream-white single-piece business dress with a sleek black belt. Nguyen wore a blue business shirt and a long black skirt and carried two laptop bags and a note-taking-tablet.

Within ten minutes, they'd boarded a hypersonic chartered jet Zula T-575 traveling to New Manzuito.

New Manzuito was a new city built on an artificial island in China's territorial waters, a cluster of skyscrapers on the easternmost tip of the Chinese mainland. This city was China's newest trade and commerce hub. A consortium of twelve top investors from China and two from India were expected to be present. They would listen to pitches from five of the world's most power-packed startups, each eyeing their next rounds of funding. Vedvance was one of them.

The usual journey time between L.A. and New Manzuito with normal airplanes was around nine hours, but the Zula T-575 effortlessly flew at Mach 5.75. Their destination was only two hours away.

All of them put on their seat-belts, and the jet plane went from zero to top speed within seven minutes. Rubina hated the deep acceleration. She often joked that she would prefer to be anesthetized until it was done.

As soon as the jet stabilized, Vedika turned to Rubina and observed her.

Rubina was swiping her finger on the short computer screen embedded in her arm, checking her emails. Rubina noticed Vedika observing her and chuckled. "What?"

"Just admiring your beauty."

"Come on, Ved. What is it?"

"I should have told you, Ruby."

"Told me what?" Concerned, Rubina touched the side of her forehead, and her eye-lens changed from the reading lens to normal.

"I have agreed to an interview with an NBWC journalist." Vedika was smiling.

"Oh, okay. I thought it was something about last night." Ruby was relieved. "But why NBWC? They write so much crap about startups. Scrutinize our every action." Rubina went back to her study.

"Well, they have been asking for it since forever. And we've been tied up for the past three weeks. Now we have time."

"When? Where is the time?"

"Well … now?" Vedika gave a sheepish smile. "Rasheed Jain, the Chief Business Reporter with NBWC, will join us via I.R.E. call."

Rubina was livid. Vedika had agreed to an interview on board the jet. "I thought I had some time to myself, at last. But I was wrong!" Her face turned a little red with anger.

"Babe, we needed to do this, now or later. I'm sorry. I should have told you."

"No, don't say sorry. Please reserve that word for unintentional mistakes. You kept me in the dark on purpose! You knew we had such a key meeting as soon as we boarded. We could have prepared for it."

"We're over-prepared."

Rubina kept quiet. She knew once Vedika had made up her mind, it was tough to change her decision.

Nguyen placed a small hemispherical I.R.E. device on the table in front of them and dictated a 4-digit pin. The device caught her voice and dialed the conference. Vedika and Rubina both quickly adjusted their clothing and sat up straight.

A bulb in the device illuminated the space where they

were seated. They were about to be broadcasted live to the newsroom. Another light-bulb on the exact opposite side projected a 3D hologram on the empty chair in front of them.

After exactly seven seconds, the image of a man in his late forties appeared in front of them. The 3D hologram was so clear, it was as if the man sat right in front of them. He started speaking with enthusiasm, but they couldn't hear a sound.

Vedika and Rubina indicated to him that they couldn't hear him. Embarrassed, he adjusted some equipment and then spoke.

"Can you hear me now?"

"Yes, we can, loud and clear. Can you hear us?" Rubina said.

"Yes, ma'am. All good. Thanks for agreeing to meet us. My name is Rasheed Jain. I will be your interviewer today."

"We are glad to be here."

"Tell us more about this revolutionary product Vedvance is building. I am sure you have repeated this sales pitch several times, but we would like to hear it right from the horse's mouth."

"I'll start off with an example." Vedika took the lead. Rubina always let her. "Do you know what a factorial in mathematics is?"

"Umm, I did, but I forgot." Rasheed had taken courses in mathematics and business statistics to get better at his job, but these areas were not his forte.

"A factorial of a number is multiplication of that number with all numbers below it, leading to 1. So factorial of 2 is 2 multiplied by 1, i.e. two. Factorial of 3 is 3 x 2 x 1, which is six, and so on."

"Okay?" Rasheed was curious about her direction.

"For humans, it is very tough to calculate a factorial even up to twenty. The brightest math prodigies have claimed to have mentally calculated a factorial up to hundred. But that's it. Whereas a computer today can calculate factorial of one million within a microsecond."

"So, you're saying …"

"Wait, let me finish," Vedika snapped. "But despite their super-fast intellect, computers and artificial intelligence have limitations. Despite our best efforts, we have not been able to build an A.I. which thinks the way a human does. Billions of dollars have been spent in making A.I. more and more emotional, but there always are edge cases which we can't cover. Deep learning strategies, convoluted neuron structs, and million layered neural networks all have failed. They've made A.I. a bigger storehouse of pre-configured decisions. Machine learning algorithms running on top of pre-configured decisions can't compete with our brains."

Rasheed was nodding as if he understood every word of what was being said. He didn't.

Rubina stepped in. "All through this, man has been pitted against the machine. How much faster can we make the A.I. in comparison to humans? There have been chess players beating computers. Science fiction writers have filled the market with works where A.I. overtakes humans. It has always been us against them.

"We are trying a very different paradigm. Us *and* them. Human and machine combined." Rubina brought her both hands together and interlaced her fingers. "Human-machine singularity."

"Singularity. Yes, that's the word we have heard many times. Tell me more about it." Rasheed was double-checking the list of questions on his tablet.

"Man and machine integrated into one body. So that humans have complete access to machine-level intelligence. At the same time, A.I. will have access to human emotions. And it can learn from them on a day-by-day basis and correct itself."

"And one day, it takes over," Rasheed said with a serious face, then laughed. The conversation had become too intense.

"We will control it." Vedika smiled. "We will have mechanisms built. Something we call 'HOA', the 'Human over A.I.' protocol. This would be hard-coded in the technology we build."

"So what is the physical manifestation of this tech? Is it a microchip which will be placed inside our brains via surgery, or will it be a wearable gadget, like the old times?"

"That's a trade secret." Rubina winked.

Vedika wanted to get Rubina to handle the media more often, so she withdrew herself from the conversation and let Rasheed talk to her. She looked outside the window.

The T-575 was slashing through dense dark clouds. She thought she saw a shadow on the wing. Her goosebumps returned as she saw Nefe standing on the wing, looking right at her. This time, she could see Nefe's whole body. Nefe stood with her arms crossed, a sinister smile floating on her face. Vedika blinked many times, even rubbed her eyes, but this hallucination was not going away.

She turned back to Rubina. "Ruby, do you ..." But she stopped herself, realizing that there was a reporter present.

Rubina stopped her conversation and looked at Vedika. Her face had turned pale, and her posture was stiff. Rubina realized Vedika had the same expression of horror on her face as the night before.

"What happened?" Rasheed asked.

"Nothing." Rubina gave a fake smile. "I just forgot that I need to do some last-minute prep for our upcoming meeting. Can we continue this conversation some other time?"

"Absolutely. I have material for not just one, but a series of talks." Rasheed wanted some kind of commitment for more time. Landing an interview with two of the most-talked-about entrepreneurs of the tech-startup world wasn't easy.

"We will stay in touch with your office. Thanks for today." Rubina asked Nguyen to end the call. She swiftly disconnected the device. Rasheed's holographic projection disappeared.

There was an uncomfortable silence in the cabin.

"What is it, Ved? Talk to me."

Vedika closed her eyes. When she opened them, Nefe was sitting in the seat in front of her. The whole cabin was empty. Rubina, Nguyen, and the air-hostess all were gone, and the table was empty.

"Who are you? Where is Rubina? What have you done to her!" Vedika blurted out, leaning back into her seat in mortal fear.

Smiling, Nefe sat with her arms crossed. "Questions, questions, questions. 'Who are you? What did you do?' Blah, blah. You, humans, are full of questions. And emotions. That's what we love about your kind."

"You are only my hallucination. You are nothing." Vedika gulped, trying to be brave.

"Oh, so that's how your brain is dealing with possession. Interesting."

"Possession?

"Yes, my dear Ved. I am slowly creeping inside your brain. Possessing your living body. Encroaching on your space, one step at a time. When I am done possessing you, your life, your wealth, your power, your everything, will belong to me. Your business will be mine, your wife will be mine, and your Concordia VX will be mine."

"How do you know about Concordia? It's our trade secret."

Nefe sniggered. "I'm in there, Ved." She knocked the side of her forehead with the tip of her index finger. "Inside your brain, I have access to everything."

An evil entity had invaded her privacy so deeply that she did not know how to respond. "Why are you doing this?" Vedika had tears in her eyes.

"You are building something incredible. But you are going to use it for all peaceful purposes. Which, if you ask me, is a complete waste of such a powerful weapon. But I will use it for something far better. I will start a poultry farm with it."

Rubina's voice distracted them. "Ved, Ved!" the voice echoed in the cabin. Vedika looked all around, but could not see Rubina.

"Your wife is calling you. But we will keep having these conversations until we are united, as one." Nefe snapped her fingers, and Vedika's whole body jolted.

When she opened her eyes, Rubina was by her side, and Nguyen and the air-hostess were sitting close to them. All three of them were looking at Vedika.

"What ... happened?" Vedika tried to speak, but her throat felt hard. The air-hostess handed a glass of water to her.

Rubina wiped her tears away. "What happened to you, Ved? I was so terrified."

"Your eyes moved rapidly, but you were not responding to us." Nguyen, too, was shaken. The Vedika she knew was a tough, hardened woman. Someone always in control. And yet…

"That's it, Ved. We are turning the jet around. We are going to get you checked up. Nguyen, can you please ask the pilot to turn around?"

"No! Not now. I'm fine!" Vedika almost shouted.

"But …"

"I said, there will be no change. We will go ahead as planned. I'll get myself checked up, but after this meeting." Vedika wanted to hug Rubina and cry but suppressed her sadness and fear. She didn't want to break down in front of others. She was shaken, but not broken yet. She had been fixing tough problems her whole life—though this was something beyond her comprehension. She had never believed in ghosts and supernatural. This was unlike anything she had ever encountered. If she talked about it, she would be labeled ill. *What will I do?* That question was piercing her from within.

Rubina wanted to say something, but Vedika pressed her hand tightly. No one said a word for the rest of the flight.

3
TEJ

**3057 BC | Deep in Dandak forest,
20 KMs from Rigu's Ashram**

Defe opened her eyes. She sat in an open clearing in the jungle. Jarna and Miran were sitting beside her. They looked at her in anticipation.

"Is your possession complete?" Jarna could not control her.

"Almost. Possessed her for a few hours. As usual, she blacked out. I initiated some key decisions using her resources. But the bitch is tougher than I thought. It's one of the longest control-transitions I've ever had. I am seriously jealous of the time crawlers. Their act of possession comes in a single stroke. But I'm close. One more trip and she will be mine." She looked at Miran. "Where are we on finding that village?"

"Tej's village? Yes, we found some documents in Rigu's Ashram before we burned the place down. In fact, a lot of events have been very well documented there. One of the documents had the address and map to Tej's village, Sarp-Nagar."

Miran offered a piece of paper to Nefe, but she gestured for her to keep it.

"Let's leave for the village," Nefe ordered.

"Right now? We finished a major raid. The whole coven is tired. Even the familiar army is exhausted."

Jarna was right. Their familiar army, comprised of normal humans, had been raiding villages and ashrams for the last three days, just looking for Kuntala. They were exhausted. But Nefe's orders were cast in stone, and no one dared to say no.

Jarna met Nefe's iron gaze. She let out a frustrated breath and walked out of the room.

772 BC, Babylon

A bazaar bustled with activity as shop-keepers yelled at the top of their voices, selling goods. Thousands of Babylonian citizens, as well as tourists, thronged the market. Tej was inside the body of medieval seventeen-year-old boy Areeb, walking through the bazaar. Alongside him was an old woman with a wrinkly face and rugged clothes, walking with the help of a wooden stick.

Possessing the body of this woman was Monothiaz, an ancient demon of time. She was also the master of multiple possessions—she could possess and control several human bodies at once. Tej had asked her to teach him multi-possession, and she had agreed.

"Lady Monothiaz, I don't like possessing live bodies. It's against my values." Tej asserted.

The lady looked at him and smiled, but kept walking. "I sensed this hesitation in you the first time you approached me."

"Does it not feel wrong to you? Us time-demons entering a body, repressing its original consciousness? It feels immoral."

"Tell me something, boy. When a surgeon cuts into a human body, it's all good, but when a killer does, it's all bad. Why?"

"Well, the doctor doesn't want to hurt the human."

"But he *is* hurting the human."

"Yes, but the doctor wants good for the patient."

"Exactly, my boy. Intentions. When you do something with a good intention, then it can't be wrong. That's how you decide what is right versus what is wrong. A mere action in isolation cannot be classified as good or bad—not without the context in which it was taken. The same applies to human possession."

Monothiaz stopped at a shop, picked a juicy red fruit from the counter, and took a deep bite. The juice from the fruit dripped down her chin as she chewed the bits. The owner of the shop came running out, screaming, asking her to pay for it. She inserted her wrinkly hand in her pocket, took out a few coins, and gave them to the shop-owner. His frown immediately morphed into a sheepish smile, and he started saluting her. She'd paid double the price.

"You want some?" She offered Tej the fruit.

"No."

She started walking again. Chewing and speaking at the same time. "When you came to me, asking me to teach you, I agreed."

"And I am thankful for that."

"You should be. In thousands of years of my lifespan, I've never had a protégé. Never." She emphasized the last word, still chewing on the fruit bits.

Tej was speechless. He only had gratitude in his eyes.

"And I agreed to teach you because I saw the good in you. I knew that you'd never use these powers irresponsibly. You will always let your truest intentions rule your actions. In those intentions, I trust." Monothiaz smiled.

"I am honored to be your mentee. But why are we here today?"

Monothiaz chuckled. "You are learning multi-possession, and I brought you to a place full of people. What do you think?"

Tej grabbed his hair and looked around. "Oh, wow. No. I can't do it."

"You can, my boy. Did you not control those hundred dancers yesterday? Oh, that dance was near perfect. You were in complete control of the hive mind you constructed."

"Yeah I did that, but that was a hundred human brains. This is a level up."

"The lesson and the principal behind multi-possession remains the same. When you walk, you don't control each of your limbs individually. You control them together. In the same way, when you multi-possess, you don't control every subject individually. You control them together. Go become the hive-mind; let it play out."

"I don't know ..." Tej was intimidated by what his teacher was asking him to do.

Monothiaz was not amused. She threw her stick away and grabbed Tej by the shoulders. "I didn't ask you this earlier. Why did you want to learn multi-possession? Why did you come to me?"

Tej had made up several reasons in his mind when he first visited Monothiaz. But she never asked him, and he kept mum. Now she'd confronted him directly.

"I … I … just wanted to learn something new," he stammered, his forehead drenched in sweat.

"No, that's not correct. Tell me the truth, or you shall never see me again." She let go of his shoulders. She frowned, her eyes burning with anger.

"I came to you because I was afraid. When I battled with Kumbh, I was aided by several people—Rigasur, Manika. They taught me about my powers and provided me vital information. Without them, I would have lost, failed badly. I don't want to be in that position again. I want to be able to fight my own wars myself. I may never go and pick up a battle with someone. But if anyone comes and hurts me or my family, I will retaliate with equal force." Tej's heartbeat had shot up, his fingers instinctively curling into fists. He could feel a bitter taste in his mouth—a taste that reminded him of the days of slavery under Kumbh. Of watching his mother dying piece by piece. He'd been a helpless kid back then—not now.

Monothiaz calmed down. She had hit the right chord. "So you are learning this because one day, you will use this power to protect your loved ones. You will use it because someone's life will depend on it."

"Yes."

Monothiaz was in no mood to listen to any more excuses. "Then, my boy, do so now. Possess these thousands as if the life of a loved one depends on it. Do it!"

Her words invigorated Tej. He felt as if electricity was running through his veins. He closed his eyes and focused on all the people around him. Merchants, customers, old people, and young, men, women and children; all going around, doing their business. He could feel all of them. Some happy, some sad, some frustrated, some hopeful. He was getting in there, creating his hive, reaching each one of them—linking them all together.

He opened his eyes and looked around. The market was no longer noisy. Every person there was standing still as if frozen. He looked at Monothiaz, his eyes asking her a question.

She had tears in her eyes. "You have done it, my boy."

Year 3057 BC | Sarp-Nagar Village

Tej and Manu Kumar lay in the bed, wrapped in sheets. The night was still young, and the moonlight was sneaking into the shed through the gaps in the roof. A small earthen lamp flickered on the ground near the door. Manu was moving his fingers across Tej's athletic abs. Tej stared at the roof.

Manu sat up. "So, you no longer need to go to Monothima?"

"Monothiaz," Tej corrected reverently.

"Whatever her name is. Do you still need to visit her every now and then?"

"No, my training is complete. She says I am ready."

Manu paused for a moment, chewing his lower lip. "I am going to ask you something. Please don't mind."

"Hmm." Tej groaned. He was in another world.

"You were calling out a name in your sleep. A girl's name."

"That so?"

"Yes. You said 'Kaalpriya' a few times. Who is she?"

Tej winced. "She was my daughter."

"What crap, Tej. You said you never married. Where did this daughter come from?"

"She existed once, but no longer. My wife and daughter. Time took them away from me. They no longer exist."

Manu scratched his head. "Is this another of your time travel things? They always end up confusing me."

"Yes."

"But if you are a time traveler, why don't you go visit them?"

"I told you, they don't exist anymore. I can't … you won't understand." Tej swiftly got up and donned his rugged hunting trousers.

Manu realized he had troubled Tej with his badgering. "What happened? Where are you going? I did not mean to offend you, love. I am sorry."

Tej was a little agitated but took a deep breath. "No, I'll take another round of the fields. Some kids spotted two foxes near the northeast corner this evening. I'll check that area out."

Tej picked his stack of arrows and tied them to his torso, adjusting the stack at the back. He picked up his bow and pulled on the string a little, causing a slight vibration.

Manu sat on the bed, dejected. He'd managed to piss off Tej once again.

Tej saw Manu like that and smiled a little. He got down and kissed Manu on the lips. Manu blushed and grinned ear-to-ear.

As Tej approached the door, he heard a commotion outside. Manu rose as well and tried to open the window doors, but Tej gestured against it. The sounds indicated that many men and women were crying as if asking for mercy. He was glad that they were at their hideout. This cottage was separated from rest of the village, way behind the bushes, away from the cluster of houses where most village-folk lived. Whoever was new to this area wouldn't know about this secret place, since even the villagers were unaware of its existence.

"You stay here. Don't move even one inch," Tej whispered sternly to Manu and rushed out.

The sounds were coming from the center of the village. Tej ran in the direction of the sound but slowed his steps as he saw a set of soldiers circling several villagers. They'd made a large perimeter around a bonfire. Three Wiccans standing near the fire were also visible. He hid behind a large tree and watched.

Five of Nefe's army-men had put five villagers at knife-point and were ready to slash their throats. She was addressing the rest of the crowd.

"I will be honest here. I love you, villagers. I have always cherished the routine, slow, moribund lifestyle which your villages follow. I have nothing against you and your peaceful austerity. I am looking for only one person, Tej. He has something that I need. So please, tell me, where can I find Tej?"

Tej stiffened. *Who is this Wiccan? And why is she looking for me?*

"I have wasted enough time searching through villages, hermitages, and whatnot. I want to rely on word-of-mouth. Speak up, or else these five poor souls will drop dead right now."

The five army-men holding the hostages tightened their grips on the knives. The hostages were now perspiring and praying for their lives. One of them even wet his pants. Their family members started wailing and crying for mercy, but Nefe was not moved.

An infant nearby started crying, and it caught Nefe's attention. A woman held the small baby, who was crying profusely. Nefe walked up to the woman. "What's the baby's name?"

"Div … Divita," the mother replied with a gulp.

"Divita. Beautiful name. How old is she?" Nefe asked as softly as she could.

"Fourteen months."

"Can I hold her?" Nefe almost pleaded.

The woman stood stiff. Two of Nefe's men came and stood behind the woman. With trembling hands, she handed over her baby to Nefe.

Nefe took the baby and started shushing it. She walked towards the area where the five men were held at knife-point. The mother tried to say something but Nefe's men gestured for her to stay quiet.

"Let these idiots go. We don't need them anymore," she ordered her men. The five men were let go, and they ran to their families.

"I can sense a time crawler's presence here!" Nefe screamed. "Tej, I know you are somewhere here. Show yourself. I can play these games all night. And I will take as many lives as I have to."

Tej was undecided. He drew one arrow, but how could he shoot? Nefe now had the infant in her arms.

Nefe paused for a few moments, looking around. "All right, then. Let the games begin." She placed the infant on the ground. She snapped her fingers, signaling for her men to bring a medium-sized circular bamboo box. They set the box on the ground and stepped back. Nefe got down on her knees and opened the box. A venomous king cobra slid out of the box, onto Nefe's arm. Nefe tapped on the snake's forehead, and it hissed.

"Either you show yourself to me, Tej or this poor baby dies!" she shouted, then let the snake slide onto the ground, in the direction of the baby.

The baby's mother came running, but Nefe's man caught her and dragged her away. The mother shrieked, pleading for mercy for her child.

The snake slowly moved towards the baby. The villagers gasped. Many women and children were crying. Nefe was laughing hysterically.

The baby on the ground was crying too, thumping her tiny wrists on the ground. Those thumping vibrations guided the snake towards the baby. The snake reached the baby and was about to strike when Tej came tearing through the crowd and picked up the serpent. The snake hissed and dug its fangs into Tej's left arm. Tej cried out in pain and threw the snake onto one of Nefe's guards, who started struggling, trying to get it away.

Tej immediately drew his arrow, placed it on the bow, and aimed it at Nefe. "Let the mother of this baby go, or this witch dies!" he screamed.

Nefe signaled for the men to leave her.

She came running, picked up her baby, and ran away.

Nefe clapped. "Tej, we finally meet. The man with a potent venom in his bloodstream, who doesn't even flinch at the most poisonous snake-bites? Oh, not a man, forgive my mistake. You are a time-crawler."

"The word is time-demon. Doesn't matter. Who are you, and why are you here?" Tej tightened his grip on the bow.

"I am here to thank you, first of all, for taking down Kumbh. He was a big blockage in our plans. That makes us allies."

"Were you working for Rigasur?"

"Oh, no, the other way round. He was the one working for me. And you were an integral part of our plan.

Although I did not like the way he used you. That was bad." Nefe pouted, feigning disdain.

Tej did not flinch. He could never forgive Rigasur for what he did. But for now, he needed to deal with the devil in front of him. "Either way, I cannot be seen as an ally with someone who is ready to shed blood at the drop of a hat. You were in bed with Rigasur all along, and he's my enemy."

Nefe bit her lower lip and smiled. "In bed with him? I like the analogy." She paused, eyeing Tej. "Look, I know we started off on a wrong foot here. I am not as bad as your first impression suggests. At times, the moon's movements mess with my head." She walked towards Tej.

"Stay where you are!" Tej warned.

Nefe kept walking till she reached him. She let the tip of Tej's arrow dig into her breast. "Why don't you shoot right now, Tej?" she whispered.

Tej was confused. There were a lot of guards around. Even if he could somehow subdue or kill this witch, her soldiers would shed a lot of innocent blood. He was in no position to get into a combat. And there was something about Nefe which was bothering him. She had no fear in her eyes. All he could see in her eyes was madness and pure evil.

Nefe broke the silence again. "I will leave, Tej. But tell me where can I find Manika."

"Manika? I haven't met her for some time now. What do you want with her?"

"I need Kuntala, but Manika knows where Kuntala is. And you know where Manika is. Phew. A pretty long chain of who knows whom. But I am ready to walk that path."

Tej was bewildered. *What does this witch want with Kun-*

tala? He had heard Kuntala's name a few times at Rigu's ashram. She was a legend among time-readers, the first time-reader who'd clearly time-read Kumbh's apocalyptic plans. She was one of the finest disciples cultivated by Rigasur, but he was told she'd later lost her mind and left the ashram years back.

"Look ..."

"Neferia; my name is Neferia. But I'd rather you called me Nefe."

Tej lowered his bow and arrow. "Nefe, I know nothing about Manika. I am being honest here. I don't know where she is."

"Yes, you may not know. But I bet you know all the places she can be found. Give me a list of places, and I will leave."

Tight-lipped, Tej nodded in negation and shrugged. "I have no clue. We weren't that close."

Nefe rubbed her eyes and sighed. A look of disappointment floated on her face. "You know what, Tej? These surroundings are at fault. A village in 3000 BC, a cloudy night, frightened villagers, crying babies. Why don't you and I go to the future? 2057 AD. Two hundred kilometers south of Asia's lowest point, there is a sky café. Five kilometers up in the air, forever floating, they serve the best coffee on the globe. Another restaurant in the same establishment has a fancy cocktail bar and a ..." Nefe came closer to Tej, "... a strip club, too. A lot of handsome naked hunks can be found dancing to the latest tunes. You and I share a similar taste in men, I reckon. And while we are partying, we can talk about some of these things. Can't we?"

He drew his knife and put it across her neck, then grabbed her by the waist so she couldn't move.

"All the soldiers, drop your weapons! Drop them now or she dies!" Tej shouted. "Ask them to do it," Tej whispered in Nefe's ear.

Nefe was fuming with anger. "Enough of these games!"

Tej felt an invisible force clasping his hand and twisting it. The knife fell. Nefe moved away and turned around. Tej was trying hard to gain control over his hand, but two kicks to the backs of his legs threw him to his knees.

"I wanted to be your ally. I extended a hand of friendship, but you spat on it. You are not worth it, Tej. You time-crawlers have always deceived me. Rigasur tried to play the same game. Now I want answers, and I want them right now. Bring the other-time crawler," Nefe shouted.

A young boy in his late teens came running and bowed to Nefe. He wore the same garb as Nefe's soldiers.

"Take him to the Truth and Confessions Unit in Cape-Town. September 19th, 2057. Pod number seven-seven-nine. That should be empty on that date. And ask Morgan to put a helmet on his head. I want this one captive for a while," Nefe ordered.

The boy nodded, then came near Tej, and sat on his knees. He started reciting a mantra, which Tej could not hear properly. The boy took out a green *bhasm* powder from his pocket and applied on Tej's palm.

Tej's heartbeat sped up. He realized that the boy was a time-demon too, and was going to perform a demon invocation spell on him. He knew he had to get out. His eyeballs turned pink as he prepared to go to his destination.

"Tej!" Nefe screamed and pointed her finger at him. "Don't you dare leave this body! I will destroy this whole village. Men, women, children, animals. I will wipe this shithole from the face of the earth!" Her whole body was trembling with fury.

Tej relented. The boy slashed Tej's palm, then his own palm, and connected them. As he looked in Tej's eyes, both of them dropped to the ground. Tej was no longer in his body.

Nefe turned around. "Give the 'green-dose' to each of these village idiots. I am hungry for some pain and screaming," She ordered Jarna, then sat down on the ground, her eyes closing.

4
RESCUE

2057 AD | Vedvance tech, secret truth, and confessions unit, Cape-town

Tej opened his eyes and looked around. He was in a dark, dingy place, and he couldn't see. His body was aching with pain. His hands were tied to the roof, and his feet were barely touching the ground.

Tej heard a voice.

"He's awake. Let's start the next round."

A switch flicked, and bright light from a large bulb hit his eyes. He couldn't keep them open. He saw two burly men walking towards him. They carried steel rods, one with sharp spikes. Tej realized he was in the body of a thirty-year-old man. He tried searching the brain for any memories, but it was a clean slate—as if the whole memory-area had been wiped out.

"Hey, Cinderella. You slept for hours this time. What happened?" One of the men grabbed his hair and pulled his head back. He was Morgan, Nefe's henchman. He had a rugged face full of scars, and he smelled of tobacco.

"Get the helmet, now," Morgan ordered the other guy.

"Oh, he won't run. Boss has his whole village on the hook." The other man smiled. He was Jack, a man several years younger than Morgan.

"I said, get … the … helmet."

Jack shrugged. Opened a bag on a table nearby, he took out a metal cap fitted with a small circuit and straps. He strapped the helmet on Tej's head.

"All right. Now, don't even think of leaving this body. This helmet detects any significant changes in your brain activity. And when that happens, it shoots a strong electrical charge through your brain. So even if you think of leaving this body, you will receive a shock. Believe me, you won't love it when that happens."

Tej was still hazy and his throat was parched. "Can I get some water?"

"Forget water. I will treat you to legacy wine. Just answer my questions." Morgan smiled.

"What is this place? Where am I?"

"You're supposed to answer my questions, not ask me some."

"Okay, shoot," Tej replied calmly.

"Where is Manika? Or Kuntala? If you happen to know them."

"Huh? I have never heard those names, ever." Tej had decided not to tell them anything. He knew only one way to respond to torturers: make them think that their ability to inflict pain wasn't working. That plan was ridiculously tough, but the only way to fatigue them. He knew he would have to endure a lot to bring them to that stage. "Though the names sound lovely. Manika, Kuntala."

Tej laughed.

"Is this a joke to you, buddy?" Morgan laughed, too.

"Yeah, sounds funny."

"Funny?" Morgan smashed the iron rod into Tej's stomach with full force. Tej screamed in pain. The spiked rod pulled off some strings of flesh as Morgan removed it. As immense pain numbed his senses, Tej couldn't breathe for a moment.

"Still funny?" Morgan asked.

Tej let the pain die down a bit and then laughed. "Oh, God. No, that was …"

"That was what?" This time, Jack readied himself for the blow.

"Wait, don't hit me again," Tej addressed Morgan.

Morgan smiled. "This one broke in one shot."

Tej then turned his gaze towards Jack. "Hey, you. *You* hit me this time. This guy hits like a little girl."

"Oh really? I hit like a girl?" Morgan struck Tej with his rod. Tej's screams filled the whole room. After a few blows, Morgan stopped and threw the rod to one side.

Tej was now laughing. "Hey girl, you broke the rib-cage of this body."

Jack brought his face near Tej's. "What are you made of?"

"I am a time-demon, you idiot. This body doesn't belong to me. The pain is temporary. I shut myself off from the body, and its empty brain takes the pain."

"Then why do you scream?"

"Reflex action, maybe. I don't know. I don't feel a thing."

Morgan and Jack stiffened. They had tortured time-demons before. They knew that pain affected them. But Tej was reacting to the beating in an odd way. Such a severe thrashing had brought down many.

"I know how to break him. Put a towel on his face." Morgan went to the corner of the room and picked up a huge jug of water.

Jack took a thin towel and covered Tej's face. Morgan started pouring water on the towel. Tej struggled to breathe as the water entered his nose and mouth. He vigorously shook his head and torso, gasping for air. Morgan kept emptying the jug.

"That's enough." Jack tried to stop Morgan, but he continued until he emptied the whole container. He waited a few seconds for Tej to catch his breath, then removed the towel.

Tej coughed as leftover water drained out of his nose and mouth.

"I have a few big containers of water here," Morgan mocked. "Still going strong, demon boy?"

Tej caught his breath and spoke. "Thanks, I was thirsty anyhow." He paused and caught his breath. "I have a serious question for both of you. What are you going to try next? Are you going to fry me in boiling oil? If so, please do. I'm itching for that."

"No!" Morgan shouted in anger, lifting his rod again.

"Wait, let's put him on ice and try the rods again," Jack said.

"Good idea." Morgan took a knife and cut the ropes that tied Tej to the roof. Tej dropped to the ground and cringed in pain. His ribcage was intact, but the flesh around that area was swollen from the beating.

"I'll go get ..." Jack couldn't complete his sentence and vanished into thin air.

"What the hell!" Morgan exclaimed. But within two seconds, he, too disappeared, as if he was never there.

Tej was too dazed to even express surprise. A device started to beep somewhere near him. He looked around, but couldn't see anything in the room except torture equipment.

He noticed his left arm was glowing. He touched it with his right hand, and a small rectangular holographic screen opened up. The screen had a white background and two buttons—"Pick up" in green and "Reject" in red. Tej tapped the green button.

Hello Tej, are you there?

It was strange—Tej could hear the voice directly inside his head.

Say something, dammit.

"Yes, yes, I am fine. Are you in my head? Am I hallucinating?"

No, you are not. You are in a time-prison.

"What?"

Yes. Now, do exactly as I say, because some more men are coming your way.

"Who are you? What exactly did you do?"

No time for questions. Can you walk?

"I'll try."

Okay, go to parking level twenty-two. You will see several cars. Sit in the green car and drive off. When you get out from the basement, drive straight out the building gate. Don't stop for anything. I'll repeat, basement 22, green car, don't stop for anything. I will contact again once you are out of the building.

"What?"

The call disconnected, and the screen vanished. Tej shook his head. He picked up the steel rod for support, stumbled, and stepped out of the cell.

It appeared he was in an old building. The gallery walls were stained with blood, and the paint was chipped.

The partly-lit lights on the roof were blinking.

Tej kept walking with the help of his stick. He managed to reach the end of the gallery, where he found an industrial lift. He stepped inside and looked for buttons, but there were none except one flat dark-red button.

He pressed the button. A small red light lit inside the button, but nothing happened. After two seconds, he heard a robotic lady voice. "No input received." He was sure it came out of some speaker from inside the button.

Tej again pressed the button, but the result was the same. He pressed the button again and shouted in anger, "Take me to basement twenty-two, dammit."

"Input received," the voice quipped, and the lift started moving down.

Tej fell to the lift floor. He was tired, angry and in deep pain. His torturers weren't there, and he was free to express his mind-numbing agony. The bleeding from his wounds had miraculously stopped, but the skin was turning brown.

The lift stopped, and doors opened to a massive parking lot. Tej managed to crawl out of the lift. Staying there for a few seconds, he heard a few noises from far above. *Perhaps these were the men the voice on the phone warned me about.*

He picked himself up with a struggle, and hurried off to the parking lot, searching for a green car. All the cars in the parking lot seemed exactly the same. They were all white, with shining bumpers and curvy aerodynamic designs. He walked through a few lanes, then hit the jackpot. There was one green car among thousands of white cars, visible from a distance. He hurried towards that car, hearing boot-steps approaching.

As he reached the car, he heard the car engine rev up. It reversed itself from the parking lot and came into the driving lane.

Tej peeped inside the car, but there was no one inside.

"Is there anyone in there?" He received no response. This car had the exact same curvy, aerodynamic design as all the other white cars present here, except it was green. Tej opened the door and sat inside.

There was no steering in there. Tej was baffled. "What the hell?" There was again a red button inside the car, similar to the one in the lift. Tej pressed it, and the whole dashboard lit up.

"Please enter your destination, sir," a robotic voice emanated from somewhere in the dashboard.

"I don't know," Tej blurted out.

"All right. I can take you away from the premises while you make your mind up. Just relax and enjoy the journey."

"Sure, yes. That would be great."

The car whirred with speed and started driving up, on a circular ramp, climbing twenty-two floors. Tej felt vertigo as the vehicle sped on the circular track. At last, the car emerged from the basement and rushed out of the building.

"Take a right here," Tej remembered the voice asked him to go right.

"Sure, sir." The car took a sharp right out of the building's main gate.

Tej noticed that the sky was dark blue. There was a miles-long empty road ahead. On both sides of the road, he could only see empty, barren stretches of land.

Tej realized that the metal helmet his torturers had put on his head was still strapped on. He unstrapped it and threw it out of the window.

He tried to leave the body, but couldn't. He imagined

his destination, his village back in 3057 BC. He even tried reciting the mantra, though he had not needed it for his past two travels, it proved futile.

"Would you like to listen to some music, sir?" the soothing mechanical voice from the dashboard broke his attention.

"What? Music? No. I am good."

"Psychology studies have indicated that listening to music can lighten the mood, sir," the voice insisted.

"I was thrashed by God-knows-who. My whole village is under the trap of a strange witch. And I am trapped in some kind of time-prison. And you want to lighten my mood by playing music?"

"I'm sorry, I could not understand your input, sir. Shall I play some music?"

"What the hell. Yeah, play something?"

"What would you like to hear, sir?"

"I don't know. Play 'Clocks' by Coldplay." Tej's previous host, Ravi, was a fan of the band. Tej himself had only grown up listening to the flute music in his village, most of it played during weddings.

"A very good choice, sir. You have a taste for the old hits. I will have to search my archives for it. Please hold on."

"Whatever."

After five seconds, the song started playing in the car, and Tej sat with his fists against his forehead. He realized that his left arm was again vibrating, and the green and red buttons had returned. He clicked on the green button and again heard the voice in his head.

The voice was saying something, but he had a hard time hearing it because of the music from the car's dashboard.

"Stop the music, will you? I am on a call."

"Sure, sir." The music stopped.

"Sorry, say it again," Tej addressed the voice in his head.

Are you being followed? It was the voice of a man.

"I don't think so."

Can you please confirm?

Tej looked back. There was nothing. The building was far behind him, though he could see a dust cloud near the building. "I am not sure. I don't see someone immediately following me."

All right. I couldn't introduce myself. I am Mozeek. I am sure you will have heard a lot about me. The man sounded as if he was smiling.

"Ah … no, I haven't."

Mozeek, the dark-net expert, most notorious hacker. Ring a bell?

"No, never heard the name." Tej felt guilty.

Oh, then you must have heard of me as the great King Mozakira. The true emperor of Abreen. The man on the other end was elated as he introduced himself.

"Mozakira … Mozeek." Tej acted as if he was trying to recall the name, but he had never heard either of them before. In fact, he had several questions of his own, but he did not want to immediately shut down the excited voice. "I am sorry, sir. I haven't heard of either of these names."

That's strange. Every time-demon knows Mozeek. This man claiming to be Mozeek now sounded dejected.

Tej felt bad. "I am very sorry again, sir, Mr. Mozeek. I have actually spent most of my life in 3000 BC. Maybe that's why I haven't heard about a great person such as you."

Hmm. Mozeek was not impressed. *Then why were you looking for me?*

"Sir, I wasn't. Now please tell me, how can I get out of this time-prison? My whole village is in danger," Tej almost pleaded.

Sure. I will help you. Open the storage part of the dashboard. There will be a wristwatch inside. Take it out.

Tej fumbled with the car's dashboard and managed to open a storage unit. There was a shining golden wristwatch inside. He took it out and put it on his hand. The watch was not working, though; its hands were still. It was stuck at eight hours, nineteen minutes.

"Sir, this watch is not working. Its hands are not moving."

Yes, because you are in a timeless zone. Time-prisons are usually constructed by cordoning off a specific area of virtual reality and removing time from it. You are currently inside a crafted virtual reality capsule called Pod 779, where time is absent. But when things come to Mozeek, nothing is unhackable. You are lucky that I was able to find your signature among the complex dark-net maze it was embedded into. Mozeek sounded self-congratulatory again.

"Okay. Thanks again, Mr. Mozeek, but how do I get out?"

Yes. Coming to that. This road is very long, and no one can design huge timeless zones—which means this whole road cannot be timeless. Continue driving down this road, and at some point, the hands of the clock will start moving. That means you would have entered a zone which has time. Then you can leave this body and come to meet me. Wait for me at the Creexathon Sky-park, Los Angeles on December 23rd, 2057 at 5:30 PM. If you are not followed, I will meet you there.

Tej didn't know what to say. He was eager to go back

to his village, but this man Mozeek wanted to meet him. "Well sir, with all due respect, I would like to leave this place and go back to my village. They are in deep trouble, sir."

Are you sure you were not looking for me?

"No Mr. Mozeek, I wasn't."

Hmm. I think I pre-intercepted the time-wave. The event after which you look for me hasn't happened yet. All right, from my side, you are free to go.

"What, sir?"

Don't worry about it. I cannot influence your decisions by giving you information on events which haven't happened yet.

Tej was too tired to make sense of what Mozeek just said. He thanked Mozeek and disconnected the call. He asked the car's computer to speed up the vehicle, eager to leave the timeless zone.

A few minutes later, he looked in the rear-view mirror and saw a caravan of cars at a distance. And they were catching up.

"Hey, Mr. Computer. Do you have a name?" Tej addressed the car's dashboard.

"I am an A.I., sir. I do have a name, but it's a complicated 256-letter name. I am afraid you won't be able to pronounce it."

"Okay, but you would have a nickname."

"Yes, sir, Mr. Mozeek calls me Pablo sometimes."

"Great. Pablo. Can you drive faster?"

"But sir, we are already at 220 in the 225-zone. Any faster, and we will be breaking the traffic rules."

"To hell with those rules. How fast you can go?"

"I can go to 355, at max."

"Do it. Go to 355."

"Sir, I would advise against …"

"PABLO, DO IT!" Tej thundered.

"Sure, sir."

The car immediately stepped up the speed. Tej felt a jolt as the inertia pushed him back. He could see the speedometer on the dashboard displaying the speed, but it was in Roman numerals. He couldn't decipher the exact number, but he realized the car was faster.

The vehicles chasing him were catching up. Tej looked at the wristwatch. The hands were as still as stone.

"Come on, come on."

"I am already at max speed, sir."

"I was not talking to you."

"Apologies. Should I play some music, sir?"

"Shut up, will you? Going forth, only respond when I say the word 'Pablo'. Okay?"

The dashboard went silent.

"Okay?"

The dashboard was still silent. Tej got worried.

"Pablo?"

"Yes sir, I am here."

"Good. Be there." He looked at the watch, which still showed 8:19.

Suddenly, the rearview window of the car shattered as several bullets passed through. Tej immediately ducked.

"Is there a weapon in the car?"

Pablo was silent.

"Pablo. Is there a weapon in the car?"

"No, sir. This vehicle is not fitted with any kind of weaponry. Mr. Mozeek designed it solely for extraction purposes."

There was another round of fire. Tej stayed down. He didn't want to be captured again.

"Come on, please," he pleaded to the wristwatch, but

nothing happened.

He tried to get up and look at the cars following him, but as soon as he did, there was another round of fire. He dug his gaze into the watch. He had just lost all hope when the second hand moved a little.

He got goosebumps. He was out of the timeless zone. The second hand was now moving.

"Pablo?"

"Yes, sir."

"Keep driving for thirty seconds more, and then come to a rapid halt. Can you do that?"

"Sure, sir. I would advise against ..."

"Do it!"

"Sure, sir. The timer starts now."

Tej started reciting the mantra and imagined his destination: his village, his body, and chose to travel to the morning after. Going back to the same moment was not safe. Within a second, he was gone. The body he was inside collapsed on the car seat.

Pablo kept driving for exactly thirty seconds before slamming the brakes. The car almost titled to the right. All the cars following it couldn't anticipate this move and came crashing into it, one after the other. As they collided with each other, a few of them exploded, consumed in smoke and flames.

5
TRANSFORMATION

3057 BC | Sarp-Nagar Village

Tej woke up in his body. As a reflex, his hand went to his rib-cage where his torturers wounded him, but his body obviously bore no signs of those wounds.

He looked around and realized he was lying on a hard bed in the village infirmary, a huge shed with a jute roof and bamboo walls. Around him, village folks were lying on hundreds of beds. Tej got up and checked the pulse of the person lying on a bed next to him. He recognized Sampat, a farmer who lived two blocks away from his house. Sampat's pulse was weak, and he had a high fever. His forehead was covered in sweat, and he was murmuring something in sleep. Tej tried to wake him up, but couldn't.

Tej moved to other beds and found most of the villagers in the same state. His foster-father, foster-brother, even Manu, all were there. Breathing, but unconscious. He stepped out of the infirmary. A few villagers sat on the central meeting place, called the *chaupaal*.

As he walked towards the chaupaal, he could see astonished people looking at him. Some gasped. Village headman Dharma, a man in his early seventies, stood up. He had a long white beard and a wrinkled face. He was draped in a shawl and wore a big white turban. "Tej, can you please keep your distance?"

"Why?" Tej stopped walking.

"You had a fever. All the villagers in the infirmary, their bodies were hot. They are asleep and are not waking up. This is some kind of a strange disease or magical spell, cast by that witch. We took a risk to move you and others to the infirmary, but it's better if you maintain your distance."

Tej saw the same resistant gaze in the eyes of the others. He could understand their fear, but he needed more information. "Where's that witch? Is she gone?"

"No one knows." Dharma sat down and clasped his head in his hands. "She and her army are no longer in the village now. No one is sure what she did. Her army was forcing people to drink a green liquid. Maybe they put some liquid in you, too."

"No, they didn't." Tej knew he had not been rendered unconscious because of the liquid.

"Then why were you asleep?" Dharma argued.

Tej wanted to talk about his torture in time prison, but decided against it. This was not the moment for him to come out as a time traveler. And he was not even sure if villager folk would understand those concepts. They might end up ostracizing him and his family, and throw them out of the village. He shrugged. "I don't know."

"Have the others woken up?" an old lady sitting on the ground asked. There was a faint hope in her eyes.

"No." Tej wanted to ask the whereabouts of his mother but had a feeling he was not welcome there. Some of his friends, loving neighbors and acquaintances were all in the crowd, but they looked at him like an outcast.

He ambled over to his house and knocked on the door.

An old lady in her early sixties, his foster mother Sarla, opened the door. As soon as she saw Tej, she burst into tears and hugged him, then showered a few kisses on his forehead and cheeks.

"My boy, you're all right! Is your father coming too? Has he woken up too? And what about your brother?" Sarla ran outside and saw no one. She turned back and looked at Tej in anticipation.

Tej nodded in negation. His foster-father and foster-brother both were also in the infirmary. Sarla came inside and sat on the couch. Her hopes had gone up but came crashing down. She sat and stared at the wall.

"I will fix this, Mother."

"How? Did you not see that witch? She is so powerful. Villagers are saying she has them under their magic spell. That green liquid she gave them was some kind of magical poison."

"There is nothing like magic, Mother." Tej was about to quote the same line Rigasur had told him once but kept silent.

"I don't know what to believe in, whom to go to." Tej's mother walked to the worship room of the house, where several idols and religious photos were kept. She touched her forehead to the ground and bowed in front of the gods. She stayed there, crying in silence.

Tej needed more information, and he knew whom to go to. The witch with the scar asked for Manika, and Manika should have some answers. He rushed out and looked for a stable nearby. He picked the best horse he could and started to ride towards Rigu's ashram.

2057 AD | Los Angeles

Vedika asked her driver to pull over near the glitzy massage parlor 'Maroon Depth'. She stepped out of her car and applied lipstick. Her dazzling party attire included a long single-piece black dress with a deep V-neck and a designer belt made of pure gold. She had done a good job of hiding the thin red scar running from her eye to her cheek. The scar followed every human body Nefe possessed.

Nefe had complete control of Vedika's mind and now repressed her original consciousness. Vedika's security officer Marcos wanted to accost her inside, but she signaled him to stay put.

"Ma'am, going in such a place alone is not recommended," Marcos cautioned.

"Come on, Marcos, what do you mean, 'such a place'? I'm just going to have some fun. Stay in the parking lot; I'll call for you. And if Rubina calls, tell her I am busy in a meeting." Nefe winked and went inside.

Marcos was appalled at Vedika's transformed behavior. He had been heading the security detail for Vedika for three years now. He had seen how close-knit Vedika and Rubina were. He occasionally saw them stealing glances, blowing kisses. He even found them locking lips when they thought no one was watching. He always viewed them as a married couple who were deeply in love with each other.

But today, Vedika asked to be driven to a known men-harem. The massage parlor was an obvious front. It provided multiple sexual partners for women who could pay big bucks for both handsome dudes and water-tight privacy.

Vedika was clearly betraying Rubina's trust. But this was their own personal matter. Marcos was an employee, after all. He shrugged and sat in the car, waiting.

Nefe entered the establishment, where the girl at the reception greeted her.

"I am looking for the Platinum Pamper." Nefe smiled as she placed her arms on the reception and rested against it.

"Excellent choice, ma'am. That will be twenty thousand dollars for four hours. There will be a three thousand dollars charge per extra half hour."

Nefe was furious. She grabbed the receptionist by her collar. The girl gulped in fear. Nefe looked her in the eye. "I thought your eye-scan system imaged my retina at the front door."

"Yes it did, ma'am."

"Then you have my credit-line details. Correct?"

"Yes, ma'am."

"Then fucking bill me. Don't read out the charges." Nefe let go of the receptionist's collar with a jerk.

The receptionist vigorously nodded. "My apologies, ma'am. Rodrigo, please escort Mrs. Vedika to the platinum suite."

Rodrigo the parlor-manager guided Vedika into a large plush room with maroon walls and red curtains.

After two minutes, seven muscular men sauntered into the room. They stood on a dais in a straight line, each of them wearing nothing but red underwear. They were all blindfolded. The men stood straight, with their chests out. The bright lights from the ceiling illuminated their well-oiled muscular torsos and legs.

"As part of the platinum-pamper package, you can choose from this line-up, ma'am," Rodrigo said as he bowed a little.

"I want all of them." Nefe laughed.

"Well, my apologies, ma'am—as part of this package, you can have only two of them."

"I am just kidding, Rodrigo." She winked.

Nefe walked along the line, smelling each of them— she even caressed their clean-shaven chests. She chose the third and seventh man from the queue. They both removed the cloth tied around their eyes.

Rodrigo led Nefe and two men into a large suite. The suite had a huge king-size bed, a full bar, a jacuzzi, and an indoor hot-water swimming pool. He closed the doors behind him as he left.

"All right, boys. Pants down. One of you can start rubbing my back. Regarding the other one, I have naughtier plans for you." Nefe winked and started loosening the belt around her waist.

Three hours later, she lay in bed, wrapped in nothing but sheets. After several sessions of intense sex, she was panting and drenched in sweat. Each of the men lay beside her. They were perspiring, too.

"You both were amazing. I loved it."

Both men sat up. "Thanks, ma'am."

"Now get lost, before I'm tempted to ride you again." She laughed.

Both men left, and Nefe poured herself some wine.

She heard a voice inside her brain. "Nefe, where are you?" It was Jarna's voice. Jarna was contacting her through their shared consciousness.

"Oh Jarna, I am enjoying the wealth, and the pleasure

which comes with it." Nefe took a deep sip from her glass.

"Rubina knows about this, Nefe."

"How come?" Nefe was slightly worried. *This could complicate things.*

"I don't know; perhaps your head of security told her."

"Son of a bitch," Nefe mumbled. "I am taking him to Vedika's house, and after that, I want you to take care of him."

Nefe hit the shower for a good fifteen minutes, then dressed up. She called Marcos to bring the car over to the front gate.

She walked out, and the receptionist came running to her. "Hope you had a good time ma'am."

"Yes, I did." Nefe smiled and stuffed a five hundred dollar bill into the receptionist's shirt. She was delighted.

Nefe walked outside and sat in the car. She did not speak for the whole way. When the car reached their apartment building, Marcos came and opened the door for her.

Nefe came out and looked at Marcos in the eye. "You told her, didn't you?"

Marcos had been dreading this moment for the past few minutes. He stammered, "I … ma'am. Actually, Mrs. Rubina called me, and she said you were not reachable. And I couldn't lie."

"You are fired!"

Marcos stood like a wax statue. Three years of impeccable service, and he had been let go in a second. Nefe walked to the parking elevator and stepped inside.

"Which floor, please?" echoed inside the elevator.

"Two-two-three," Nefe said. The elevator started

going up. Through the glass walls of the elevator, she could see Marcos still standing near the car with his head down. Two men wearing black masks were approaching him from behind. One of them put a black cloth bag over Marcos' head. He struggled to get free as they both dragged him away. Nefe smiled as the elevator moved up slowly.

When Nefe entered the house, she could see Rubina pacing around in the living room. She clearly had been crying. Her eyes were wet, and her face was red.

"Hey, Missy, what's happening?" Nefe tried to hug Rubina, but she gestured her to stay away.

"You went to a male brothel? Really?" Rubina scowled. She felt betrayed beyond her wildest dreams.

"Oh, come on, it's just a cute little massage place, Ruby."

"Don't call me Ruby. You have lost that right."

"Why? Because I went somewhere to relax? Haven't we gone to spa therapy and massages ever?"

"We have done a lot of things together. But what we have never done is share our bodies with an outsider."

"You're stretching it." Nefe again tried to hug Ruby.

"DON'T you touch me! Not only are you not ashamed of what you did, but you are also, in fact, trivializing it! When did you change so much?" Rubina's throat choked with emotions, her tears flowing again. She'd put so much into her relationship with Vedika, and she'd ruined everything.

"Wow. If men do it, they're called studs. But when I do it, I've done something wrong." Nefe sat on the sofa and took out a cigarette to smoke.

"Oh, don't you dare spin it that way. It's about our relationship, our marriage, the sacredness of it. You have violated this relationship. You have ruined our future."

Rubina saw Vedika lighting a cigarette. Vedika never smoked. Rubina got down to her knees. She was broken from inside. "What has happened to you? Who are you? You're not the Ved I loved."

"I'm the same, Ruby. You are the one who needs to change," Nefe spoke nonchalantly as she let out a huge puff of smoke.

Her words of indifference hurt Rubina even more. "That's it, Vedika Sharma. That's the end of our relationship. My lawyers will file for divorce tomorrow morning. We are going to split everything."

"What happens to our daughter, Ruby? Think about her."

"You should have thought about her before cheating on me."

"No, I was saying, will she even live to see us getting divorced?"

"Are you threatening to …? How could …?" Words dried on her tongue. Vedika kept smoking with aplomb.

"What the hell is wrong with you? How can you even think like this? This is Jess we're talking about, our daughter. You explain to me right now what is happening here." Rubina looked into her eyes, and all she could see was hollowness and malice. She had forgotten about Vedika cheating on her. She was very worried about their daughter.

"You know what? You just threatened my daughter. I cannot forgive that, ever. I will call the police right away. They will arrest you and take both of us into protective custody."

Rubina swiped the back of her left arm with her right index finger, and a holographic 3D screen of the wrist-o-phone appeared with a dial.

"Call pol- ..." Rubina felt a tight grip on her neck. An invisible hand was smothering her. She couldn't speak and turned around with difficulty. Vedika was smiling.

The autocomplete on the phone buzzed. *Did you mean, 'Call Police'?*

"No, disconnect," Vedika spoke in Rubina's voice.

Rubina's eyes widened with shock. The 3D hologram wrist-o-phone screen disappeared. Vedika doused the cigarette and sauntered towards Rubina, a smirk on her face. "I didn't want to end your life, but you have complicated things. I have too much riding on Vedvance right now. I don't want unnecessary delays."

Rubina was still choking and unable to speak. She felt her body rising in the air. Her feet were no longer touching the ground.

"Don't worry. I will not kill your daughter. I have arranged for her to be sent very far away so that I can live my life in peace." Nefe came close to Rubina and ran her fingers through Rubina's hair. "When Vedika's body gets old, Jess' body will still be young. Then I will possess her. It's easier for me. Same family, same DNA, same inheritance."

Within two hours, the news spread like wildfire: Rubina Vance, the co-founder of Vedvance Corp, had been found dead. Her suicide letter floated around the internet.

The next morning a teary-eyed Vedika addressed a press conference at the city center. She wore a black dress and sat with a glum face as she addressed several reporters.

"With Ruby gone, I feel as if half of my life is gone— as if one half of me is dead. Ruby had been dealing with several mental health issues for a long time. We never wanted it to become public knowledge, because it was our private life. But with her gone like this, I want to say it to each one of you. If your spouse or loved one is undergoing mental health issues, please don't ignore it. Please help them pursue proper therapy. Once they are gone, you are only left with a memory." Vedika burst into tears. A couple of people near her consoled her and offered her water.

Wiping her tears, she continued, "Today, I'm announcing that Vedvance will begin research on another VR-product called Mental Health Labs. In these labs, we will use powerful A.I. simulations to treat mental health patients and trauma victims without using any medication. This is something Ruby always wanted to do, but we kept delaying it. I will delay it no longer. Treatment in these centers will be free of cost, so please do sign up. Steve will share more details on that." Sobbing, she got up and left the press conference, while reporters fired a volley of questions.

A neat-looking company spokesman, Steve, took on the stage. With a feigned expression on his face, he spoke. "Mrs. Sharma will not be taking any more questions today. You all can appreciate that this is a difficult time for the family. I urge you all to keep her and her daughter in your prayers. Later this week, we will be sharing a detailed press release with more details around the Mental health Labs program, the MHL initiative."

6
KUNTALA

3057 BC | Rigu's Hermitage

Tej reached the hermitage and got down from the horse. He was appalled to see that the grounds once housing the ashram were now burnt land.

He ambled the whole periphery of the ashram. Gardens, fences, sheds, brick wells; all were charred and destroyed. In several places, he could see burnt remains of humans and animals. It was clear that no person or thing had survived the fire.

Manika? Is she dead too? No, she's a time reader. She can see her death approaching. He realized he was talking to himself. It occurred to him that there was one more place he needed to check. He climbed the horse and rode towards the secret ashram.

A few minutes later, he entered the secret ashram. The gates were wide open, and the whole place had a deserted look. He was about to turn around when he noticed the ashram's well. As his throat was parched, he got down the horse and walked to the well.

He threw the bucket in and hit the water level with a splash. As he pulled on the rope, he sensed someone behind him. He swiftly turned back, and a woman wielded a wooden stick on him with her full force, intending to hit his head. Tej brought his arm between them, and the stick broke into two pieces. He winced in pain.

The woman was Manika. Her clothes were disheveled, her eyes were swollen, and she looked dead tired.

"What the hell, Manika?"

"I am sorry, I am so sorry, Tej … I thought you were … I am sorry." Manika burst into tears and embraced him tightly.

"What happened?" He had never seen her like this.

Manika did not say a word and kept crying. Tej kept patting her back, trying to console her. He had come to her seeking her help, but it seemed she needed help from him.

After a few seconds, she calmed down. After Tej got water, he also poured some for his horse. Manika led him inside one of the sheds at the very end of the ashram. Tej saw that she had collected a heap of sticks, stones, knives and sharp farm equipment inside the shed. It was evident that she was afraid for her life.

They both sat down on the cot. For a few minutes, no one said a word. Tej was waiting for her to say something. He was about to ask her when she spoke.

"They burnt everything. Everything."

"Who?"

"A witch's coven and their army."

"Neferia? Nefe?"

"I don't know. Whenever I try to time-read them, I get nothing. As if they don't exist."

"This witch Nefe visited my village, too. She was desperately looking for you."

Manika sat silent, looking into oblivion—as if she knew something Tej didn't.

Tej continued speaking. He just wanted to let it out, speak to someone who would understand. "One of the time-demons in her service took me to the future. I was tortured. They wanted to know your location. I somehow escaped and came back. Now she has put several of my village people under some kind of virus or spell. My father, brother, and friends are in there too. Why were they looking for you? What do they want?"

"They were not looking for me. They were looking for Kuntala." Manika raised her eyebrows as she looked at Tej. Tej remembered the witch had mentioned Kuntala's name too.

"I couldn't sleep that night," Manika continued. "I had a strong feeling something terrible was about to happen. I got up and took a stroll along the ashram periphery when I saw several men and women entering the ashram. They were all wearing demon masks. I hid behind the bushes. They first went to the chamber of time travel and then spread throughout the ashram. They started knocking on the doors. I overheard them saying they were looking for Kuntala. I knew Kuntala was being kept in a cottage away from others.

"I took a large route around the ashram periphery, woke up Kuntala, and we both ran away. When we were further away, we heard a commotion from the ashram and saw smoke and fire emanating from it. They were burning the place down. We kept running until we got here."

Tej was trying to picture the whole thing and contemplated visiting Rudrakshini. *She was a necromancer; she would definitely know what to do in this situation.* She was the only person he could look up to. "Kuntala was with you? Where is she now?"

"She is right behind you."

Tej turned back and was startled to see a woman standing behind her. "God, you scared me!"

Kuntala was in her early forties but looked much older. Her hair was tousled, and she wore a white saree. With a deadpan expression on her face, she walked slowly forward and sat on a chair nearby, staring into the oblivion.

"Kuntala, I've heard a lot about you. You are one of the best time-readers. Can you please tell us what's happening?"

Kuntala didn't move a muscle.

"Kuntala, can you hear me?" Tej was getting impatient. "What's wrong with her?"

"She won't speak," Manika interjected. "She hasn't spoken to anyone in decades. She used to be Rigasur's favorite time-reader."

"What happened then?"

"One day, she did a time-reading on Rigasur. Knew who he was. Then word reached him, and he imprisoned her. Long periods of solitary confinement pushed her brain elsewhere. She's been tongue-tied since then."

Tej looked at Kuntala again, this time with pity. "If they were looking for Kuntala, then she definitely knows something about this witch. I can go to the past and do a pre-dead-brain-feeding of her brain. That should work."

"No, Tej, there's no use doing pre-dead-brain-feeding of a time-reader. We see so many visions, so many alternate futures. You won't know which vision is true and which is false. You'll be lost in the maze of countless, near-identical futures, most of which never materialized.

Such convoluted knowledge would drive you nuts."

Tej rubbed his face. He could see no clear path forward. He knew zilch about his enemy. "How do I cure my villagers, then? The witch made them drink some kind of green liquid."

"She's not a witch," Kuntala spoke in a hoarse voice. Tej and Manika looked at her. She sat still with the same deadpan expression, but now her eyes were blinking. She also cleared her throat a few times. Those were the first words she'd spoken in a very long time.

Manika got up. "Kuntala did you … did you just speak?"

"Yes, I did. Nefe is not a witch. Witches don't keep large armies, and they don't go around raiding villages and torturing people. Witchcraft is just a disguise—a façade built to hide her true cause. She's not from this world. She is an alien. The three women you saw were not witches; they are all aliens. They call themselves Kshins."

Tej and Manika stole a quick glance. Kuntala had not only spoken after years of silence, but she was saying something which made little sense.

"Is she all right up here?" Tej whispered to Manika and pointed to his head.

Manika angrily signaled him to stay quiet. Although she had never seen Kuntala speaking she respected her. Not because Kuntala was a powerful time-reader, but because she had the guts to face Rigasur when no one else did. It was Kuntala's misfortune that she was the only person to do so and she paid a heavy price. For Manika, Kuntala was a lost legend.

Manika tried to make conversation. "Tell us more, Kuntala. These Kshins, I was not able to time-read them.

I tried multiple times."

"Not everybody can. They have some kind of sub-atomic quantum-veil around them. This veil prevents clairvoyants of any kind from experiencing them. And even if someone does manage to experience them, it can get very risky for the viewer."

"Risky?" Manika gulped. She had just enough trouble in her life. She wanted no more. Tej listened quietly to the two ladies.

"Manika, do you see the quantum-veil too?"

"Yes. Whenever I focus on them, I get a blank white wall staring at me. My vision can't get past it. This never happens when I time-read other people." Manika was relieved. If a time-reading legend such as Kuntala couldn't read these Kshins, then Manika stood no chance. "But you said it's risky to time-read them. Why?"

Kuntala took a deep breath, contemplating something. "Tell me something. Whenever you go to a time-vision, do the elements in there ever interact with you? Can people in a time-vision see you and talk to you?"

"No Kuntala. That has never happened. Guru Rigu—I mean Rigasur—taught us that time-visions are static. We are just looking at them as if we are looking at pictures. Neither we can alter their course, nor can they have any impact on us."

"The thing is, I can go past the Kshins' quantum-veil. I have done that before. I can time-read Kshins. But whenever I try to time-read them, they can see me."

Manika stiffened. Tej, too, shifted in his seat. This was unheard of.

Kuntala continued, "I went past the quantum-veil and saw their true face ten years back. And that is why Rigasur punished me. He tortured me, kept me in solitary confinement. He warned me if I tried to do that again, he would kill my whole family. He was working for the Kshins."

Tej and Manika looked at each other in shock. These Kshins were connected to Rigasur, too. It seemed that the root cause of all the darkness in their past, present, and future was tied in some way to these aliens.

"I will try to read them again. But I am not sure if I will come back from this vision alive."

"No, Kuntala. Please don't put your life in danger. We will find another way out." Manika didn't want to lose Kuntala. "Why don't you say something, Tej?"

"I … I mean yes, I will meet Rudrakshini Devi. She can be rude on the outside, but she is a kind-hearted person. She will definitely help us," Tej blurted out. He desperately wanted Kuntala to help him, but not by putting her own life at stake.

Kuntala smiled and looked at both of them affectionately. They were kind souls, which she was not used to. She softly touched Manika's face. "It's not about me, or you. The Kshins came looking for me because they know Rigasur is trapped. He was one of their pawns. Rigasur kept me alive because he had a selfish angle for time-readers. He was sure that I was of some use to him. But now that he's gone, the Kshins just want to tie up all the loose ends. And since I was able to read them ten years ago, they think of me as a potential threat."

"So? You will go and serve yourself to them on a platter? No."

"Manika, I don't know a lot about them, but one thing is clear. They are a technically advanced, superior race, and a darker evil than Kumbh or Rigasur. They will find me regardless—if not today, then tomorrow.

It's only a matter of time. I can't keep running like this. I will time-read them now. I will eavesdrop, try to keep a stealthy profile. Perhaps this time, they won't see me. And if I can gather some more intel about them, it can prove valuable to us."

Manika was still not convinced.

Kuntala looked at Tej. She stared into his eyes as if looking for something. "A lot of wrongs have been done to you. But all I see in your eyes is truth and mercy. I see in your eyes a hope which I could never cultivate within myself."

"I …" Tej fumbled. He did not know what to say to a direct compliment. "My only thought right now is, how do I get my village folk back to health? A lot of people are in pain."

Kuntala closed her eyes and after two seconds, opened them. "Nefe has used very old alien tech, an artificially designed virus, which has sent your village folk into nightmares. It's tied to her powers and is slowly corroding their bodies from within. She may have an antidote, though I am not sure."

Tej was speechless. How could he find that antidote? "We need more information, Kuntala-devi. If these aliens are our enemies, then we need to know more about them."

"I will get that information. But I want a promise from you, Tej."

"A-anything, Kuntala-devi." Tej stammered a little. *What is she going to ask for?*

Her eyes glittered with iron resolve. "Promise me you will not rest until you defeat these aliens. Promise me that you will take them down in the same way you defeated Kumbh and Rigasur." Years of suppressed anger was raring to come out, but she was in total control of her emotions.

Tej took time before he spoke his next words. By now, he had assessed how ruthless and formidable the enemy was. He decided that he would not say something for the sake of it. He was not going to make a light promise in the heat of the moment. "I will fight them with my life, Kuntala-devi. But with all due respect, I have seen their immense powers. I am only a speck of dust compared to these aliens. How can I even begin to think that I can fight and defeat these supernatural beings?"

"A small matchstick can burn a whole forest. One only needs the right kind of fuel. Be that matchstick, Tej."

Tej pressed his lips together. He had nothing but respect for this brave woman. She was about to enter a very evil place, knowing very well that the repercussions were most likely fatal. Yet in her eyes, he saw no fear, no dread.

Kuntala relaxed on the chair, closed her eyes, and started focusing.

2057 AD | Vedvance headquarters, Floor 217, Main Conference Room

At the same time in the year 2057, Vedika sat on one side of a long table, along with five of Vedvance's top executives.

"My possession of Vedika Sharma is complete. Her consciousness is somewhere in there, banging its head against the dark walls." Vedika chuckled. "I hope each of you has also acquired total control of your hosts. We are on one of the critical paths from next week. I want no slips. Clear?"

"Yes, Nefe!" all five of them spoke in unison as if replying to a military commander.

"Only one thing worries me—that time-crawler Mozakira. He knows a lot about us, and he's been out of grasp for a long time. I don't want any interference to the critical path."

"I will take this upon myself to track down Mozakira and finish him off," one of the executives said.

"All right, Jarna. You know what you are signing up for. I don't forgive losses."

"I know, Nefe. I won't disappoint you."

Nefe smiled at Jarna, and the expression on her face turned serious. A woman wearing a white saree was standing behind Jarna: Kuntala. Nefe had briefly seen her once, in her young age.

Nefe got up and walked to her. "Wow. After ten years, we meet again."

All of Nefe's executives got up. Kuntala tried to move, but her whole body stiffened.

"No, my dear. You cannot go anywhere now. You are completely under my control." Nefe went ahead and grasped Kuntala's neck. Kuntala's body started disappearing and re-appearing. She seemed to have stuck between both the time-slices as Nefe smothered her.

In 3057 BC, Kuntala's body was getting small jolts. Her eyes were closed, but her limbs were stiff. She struggled as if having a nightmare. Tej and Manika watched helplessly.

"Who the hell is she?" Jarna came forward and stood on Nefe's side.

"She is the clairvoyant we have been looking for: Rig's favorite time-reader, Kuntala." Nefe's gaze was dug into Kuntala's eyes. "We raided three villages for you, my dear. Killed a hell of a lot of humans. So much bloodshed, so much pain. I loved consuming all those cries and anguish. All that fear is now running through my veins." Nefe brought her face close to Kuntala and whispered, "Time to meet your creator, if there is one."

"Mo … Moza … Mozakira." Kuntala managed to speak one word as Nefe tightened her grasp. That was the only information she'd heard that made sense. She hoped that word reached Tej and Manika. Nefe strongly crushed her neck, pulverizing Atlas, Axis and other five cervical vertebrae. Kuntala disappeared.

Tej and Manika sat in shock. They had witnessed an invisible supernatural force murder Kuntala right before their eyes. But before she died, she had managed to say one word: "Mozakira."

Tej recalled that the strange voice from the car's radio also claimed to be Mozakira, a.k.a. Mozeek.

Tej got up, furious, feeling as if an electric charge was running through his body. He was reeling in anger at these Kshins. He had already seen Nefe's cruelties. He was raring to go to the future, find Mozeek, and get to the bottom of it.

He looked at Kuntala's body and mellowed out. He knew he would have to perform Kuntala's last rites. She deserved a proper funeral. "I'll get some wood." He walked out. Manika, traumatized, didn't even move a muscle.

7
KSHINS

23rd December 2057 AD, 4:45 PM |

New Los Angeles

A crowd of hundreds of people had gathered at JVK's Multi-Faith Center of Worship—an MFCW in short. The federal government created MFCWs for people who believed not in a single faith, but many religions and practices. The multi-faiths could come here and worship their gods, deities, or books in their own way. Spiritual atheists were also welcome to walk in and meditate.

That day's occasion was the funeral ceremony for a nineteen-year-old girl, Rosy. She'd died two hours before due to an overdose of blood pressure medicine. Her pale body lay in a golden casket, and people were arriving and paying their respects. Around one hundred of her family members, faith group buddies, and friends had gathered in the MFCW. Five hundred people attended the funeral via their virtual reality I.R.E. presence.

James Vasudev Khan, the co-founder and lead pastor

at JVK's MFCW, rose and climbed onto a small dais next to the casket. He bowed to the audience, then began to speak into a microphone.

"Oh, my dear friends. We are here to celebrate the future journey of one of our departed souls, Rosy. Rosy was born as Rosina Belthraz. She later converted to the multi-faith and called herself Rosina Belthraz Kyoning. She was a Catholic-Buddhist, and also observed ancient Indian pagan practices. Rosy, if you can hear us, I want to tell you that we are all very excited for your journey to the next life. If you can hear us, we …"

"I can." A loud voice resonated through the center of worship.

People gasped to see that Rosy was now sitting up in her casket. James also took a step back in fear. Rosy climbed out of the casket and started walking towards the seats, where people were sitting. She wore a light pink frock with floral designs. Her skin was pale white, her eyes were swollen, and she walked in a crooked fashion, like a zombie.

As she walked through the aisle, she caused a mini-ruckus as people started screaming and running. Folks sitting near the aisle panicked and tried to run towards the inner chairs. While some froze in their seats, others ran out of the MFCW. A small boy even fainted in his mother's lap. Some brave ones were live-streaming Rosy's dead-walk on their phones, tablets, and mobile-eye-lenses.

As Rosy reached the door of the center, her brother Wilkin mustered his courage. He sprinted towards the door and called out her name. He was stammering with fear. "R-Rosy, where are you going? You … you all right? Doctors declared you dead."

Rosy stopped walking and turned around. She looked at Wilkin, giving a blank stare. He froze. She spoke in a heavy voice. "My apologies. I will return her, in one piece. Please don't follow me."

"What?" Wilkin was baffled. Her last sentence was more of a stern warning.

Rosy turned back and kept walking.

Creexathon Sky-park, Los Angeles 05:15 PM

News that a girl had miraculously come back to life two hours after death had spread like wild-fire. More than four hundred news and radio channels were now broadcasting this news. Some sensationalist media outlets were calling her the "MFCW-Zombie-Killer".

She had boarded an A.I.-driven sky-taxi, which had dropped her at the entrance of Creexathon sky-park. Creexathon was located five kilometers up in the air. It was one of the well-known entertainment zones called sky-parks, which air-floated all around the year. People visited it for movies, games, coffee-shops, retail purchases, and similar things.

The security A.I. at the entrance of the sky-park had let the MFCW-zombie-killer in. Her fingerprints swiped at the main gate, Authorities scrambled a small police-task force. Their mission was to enter Creexathon and arrest this zombie. The sky-park and the shops were being evacuated.

Rosy was now moving towards the central coffee shop Blue-roast Café. People were scampering around her, running for their lives. The shop was very spacious but was largely empty now. She seated herself.

A humanoid-robot waiter came over and handed a digital-tablet to Rosy. It showed the menu card.

"Welcome Miss Kyoning. Shall I call you Rosina?"

"Call me Rosy."

"Noted, Rosy. May I recommend our maroon pink-roast with edible platinum marshmallows and dense cream? This drink won the 2056 Best Brew award."

"Can I get a glass of water, please, with ice?"

"Sure! Coming right away."

The robot turned and walked back towards the food counter. A man wearing a large cap and big black eye-glasses entered the café. The cap and glasses a hid a large part of his face. He wore a red shirt, a blue denim high-collared jacket, and matching trousers. He strode right up to Rosy's seat and joined her at the table.

"What the hell are you doing?" he whispered, trying to speak imperceptibly and keep his lips straight.

"Are you Mr. Mozeek?" Rosy asked, her facial expressions calm.

"Yes, I am." The man was Mozeek. He tried to repress his anger. Rosy's calm demeanor was irking him further.

"Great. You asked me to meet me here at 05:30 today."

"Yes, Tej, you were supposed to come here in a stealth mode. Not hijack a funeral, steal the body of a girl, and bring all the media attention and police forces here with you." Mozeek spoke in a single breath. He was fuming.

"But …"

"But what? Kshins are everywhere. They control most of the media houses, almost all the police. Their machine-learning algorithms keep looking at all camera feeds throughout the cities. They can detect one true anomalous incident among a thousand false ones. You were on their radar the moment you woke up on that casket, and people started streaming you live. How can you be so callous?"

"I'm sorry, Mr. Mozeek. This is the only dead body Manika could find close to this area and time. I can explain."

"Dead body? Why not take a live one?"

"I ... I can't."

"No point arguing about that. Let's exit this building." Mozeek got up.

The waiter-robot returned with a glass of water filled with ice. "Oh, Rosy. I see you have company." The robot then addressed Mozeek. "What can I get you, sir?"

"Nothing, get lost!" Mozeek almost shouted. The robot set the glass on the table and walked away.

Rosy sighed. "I don't know if it's this body or this era. I am feeling very tired."

"That is because you have possessed a dead body. Its brain is dead. Its movements, speech, and sense are completely driven by your time-demon energy. That's wearing you out." Mozeek pulled Rosy up by the arm and started walking as swiftly as he could. "You should always possess a live body. That body consumes its own pre-stored energy. Or at least a dead body which is not braindead. The brain can revitalize the organs and keep the biological systems moving."

As they reached the door, Mozeek froze. Police siren noises could be heard at a distance. Tej was rubbing his forehead. His eyes were drowsy. "What do we do now?"

"Now, we run. But we don't have time to exit the building. I didn't want their CCTV cameras to see this, but we have no choice." Mozeek took out two small bracelet-like devices from his jacket pocket. He strapped one of them onto Tej's right wrist. Then tied the other to his left wrist and pressed a button. A small black screen lit up on Mozeek's bracelet, and it started showing a countdown from thirty. The same countdown displayed on Tej's bracelet too.

"What are these?" Tej was intrigued.

"These are brain-to-brain synchronizers. These will sync the brains of our hosts within thirty seconds, and then I can take you out of here."

"Oh, like the demon invocation spell?"

"Yeah, very much like that. But far less messy. I hate all that powder and blood and necromancy paraphernalia."

"Cool, Mr. Mozeek. You are very resourceful." Tej was smiling as if drunk. His exhaustion had turned into intoxication.

The police sirens were louder now. Mozeek walked to the center of the café. Tej followed him like a robot. Fifty armed policemen came running in their direction and froze at the café gate. "Freeze! Hands in the air!"

Mozeek stopped at the center of the café and put his hands behind his head. Tej did the same. The device dials were reading 14, 13, 12.

Tej put his hands down and said, "Hey officer. Have I seen you somewhere?"

"Don't move, or I will shoot!" The policeman in the front hollered. He clasped his gun tightly. It was not every day that they were ordered to arrest a zombie.

8...7...

"Tej, don't do it!" Mozeek shouted, without moving an inch. Tej kept walking toward the police cordon.

4...3...

Tej took another step.

2...

Mozeek lunged toward Tej to stop him. Police opened fire. Hundreds of bullets slashed through their bodies, spurting blood. The police came and checked the bodies. Their dials were stuck at zero.

Mozeek's underground hide-out

Tej woke up in a hard but comfortable bed. He was in a small room which had dirty grey walls and a dim light fixed on the ceiling. There was no window and only one black door. Another empty bed beside his own sat on the right side. Two large computer screens were placed on a table to his left, along with three small cupboards.

He realized he was inside the body of a muscular man. He stood up and stumbled, but still felt weak. He walked up to a dusty mirror on the wall and cleaned it with his left hand. His host was a man in his early thirties with green eyes, a wide jaw, and light stubble. He had muscles of a bodybuilder. He wore nothing but tight black pants.

A door at his back opened, and another man walked in. Tej was shocked to see that the man was an exact twin of his host.

"You woke up so soon? That's earlier than expected," the man addressed him.

"Who are you?"

"I am Mozeek, you idiot."

"Why are we in the same body?"

"Same? Similar. These are clones. Blank-brain clones of abandoned super-soldiers."

Tej's face bore a puzzled look.

Mozeek sighed. "I'll answer all your questions. But

why did you have to pull off this stunt? You jeopardized both of us today. You ended up doing exactly what I didn't want you to do. You created so much attention with your arrival. Why?"

Tej knew there was no point going around with Mozeek on his hesitance with human possession. "The answer is simple. I would never possess a live body. That's the only rule I have. I spent my whole childhood under the repression of a tyrant. I would never repress another soul." Tej paused, but Mozeek sat quietly, listening. Tej was drowning in inexplicable guilt. "And who is this person I am possessing right now? I cannot find any memories inside this brain."

Mozeek sighed. He realized demonic possession meant a great deal to Tej. "Well, you are not possessing a live body, I can assure you that. In the mid-forties, several allied countries came together to fund a synthetic soldier program. A man named Rory Kruger, who was crowned Mr. World 2047, was chosen as a prototype for an ideal soldier. Six feet, eight inches tall, with muscular build: a top athlete. With the detailed scans of each tissue of his body, ten thousand replicas were 3D-printed. The properties of synthetic materials used to build these clones exactly matched the functions of the body. Using these, they created the skin, flesh, organs, bones and even the smallest of the veins. Each clone was given a fully functional but blank brain. It was a combined technological marvel of human anatomy studies, 3D-printing, and robotic tech. Rory-clone program was going to change the future of robotics."

"So, these are hosts something like robots," Tej interrupted. "Do they have any sentience?"

"No, they don't. Scientists planned to later insert an

A.I. into these blank brains. A few initial attempts were successful, too. Two of the Rory-clones were alive for a few months, which propelled mass production." Mozeek lit a cigarette and puffed out some fumes.

"I sense there is a 'but' coming." Tej waved his hand in the air to brush off the smoke.

"Yes, but the two clones degraded after some time. Although the brain was designed exactly like a human's brain it failed to accept any A.I. programs. The scientists failed at what biology does with ease. Seeing no progress for two years, the consortium of countries funding this program pulled the plug. These empty clones were abandoned. Ten thousand precious gems were left to rot in several factory yards around the US and Europe. Standing naked, open-eyed, staring into oblivion."

"Hmm." Tej felt relieved that he was not possessing a live body. "But why do you use these clones?"

"Three reasons: first, they are better vessels than human bodies. Humans are susceptible to ailments and wounds. Clones are not. Second, human brains have emotional baggage or trauma from death that you may have to deal with. Clones have none."

"And third?"

"I needed a regular supply of new vessels for human possession. I have been following Kshins for a long time, documenting their activities, characteristics, strengths, and weaknesses. Hence, I have to be in hiding forever. My vessels were getting destroyed in encounters with Kshins and their familiars.

"So, slowly, batch by batch, I kept stealing clones from an abandoned facility and hid them in a safe place. Now I have a few hundred. I keep possessing them and run around the world. If my current host gets destroyed,

I take a new one with ease and without guilt."

Tej smiled. He liked the fact that unlike Kumbh, Vetri, and Rigasur, Mozeek valued human life. In him, he found someone relatable.

Tej sat down on the bed. "I am sorry for all the ruckus I created, but I panicked and possessed the nearest body Manika could help me find. She's devastated, too. These Kshins, they are very cruel, Mr. Mozeek. They attacked my village, tortured the inhabitants, and kidnapped me. After you rescued me from time-prison, I went back to my village. A lot of village folk, including my father and my brother, are suffering from an alien virus."

"I know, Tej. Later, you went to Manika and Kuntala for help, but as I recall, Kuntala was killed."

"How do you know this, Mr. Mozeek?"

"I know this, Tej because I am different. I am a unique time-demon who is a time-reader too. I have both these powers."

"What?" Tej's mouth fell open.

"Yeah, we exist, the dual-power bearers. Though I have never met another like me, I have heard of them. This is why I'm famous." Mozeek grinned.

"You could have time-read me to find out." Tej returned the smile.

"I did try. But the previous few hours of lifeline until now had a Kshin-interruption. Kshins are the only species who can interact with us time-readers via our visions, which is very strange. You saw yourself how lethal it was for Kuntala. So I only chose to read selective portions of your life."

Tej winced. He could still not forget the sight of an invisible power crushing Kuntala's throat. Mozeek handed over a thick dossier of documents to Tej and asked him to read it. Tej sat down and turned a few pages.

On the spur of the moment, he looked up and asked, "I know you can time-read but how did you even know about me?"

"I saw a vision where you were searching for me. When I focused, I saw you inside that virtual reality. So, I hacked it, unplugged those guards torturing you, and sent Pablo to free you. You get on with studying about Kshins."

"Why these paper dossiers, Mr. Mozeek? This is 2057. I thought you would insert some kind of digital drive into my brain and upload all this information," Tej joked.

"Ha—I wish I could. Kshins have an army of hackers scouring the internet, and the deep-dark web. Nothing digital escapes their eyes. Any breadcrumbs we leave will lead them to this underground bunker."

Tej dug himself into the dossier, and Mozeek left. The dossier was full of pages and pages of text written in pen, as well as several cuttings from newspapers. In one of the section of the dossier, Tej saw hundreds of printouts of web articles written by someone called "The Last Kuleen. These articles had precise details on Kshins.

As per the writer, Kshins were a humanoid civilization which evolved thousands of years ago inside the relatively cold cavity of a dying star. They called their star Suryaksh, and hence they called themselves Suryakshins or Kshins. Over thousands of years of their existence, they made huge scientific advancements. Their specific focus was on their genetics and anatomical transformations—but they could never leave the cold cavity.

As Suryaksh destabilized and reached a pre-supernova stage, they had to find another home. But their anatomy was only accustomed to the cold environment of the cavity. Finding another such cavity in the galaxy had a very low probability. As a short-term solution, their scientists found a way for them to discard their physical bodies. They turned themselves into machine-generated entities with consciousness. They lived in another realm of existence, a digital reality, which the writer identified as XM-net.

All Kshins were connected to each other via XM-net, and being inside it gave them their telekinetic powers. When their spaceship landed on earth thousands of years ago, some of them ventured out of XM-net. The human body was an ideal vessel for possession.

There were a lot of technical details, diagrams, and mathematical calculations around XM-net. Tej could not understand everything, but he read on and skipped the science-rich parts. Later in the document, there was a section on Kuleens, too. But by the time Tej reached it, he had already dozed off in exhaustion.

After a few hours, Mozeek came back and saw Tej sleeping among his dossier files. He woke him up.

"I am sorry, Mr. Mozeek. I was tired."

"Nah, I know. The text isn't a very exciting read either."

"No, sir. You have done a commendable job. These details, data points, and observations are a gold-mine of data on Kshins."

"Good—I'm sure you grasped some of it. We need to move quickly. I have a plan, and if we succeed, then we stand a good chance in our fight against these aliens."

"Wait. I have a question. As per these documents, the Kshins are a race of super-beings. They are telekinetic, they can possess humans, and they can time-travel too, as we do?"

"No. They can't just jump from any time-slice to another. Their movements are restricted." Mozeek sat near Tej. "They have established a worm-hole bridge between 3050-ish BC and 2050-ish AD. Their span of time-travel is fairly limited around these years. They can't move freely through time as we do."

"Yeah, but they *can* time-travel."

"Tej, your point is?"

"My point is, how can we even think of making any plan for defeating such a formidable enemy? To me, it seems that they are invincible."

"But you took down Kumbh. Was he not much powerful than you were?"

"Yes, but I had Rigasur and an army of time-readers with me. Now all that is lost, too. And Kumbh was just one time-demon. Kshins, as you say, are an alien race born on distant stars. Hundreds of them roam around this world. It's not the same as taking down one time-demon, Mr. Mozeek."

Tej felt weak in his gut. He missed his old, uncomplicated life. After Kumbh was captured he thought he could just go back to his village life, and occasionally visit other time-slices for fun. But that was not what the universe had planned for him.

Mozeek took a deep breath, "You may feel intimidated now, Tej, but remember what Kuntala said. A small matchstick can burn a whole forest. Be that matchstick."

Tej froze. Kuntala had sacrificed her life just so he could learn more about what the Kshins were. His anger and hatred for Kshins were invigorated.

"All right, Mr. Mozeek. I'm with you."

"That's more like it, my man. Addressing the point about their supremacy—their powers are not enough for them to rule this world. That's why they have possessed people in authoritative roles. Politicians, police generals, media magnates, mafia bosses, drug cartel kingpins, hacking organization leaders. Kshins have acquired many influential positions throughout the world. But there is one pattern which has caught my eye."

"What is that?"

"They have existed on this planet for thousands of years, and for most of their time here, they lay dormant. But their rate of human possessions has increased only since the late 1980s—which means they are planning something big. And my gut feeling is that something big is around the corner."

"Interesting," Tej spoke to himself. "One more question. I read many articles written by someone called *The Last Kuleen*. Who is that person?"

Mozeek smiled. "Kuleens are a different species. They are the only people Kshins are afraid of. They are the only reason I see some light in our dark fight against Kshins. You will know more when you meet Pete Morales, the Last Kuleen. In fact, you and I together are going to rescue him from a Kshin stronghold. He is mankind's last hope against these alien bastards. Three days later, on 26th December 2057, this world will experience a total solar eclipse. That's when we hit."

"Okay? How does that help us?"

"That day, we cut off the head of this serpent. That day we kill Nefe!"

Something in Mozeek's eyes told Tej that the man

knew what he was doing. Tej believed that a man with a plan was a dangerous weapon, and he could see one in front of him. "All right. What's the plan?"

"All in good time, Tej. But first, we need to enter the inferno and find Pete Morales."

8
KULEENS

24ᵗʰ December 2057 AD, 03:00 AM

Two hundred km outside New Los Angeles, Tej helped Mozeek set up a huge piece of equipment in the middle of an abandoned football stadium. Mozeek had soldered several metal poles one after the other to create a fifty-foot-long metal pole. He was now trying to position it at a forty-five-degree angle to the ground by adding supports. After erecting the pole at that angle, Mozeek wrapped a barbed metal wire around it. He also placed a large, round disk-antenna on the top end of the pole, which was now facing the sky.

Mozeek used his rocket-powered shoes to fly around and make adjustments while Tej helped from the ground. After they completed the setup, Mozeek and Tej sat on chairs nearby and sipped hot coffee under the starlight.

"This metallic monument is impressive, Mr. Mozeek." Tej looked up at the extent of the metal structure.

Mozeek almost spat his coffee out. "This is not a monument, Tej. This is the world's biggest wi-fi receptor. This will pull wifi signals from several major city districts nearby. It will even tap into the wifi signal sent out by the geostationary satellite right on top of us. I am planning to hack into Kshin-network. I would need the bandwidth of at least five Petabytes per second for the entire three minutes. This receptor will make sure I get that."

"But if you hack into their networks, won't they get to know our location?"

"They'll detect me within thirty seconds. I will further delay them by thirty more, after which they will know my exact location. But even with their fastest choppers, they will take at least two minutes for them to reach this place. So that gives us exactly three minutes."

"Us? Where do I fit in here?"

"All in good time, Tej. But first, you must take up another body. I will help you find it."

Half an hour later, Tej was sitting on a self-driven bus en route to a suburb outside Los Angeles. He was now inside the body of a forty-five-year-old homeless man who'd died half an hour ago due to low blood sugar. The vessel had a frail body and wore shabby clothes. He had a big beard and wrinkly spotted skin. Mozeek assured him that this attire was well-suited for the mission he was about to undertake.

As per Mozeek's instructions, Tej was to show up at Vedvance MHL center at 08:00 AM and sign up as a mental health patient. There was usually a long line to get inside; hence Mozeek advised Tej to be at the premises at 05:00 AM.

Everything went according to plan. At 08:15 AM, Tej signed up as a mental health patient. He was asked to change into an orange gown, after which he underwent a full body checkup. The machine identified him as Rob Muffley. As per Mozeek, this MHL center was a fake cover for a Kshin operation to capture humans for a virtual reality program called Infernex 2.0.

All the people who showed up for free mental health treatment were plugged into Infernex 2.0. They were subject to virtual simulations of mental-trauma while Kshin scientists monitored their brain activity. Mozeek was not sure why Kshins were doing this, but he knew that Pete Morales was kept deep inside Infernex 2.0. In a way, Tej was going undercover to find and extract Pete.

Soon after his medical checkup, the personnel gave Tej strong tranquilizers. He struggled to stay awake but fell unconscious.

Infernex, Circle 1: The Accident

Tej woke up at a beach. He wore a yellow flowery shirt, a large jute hat, and red shorts. The sun was shining overhead; kids were playing beach volleyball. Several men and women were tanning their skin and sipping ice-cold cocktails. Tej realized that he was now inside the Circle 1 of Infernex. This was exactly what Mozeek told him. He would have to cross Circle 1 and Circle 2 because Pete Morales was captive inside the Circle 3.

Tej started walking on the beach and felt the softness of wet sand beneath his feet. He got down and picked up some sand in his hands. It felt grainy and wet. Whoever had designed this real experience had worked very hard to get the smallest of the details accurate.

"Hello, Mr. Muffley. Can I get you some drinks?"

Tej turned around to see a young waitress smiling at

him. She was a slender girl in her early twenties wearing a green bikini and a matching short skirt. She had several menu-cards and an empty white tray in her hands.

"Your best cocktail, please."

"All right, sir, coming up right away."

Tej nodded. The waitress went away. The A.I. had identified him as Rob Muffley, his current vessel. He kept walking.

Mozeek did not tell him what would happen or how he would cross over to the Circle 2. He only iterated his pet-dialogue. "All in good time, Tej."

He hated when Mozeek said that. He didn't like to be kept in dark.

But Mozeek emphasized that it was important for him to know only certain parts. If Tej knew what was going to happen in this circle, he would behave differently than the others. The Infernex A.I. would identify him as an anomaly, and he would never make it to the next circle. Mozeek's only advice to reach Circle Two was, 'keep your emotions in check.' The Infernex A.I. was very sensitive to even small changes in his emotions.

As he walked a little further, he saw a couple making out. He was reminded of Manu Kumar. His heart ached with longing. He missed the touch of Manu's soft hands, and his innocuous, jovial smile. In this world full of darkness, Manu was his only light. But he was now very far away. Tej curbed his tears and kept walking.

At a distance, he saw several people gathering and gazing at the sea. Something was wrong. They were all pointing at an object in the sky. As Tej went near them, he saw what they saw. A few kilometers above the sea, some bright dots were sparkling in the sky.

"Daddy, are they U.F.O.s?" an eight-year-old girl asked

her father, who picked her up.

"No, kiddo, I don't know what they are." Her father was equally flummoxed.

The dots were getting bigger in size. Someone screamed, "Missiles! They're missiles! It's a nuclear attack!" There was a sudden stampede on the beach as people started looking for their kids and families.

Tej froze among the chaos. This was virtual reality. But the people around him, were they mere computer avatars, or were they real people plugged into Infernex like he was? He couldn't know for sure. He decided to help people out. One lady, who was running and carrying her two girls, was struggling to have her ten-year-old son keep up with her. Tej picked up her son and started running with her.

The sparking dots were now clearly visible. Indeed, they were long missiles flying toward the beach, their altitude decreasing as they approached. Their heads and wings were deep red, and their bodies were shining black.

The missiles came and hit the shore, but nothing happened. They dove right into the sand. The people running around noticed that. Some of them kept running, but some others stopped. The chaos on the beach settled down. Tej and the lady he was running with also stopped and looked at what was happening.

Some brave men went close to the missiles.

"They are hollow shells!" one of them yelled.

"Yeah, they're blanks," another person added.

The confusion continued for a few seconds. After that, small slots started opening in the missiles, and swathes of small red spiders began creeping out of those slots. The spiders walked rapidly and first attacked those standing nearby. The people again panicked and started running, but the spiders were too swift.

Tej realized what was happening here. This was a test of courage and fear—not only his fear but the fear of all those who were plugged inside the Circle 1. He let go of the woman's kid, sat down on the ground, and closed his eyes.

"What are you doing, mister! Help me? Please?" the woman pleaded to Tej for a few seconds, and then she had no choice but to run. She made it only a few paces before the spiders took her down.

Several spiders climbed Tej's body, bit him, crawled on his skin, under his clothes, and entered his ears and mouth. He could taste them in his mouth, feel their limbs wiggling in his ears. He finally felt the fear, even panicked, but controlled his emotions until he went unconscious.

Infernex, Circle 2: The Nightmare

Tej opened his eyes. This time, he was standing on the edge of a cliff. This was a familiar setting. He recognized it as the cliff near his village, Sarp-Nagar. The cliff edge was around a hundred feet long, and the valley below was at least two miles deep.

Tej looked at his body and his attire. It was the same as the garb he wore back in his village, with very small nuances. The Infernex A.I. had gone deeper this time, and actually identified him as Tej. His own brain patterns were now impacting his vessel's brain patterns. Mozeek told him that Circle Two was called "The Nightmare." Tej braced himself for another test of his fear when he heard a scream.

He turned around to see Kumbh standing on the other edge of the cliff, along with his mother Dhara. Kumbh was in his old vessel, the one he remembered from his childhood. His mother also looked younger. The A.I. had re-created them just as he remembered them from his childhood. Kumbh was clutching Dhara by her hair, and she was screaming for help.

Tej could feel the goosebumps and his anger rising. His thirst for revenge from Kumbh was never sated. He took a step towards them when Kumbh thundered, "One more step, Tej, and I will throw her down." Kumbh leaned towards the cliff.

"No!" Tej screamed. "What do you want?"

"I want you to suffer, Tej." Kumbh smiled. His blood-stained teeth peeled through those ravenous black lips—the same smile that had haunted Tej for so long.

Tej knew this was a fake reality, a test. But how could he let Kumbh torture her again? This was indeed his worst nightmare. Tej hated Kshins all the more now. *Is everyone plugged into Infernex having their worst nightmares? What do Kshins gain out of this?*

Tej repressed his thoughts, questions, and instincts. "Do whatever you want, Kumbh."

Kumbh drew a knife from his belt and grinned. "Are you sure, boy?"

"Yes."

Kumbh slashed Dhara's throat and threw her down the cliff.

Tej shut his eyes tightly and collapsed on the ground. He was trying to keep his emotions in check, but a tear rolled down his left cheek. He took several deep breaths, after which he went unconscious.

This time, Tej woke up in the body of his vessel, Rob Muffely. He was out of the Infernex and was lying on a bed-with-wheels, which was slowly moving on a track. His vision was hazy, but he could see the intravenous drip inserted at the back of his left hand.

Mozeek told him that as the subjects crossed from an outer circle to the inner circle, they were physically moved by the AI using automated machinery. The chambers that housed patients from each circle were different. Mozeek knew that Pete Morales was kept along with other Circle 3 subjects, and that was where Tej hoped he was being taken.

Tej looked around and saw that his bed was in a series of several beds slowly moving along that track. He felt the liquid inside his drip was entering his body at a faster speed. He dozed off again.

Infernex, Circle 3: The Unknown

Tej woke up, but could not see or hear anything. He tried moving his hands and feet to get up, but he was confined to a dark, constrained space—inside a box with hard walls all around. His hands and legs were tied, as if with iron shackles, and his mouth was gagged. He felt a soft snake-like thing moving on his left leg, and then one on his right.

Have I been thrown in a dark box full of snakes? The snakes can't harm me, he thought and tried to relax. A swarm of ants began biting his feet. This was an eerie feeling. Tej shivered and tried to move his feet, but the bites intensified. The snakes, too, were sliding around his legs, moving towards his groin area. Tej panicked. But the next instant, all those feelings disappeared. Tej let out a sigh of relief.

There was an uncanny silence for a few seconds, after

which he felt that the surface beneath his back getting warm, and the surface behind his head getting cold. The intensity of cold and heat kept increasing until it became unbearable. He wanted to scream, but he couldn't. After a few seconds, the heat and cold went away.

Tej tried to relax and stay strong, but the feeling of being tied and gagged in a dark constrained box was inescapable.

He again felt the snakes on his legs and ants on his feet. He also heard a movement behind his head—perhaps a rodent was trying to sniff his hair. Tej was feeling a strange mix of suffocated and creeped out. Snakes were sliding on his legs and moving towards his groin area; the rodent was clawing on his head. The surface behind his back again started getting hot. He shook vigorously to shrug off these animals, but he couldn't.

He decided to move out of this body. He couldn't take it anymore. The strange pain Infernex A.I. was putting him through was unbearable. Through the darkness, the helplessness and through these animals, the A.I. was testing the limits of his fear of the unknown. As he decided to move out, he felt the guzzle of liquid in his left vein, and he woke up.

He was back in Muffley's body and was sitting on the same bed. He was sweating profusely, and his heartbeat was fast. He immediately checked his legs and feet for snake and ant bites, but there were none. It was another virtual reality nightmare.

He looked around. The room was small and had a few other beds with patients. He counted, and there were nine other beds.

He heard a crackling human voice. "Tej, are you all right?" The sound came from a console panel on the wall. Tej got up with difficulty and walked to the console. His legs felt weak.

"Say something, Tej. I have hacked their systems. We have less than three minutes now." The console crackled again.

"Yes, yes I am fine." Tej recognized Mozeek's voice.

"Great. You were given some real hard tranquilizers, I gave you an adrenaline dose, and was going to give you another. Now you need to act quickly. You should be in the room where all the Circle 3 subjects are kept. Pete Morales will be one of these. You have seen his pic. Search for him and tell me his bed number."

Mozeek had told him that people who signed up at MHL-center were divided into batches of a thousand. Each batch of a thousand was kept together and plugged into Circle 1, the outermost circle. Only a hundred top performers who handled the pain the best were chosen for Circle 2 and only ten for Circle 3. Those ten subjects were all there in this room including him.

Tej started going through all the beds and found Pete Morales lying on one. He was a man in his late forties with a balding head, a grayish-white beard, and several scars on his left cheek. He wore the same gown as Tej and had a similar intravenous drip going into his veins.

"I found him. His bed number says 10304," Tej spoke.

"Great. Here you go."

Tej heard Mozeek typing on his keyboard. He saw a liquid entering Pete's veins, and within two seconds, Pete woke up with a deep breath.

"He is up now, Tej. Kshins have already detected a breach, and their hackers are trying to find me out. They will detect me within a few seconds, and Kshins' police force will reach me within two minutes. Go out of this room. Take a left, and you will find a lift. Pablo will guide you from there. I will meet you at our rendezvous point."

"Which rendezvous point, Mr. Mozeek?"

"Pablo will take you there." The console went dead.

"What the hell?" Tej murmured.

"Who are you? Where am I?" Pete asked him.

"No time for this, Mr. Morales. You need to come with me. I am here to rescue you."

Pete nodded and got up from his bed. Owing to the adrenaline shot, he was feeling energetic.

They both rushed out of the room and stepped into the gallery. There were several other rooms in the gallery. Tej saw a lift at the end of the gallery-way and ran and pressed the button.

"Welcome, sir. Pablo reporting." a mechanical voice emanated from the speaker inside the lift.

Tej felt relieved to hear Pablo's familiar mechanical voice. He rushed Pete into the lift and the doors closed behind them.

"We are in your hands, Pablo. Get us out," Tej said.

"Certainly, sir." The lift started going up with a high velocity. "You were fifty floors underground, sir. I am taking you to Basement 10, where we have a car waiting that shall be our transport out of here."

"The same green car?" Tej joked. He realized he had been through Hell, but he had immense faith in Pablo's extraction capabilities. With Pablo, he felt safe.

"Yes, sir. But I am afraid our adversaries have detected the breach, as well as my presence. So please be ready for a rough ride."

The lift came to a sudden halt. They paced out of the lift into the parking lot. They had taken just a few steps when a blaring alarm echoed through the whole building.

Tej heard car tires screech and saw a stylish designer green-colored car zooming towards them. The car stopped near them with a sharp halt, and the doors opened. There was no driver inside.

"Hop in, Mr. Tej and Mr. Pete." The car dashboard buzzed.

They got in the car, and it sped off onto a circular ramp from Basement 10 to Basement 9, and so on and so forth. The basement had boom-barriers installed to prevent vehicular movement, but the barriers opened automatically as the car passed through them. Pablo was hacking through them.

Twenty guard robots were stationed outside the basement gate in attack stances when the green car whooshed past them like a rocket. They opened fire at the car with their automatic weapons, but it sped off on the road.

"Well done, Pablo," Tej chuckled. He saw that they were speeding out on the stylish brick road of the Vedvance MHL center where he'd signed up.

"Wasn't this too easy?" Pete murmured and looked at Tej. "But I must thank you and Pablo."

"It's Pablo all the way." Tej smiled. He wanted to tell Pete to thank Mr. Mozeek for all this, but Mozeek had sternly warned him to not disclose his identity to Pablo as yet. He explained that since he had been scheming against Kshins, they had spread false information around him being their own agent. And Pablo, being a Kuleen, hated everything marked Kshin.

Vedika sat on a sofa, filing her nails, when her six-year-old daughter Jess came running, followed by her nanny

Naaz. Jess had tears in her eyes. She tried to hug Vedika, but she gestured for her to stay away.

"Careful, kid. You won't want to ruin my dress."

"Mom Ved, where did Mom Ruby go? No one is telling me."

"She's dead, kid. She's never coming back."

Jess stood silent, crying.

Naaz was appalled at her cruel behavior with the kid. She had seen visible changes in Vedika's behavior, but this was reprehensible. She was not only avoiding the child but was being too cold to her.

"Mom, Naaz told me that you are sending me to a private school. I don't want to go."

"You have to go, kid. Mom has to do a lot of important stuff. I can't have you running around here."

"I DON'T want to go!" Jess screamed.

Nefe got up and clutched Jess by her shoulders. The kid gulped. "You listen to me, girl. I don't like anyone screaming around me. You go to bed right now and learn to be disciplined. You are going where I am sending you. Period. I don't want to hear another word."

Jess started sobbing. Nefe signaled for Naaz to take her inside. "Kids, I hate them," she murmured. Naaz and Jess walked away.

"Nefe, are you there?" She heard Jarna's voice via XM-net in her head.

"Yes, I am."

"Morales has escaped with Tej."

"Track them and keep me updated."

"I will."

"Let's wrap this up today. Eclipse is near."

"Noted."

9
CONSPIRER

The green car carrying Pete and Tej raced on the track, further away from the Vedvance MHL center building. The sun was on its way to set beyond the horizon.

"Sir, Mr. Morales. Sorry I didn't introduce myself earlier. My name is Tej."

"That's fine, young man. You saved my life, so I owe you a big thanks. And you can call me Pete."

"How do you know I am young?" Tej was amused. He was inside the body of an old man.

"I am a Kuleen. We are all empaths with extrasensory perception. That's how we can detect the presence of Kshins. The moment you woke me up in there, I read your mind. You are a young man, not more than thirty. You are not even human—you are a time-demon."

Tej was taken aback. Mozeek was right about them. Kuleens came with their own set of powers. In this fight against Kshins, they were a weapon to be reckoned with.

Pete continued, "If you time-demons and we Kuleens come together, we can take down the Kshins once and for all." Pete was gauging Tej's reactions and trying to perceive his thoughts.

Tej was cautious. "I agree, Mr. Morales—I mean, Pete. We need to work together."

Pete was reading Tej's ambivalent stream of thoughts. "You may-be a time-demon, but you are a benevolent soul. I can sense that mercy and honesty in you. Your superpower is not time travel or human possession. Your superpower is your ability to take in a lot of negativity and still do good for this world."

Pete paused and looked towards the sky. "But that is not the case with others from your species. Don't get me wrong, but time-demons are tyrants, no different from Kshins. The only difference is that time-demons are largely lone wolves, and Kshins live and die in a pack. Either way, we Kuleens will never ally with those who oppress others."

"Pete, my experience with other time demons is no different." Tej could empathize with what Pete was saying. Kumbh, Vetri, and Rigasur all fitted Pete's assessment. Tej looked in the rear-view mirror and noticed that a few cars were pursuing them.

"Someone's chasing us, Pablo."

"I noticed that, sir."

"You still don't have any weapons in here, do you?"

"No, sir. But I have something better."

A machine whirred right behind where Tej and Pablo were sitting. A thick metal rod started to emerge vertically. The roof of the car detached from the front glass and started going back. The rod grew up to around fifteen feet, and then the top half of the rod broke into three rotors. A small vertical rotator also emerged at the back of the car.

"Wow, a full heli-convertible?" Pete exclaimed. The

car was fitted with a helicopter gyro and could take flights as well.

"Yes, sir. Please sit straight." Pablo cautioned, "We will start our ascent in fifteen seconds."

Pete sat straight on his seat and asked Tej to do the same. As soon as they did that, an automated seat belt clasped them into their chairs.

The cars chasing them were getting near. One of those cars was leading the pack. Two robots brought out their torsos from that car and aimed their weapons towards them.

The rotors on the green car started rotating and reached max rpm within three seconds.

Pablo started the countdown. "Ascent in 5 … 4 … 3 … 2 … Go."

The green car was no longer touching the road—it was flying. Tej sat with his breath stuck in his gut. He was afraid enough of normal airplane flights, and now he was in an open-roofed flying car. They did hear some gunfire, but they were out of range within five seconds.

Pete asked Tej to look down and observe the buildings, parks, and skyscrapers from the top. Tej declined.

"Where are we going, Pablo?" Pete asked.

"Sir, I have been instructed to take you to a discreet location. The coordinates have been pre-configured in me, and I am flying to that location."

"Where are we going, Tej?" Pete asked Tej, who was speechless. He himself did not know. *Mozeek only mentioned a rendezvous point, but where is that point? Is this the right time to tell Pete about Mozeek?*

Before Tej could speak, Pete said, "It's all right. I know where I need to go. Pablo, turn over to the *Gribana Queen* Fresh-Brew Pub on 52nd and 3rd, please. We will get a safe refuge there."

"But sir, I was instructed to take you to a specified location."

"Pablo do as Mr. Morales is saying. After he visits this location, we will go to our location," Tej intervened. He did not want the conversation to go in the direction of Mozeek. He preferred that Mozeek reveal his identity to Morales himself, in person.

"But sir …"

"DO it, Pablo!" Tej raised his voice.

"Ok, sir. Changing location coordinates, re-routing." The car took a sharp tilt and turned toward the north-west direction.

"You should not be addressing A.I. like this. Their feelings are hurt." Pete smiled. As an empath, any aggressive behavior pinched him harder than others.

"But it's an A.I., a computer. It does not have feelings."

"A.I. is modeled in our image. It's built to think like us, and as a result, it feels like we do. It's not without feelings."

Tej felt guilty. He'd never thought about A.I. this way. His larger knowledge about A.I. was from the year 2024, and the A.I. of that age was quite rudimentary.

"Pablo, I apologize for my outburst a few seconds back." Tej did the right thing and was relieved.

"It's all right, sir."

"Tell me more about Kuleens, Mr. Morales." Tej was curious to know more about Kuleens. He was hopeful that he could join their fight against Kshins, get rid of Nefe, and cure his village of the disease. The Kuleens were a bright ray of hope.

Pete had a delightful smile on his face. In a world

where he was constantly in hiding, he rarely had a chance to tell someone about himself and his race. "Well, we Kuleens are humans with some special powers. We are strong empaths, but if required, we can even control brains. We can sense the presence of Kshins around us. And as a bonus, Kshins' telekinetic abilities are weakened in our vicinity. Consider us Kuleens a natural antibody response this planet has against Kshins."

Tej was nodding and listening with keen interest. He was also trying to divert his attention from the mild turbulence the car was experiencing as it tore through the wind columns. This travel was making him queasy.

Pete, on the other hand, was engrossed in his own narration. "Some Kuleens started developing our powers more than a hundred years back. I remember the date, too. On June 8th, 1937, the world saw a major solar eclipse. Somewhere around August 1937, we find the first mention of Kuleens."

"What's the connection with solar eclipse?"

"Solar eclipses impact both Kshins and Kuleens in exactly opposite ways. A solar eclipse strengthens us Kuleens but weakens the Kshins. We learned this around forty years back, when we organized in large groups and started studying Kshins. Our intelligence observed that humans possessed by Kshins behaved oddly on solar eclipse days, a trend which has continued to date. They do not make any public appearances or big announcements on solar eclipse days. No major Kshin activity or operation has ever been planned around a solar eclipse. I will tell you much more when we reach our destination."

After a few minutes, the car was now descending towards a building which had an aero-vehicle pad on top for it to land. Since the advent of flying cars, most of the buildings had aero-vehicle pads. These pads not only supported the landing of flight-enabled cars, but also very lightweight helicopters.

Tej was relieved when the car landed on top of the building and he could put his feet on the ground again. They alighted the car and walked towards the staircase. Two burly men stood guard with semi-automatic weapons in their hands.

Pete showed them a mark on his right wrist, which they scanned with a small machine, and the scanner lit green.

"Welcome, Mr. Morales. You can go in."

Tej also tried to tailgate Pete but was stopped by the men. One of them picked up a thick black rod and scanned Tej's body. The top part of the scanner lit yellow.

"Guys, he is with me." Pete grinned.

"But he is neither human nor a Kuleen. We are not allowed to let 'Yellows' in."

"He saved my life, folks."

"Rules are rules, sir. We are on Defense Mode 5C. Especially after you and several other Kuleens were picked up from the streets."

"Can I please talk to Beth?" Pete was furious. He never liked these enforced security rings. He got on a call with a lady called Beth and argued with her for a couple of minutes. After that, the guards received new orders, and they allowed Tej to go in.

"I really had to fight for this one, but I have a special equation with Beth." Pete winked.

They got into an elevator which had no buttons. The

elevator plowed down for a few seconds and opened in a very loud discotheque. A DJ was playing punk rock, and several people were dancing to the tunes. Pete led the way and Tej followed him until they reached a door which said "washroom."

"After you!" Pete said. Tej felt weird but entered the door.

It was a spacious washroom, albeit in a very bad condition. The urinals were broken, tiles were scarred with stains, and washbasins were leaking. Even the lights on the roof were flickering.

Pete went to the end of the bathroom, where a man-sized mirror six feet long and one foot wide was affixed on the wall. To Tej's horror, Pete inserted his hand inside the mirror. The glass surface developed a wave-like dispersion as if it was a liquid. Tej had never seen anything like that. Pete kept moving inside the mirror and disappeared. The glass surface wavered for two seconds, then came to a standstill. It looked like a spotless, normal mirror again.

Tej mustered up the courage and walked near the mirror when Pete stuck his head out of the mirror and startled him.

"Come on, buddy, what are you waiting for? This is femto-pixelated gel. Doesn't bite. Come on in."

Tej took a deep breath and first inserted his fingertip into the mirror. It felt cold. Tej saw that the surface of the glassy liquid was not touching him, but was giving space to him to enter. He took Lord Shiva's name and inserted his whole hand. He pulled back his hand and inspected it. It was still the same. *No way am I putting my head through this gel*, he thought.

He again squeezed his arm through it, but this time,

Pete pulled him from the other side. Tej too disappeared inside the mirror. He turned back to see a similar mirror on the wall on the other side. They now stood in a dark rectangular room with green lighting on the roof.

"Is it some kind of a portal to another world, Mr. Morales?"

"Portal? No." Pete chuckled on Tej's innocuous question. "The glass we came through is right on the other side of this wall. This mirror is actually a door, hiding in plain sight. But philosophically speaking, yes, it is another world which I am taking you into. You will see." Pete laughed again.

On the other end of the room was a door behind which stood an elevator. As Pete and Tej walked towards it, the elevator doors opened, and a robotic voice welcomed them.

"Level five-nine, please." Pete entered the elevator, and Tej followed him. The doors closed, and they started moving downwards at a fast pace.

The doors opened, and they entered a huge, well-lit office space. Hundreds of people were busily working on their computers. Laptops, cupboards, files, and papers.

Pete walked a few steps inside, turned around, and spread his arms to his side. "This, Tej, is our underground office. Our Los Angeles headquarter, the second-largest Kuleen stronghold in the whole United States. Let's meet Beth."

Pete led Tej through a narrow aisle between the desks and cubicles, towards a large brown door at the end. Tej observed people working on their systems, some frantically typing on their keyboards. Some were arguing with each other, and some others were sketching on whiteboards while discussing.

"Who are these people? What are they doing?"

"These people are all Kuleens. The day after tomorrow is the solar eclipse. Our teams are planning three high-profile assassination attempts on Kshin targets tomorrow, hitting them at their weakest points. Our on-ground folks are gathering intel on a major initiative that Kshins are planning. We don't exactly know what it is, but the scale of it would be global. We are calling it Operation X."

"So this your base of operations?" Tej was fascinated with the scale at which Kuleens were operating.

"One of the bases." Pete looked at Tej with pride in his eyes as they kept walking. "Kuleens all over the world have organized themselves against the silent Kshin invasion of our world. This office is just one glimpse of it."

They reached the end of the aisle where one receptionist greeted them. "Long time, Pete."

"Long time, Rebecca." He and Rebecca touched their cheeks as a greeting. Pete was joyous to be among his people again.

"Nice dress, by the way." Rebecca winked.

Pete looked shabby in his MH Labs attire and stretched his arms out as he posed for her. "Kshins gave it to me. Gotta love it. *Sin Quejas*. Listen, can we meet Beth?"

"Yes. Please wait in the Meeting room 5. Ms. Bethany is in an urgent briefing; she will see you shortly."

"Come on, Tej. We will sit and chat while Bethany wraps up her stuff."

Pete and Tej had been sitting in a small meeting room for two hours now. The room had a large grey metal table at the center, with color-matching metal chairs kept around it. There was a sixty-inch long TV screen mounted on one of the walls. The TV displayed a map of the entire world, with several red dots scattered around.

"All the red dots you see on this map are the cities where Kshins hold major positions of influence."

Tej was curious, yet slightly intimidated by this whole setup. His confidence in the Kuleens was strengthened. They were not a bunch of disorderly street rebels but comprised a powerful and organized effort against Kshins. "You said something about Operation X. What is that, Mr. Morales?"

"No. I have been speaking a lot ever since we met. Now you tell me, how much do you know about Kshins, Tej? And how did you get into their crosshairs?"

"Well, they are telekinetic, they can possess humans, and they can even time-travel. They are not from this world. And they are cruelest species I have ever encountered. That's the extent of my knowledge." Tej paused. "One of the Kshins, Nefe, attacked my village back in three thousand BC, where I am from. She tortured many of my village people, took me hostage, and tortured me for some information."

A grim expression floated on Pete's face. His eyes were wet as he felt Tej's pain.

"Whomever these Kshins are, Mr. Morales, they are no different from the tyrants I have encountered in the past. Now, several villagers, including some of my close relatives, are under Nefe's spell, caught up in some strange fever." Tej could feel a lump in his throat. Pete was also in tears listening to him, deeply feeling his pain and anger.

Pete wiped his tears. "Do you know that Kshins devour human emotions?"

"What does that even mean?" That had not been mentioned anywhere in the dossier which Mozeek shared with Tej.

"Kshins ceased existing in the physical world, and stay mostly in another plane of existence, the XM-Net. Their nutrition can't come from the resources of this world. Their food is human emotions, especially negative ones. Frustration, irritation, anger, jealousy, and their favorite is 'pain.'"

"I ... I don't think I follow, Mr. Morales. Thoughts and emotions are not tangible entities, as far as I know. How can they consume them?"

"It is a strange fact, but it's true. It's very similar to the concept of aura or bodily radiation. Every human body emits radiation. The intensity and type of radiation are different for different people, and changes with changing moods. Since Kshins were original inhabitants of a star called ..."

"Suryaksh?" Tej cut him off.

"Yes—I see you have done some research of your own. On Suryaksh, they were accustomed to consuming huge amounts of radiation. After they moved their consciousness to XM-Net, this radiation was their only source of nutrition and strength."

"But my question is, how can you even think of defeating such powerful entities? With all due respect to your setup here, what possible weapon can you build to combat such a nemesis?"

"We can't just give up." Pete smiled. "We humans have built a lot of technology. And most of it is weapons which we've used to kill each other. But for the first time in history, a lot of us humans have gotten together with a single aim: to defeat Kshins. And we Kuleens are bearing this burden because most of the humans are not even aware of the presence of Kshins. These silent invaders have kept their conquest tightly under wraps. Why tell them that you rule them? Rule them from behind democratic institutions and parallel economies."

Tej nodded. "Coming back to my question, what sword or gun or bomb could kill something which is just a consciousness?"

"Consciousness is matter, too. Even the light is made of photons. It's matter." Pete got up, picked up a marker, and went to a whiteboard fixed on the opposite wall. "Anything which exhibits itself has to be some kind of representation of sub-atomic particles." He drew a complicated diagram on the board, which looked like atomic fusion. Tej had no idea what it was. "I am, in fact, leading a team of seven quantum physicists who have successfully tested bombs based on Zason particle technology. The Zason is a more stabilized version of the Higgs-Boson, the God particle. This particle dictates the way matter is created or destroyed."

"I think I need coffee." Tej rubbed his forehead. He needed to do a pre-dead-brain-feeding from a quantum physicist to understand these concepts.

Pete chuckled. "Okay. I won't bore you with the science, but let me show you something." Pete got up and spread out his palms, asking Tej to hold his hands.

Tej felt awkward but went ahead. "Okay, now what?"

"Now I will show you the best gifts empaths have. I will share a selective memory with you." Pete tightly clasped Tej's hands and closed his eyes. Tej also closed his eyes.

"Calm yourself now, Tej, and hear the sound of a train."

"I don't hear anything."

"You will."

Tej could really hear the voice of an oncoming train. After a few seconds, he realized the voice was something different—it was a noise coming from a machine. He saw a visual of a large cube made of shining metal. One side of the cube was transparent, through which Tej could see inside of it.

Inside the cube, two small shining metal spheres were flying. They revolved around a banana placed on a black plate. The spheres were flying diametrically opposite to each other. After just two seconds, the banana started rising in the air. The revolution frequency of the spheres kept increasing until their trails formed a translucent spherical bubble around the floating banana. After three seconds, there was a bright spark, and the spheres disappeared, along with the banana. They left big circular holes in the steel box too. Tej opened his eyes.

"Did you see what I see?"

"Yes, Mr. Morales. But how could you show that to me?"

"An empathic gift—I told you. I can share memories with subjects, but they have to be receptive. But that stuff is not important. Did you see what those spheres did?"

"Yes, I did, sir. Is that the Zason weapon you were talking about?"

"Exactly. The spheres were charged in a way that their rotation produced a Zason in an altered state. In this altered state, the Zason wiped out all the matter within that radius. If a Kshin stands between those rotating balls, it will be wiped out, too. Guaranteed!"

Tej was about to ask another question when a lady

stormed into the room. She was Beth, in her late forties, pleasant face with a tough demeanor.

"Beth, my friend. Long time." Pete got up and tried to hug Beth, but she snubbed him.

"What the hell! How dare you coax me into letting an unvetted human into my premises?" she thundered.

"*Tranquila, señora.* This brave boy saved my life. I know trouble when I see it. This chap is no trouble. He's a benevolent soul. I peeked into his brain. He is good."

"Morales, you *looking* into someone is not equivalent to our established vetting process. He has to be empath-read and certified by three different Kuleens. All three shouldn't have a conflict of interest, as you have. Then and only then can he step within a kilometer of this facility. So that's the first protocol you broke. And then you have the guts to lie to the guards that it's a life and death situation to get me on the call? As commander in charge of this facility, I will not allow you to skip protocol and break rules."

Tej got up from his chair with a thought to intervene, "Ma'am, actually …"

"You stay out of this, Mr. whomever-you-are. I am coming for you after I am done with Morales."

Tej sat back into his chair.

"Look, Beth, I am sorry, okay? I should have vetted him. But Kshins took me. They tortured me for days inside their VR system. They are trying to learn about the weapon. I gave them nothing, but to be honest, they have upped their tech game. Their Infernex software is updating its algorithms at a rapid pace. A little more pressure at the right points and I might have broken down."

"You would not have. You are a tough nut." Beth calmed down. Pete smiled. Beth appeared angry, but she trusted Pete a lot more than she let on. Although she'd climbed up the ranks, she and Pete were Kuleen foot-soldiers once. They went way back.

Beth now addressed Tej. "And you, Mister …"

"Tej, ma'am." Tej got up.

"Tej, what kind of name is that? You're not from around here, are you?"

"No, ma'am."

"He is a time demon, but he's good."

"WHAT? You brought a time-demon into my facility?" Beth's eyes widened.

"I told you, he's clean." Pete relaxed into a chair.

Beth also took a chair and jammed her palms on her forehead. "You don't understand, Pete. You trust him to be good. And perhaps he is. But what if someone is using him as a pawn? What if someone is using him to get to us?"

"You are not hiding anything, are you?" Pete casually asked Tej.

A look of embarrassment floated on Tej's face. "Actually, there is one thing I haven't told you."

Pete sat up, and Beth, too, stiffened in her posture.

"I was sent to rescue you by Mr. Mozeek."

"Say that name again."

"Mozeek."

"Oh, Lord!" Pete exclaimed. Beth gave him a stern "I told you so" look. She got up, tapped her wrist-o-phone, and started speaking. He voice resounded in the room and the whole facility. "As of this instant, we are going into Defense Mode 7B. I repeat, Defense Mode 7B. Be ready for document purge and evacuation."

Tej could see frantic activity outside the room. Pete was now sitting with his face hidden behind his hands.

Beth was looking at Tej in anger.

"Mr. Mozeek said that if I told Mr. Morales about him, he would not come with me, because Kshins have spread lies about Mr. Mozeek," Tej mumbled.

"No, you idiot! Those are not lies!" Pete yelled. "Mozeek has sided with Kshins. Mozeek is a part of their organization. Many time-demons such as him are Kshin war-commanders. They share the same aim, after all. Power and repression."

Tej was thoroughly confused now. *This must be a misunderstanding.* Mozeek had saved his ass when he saw little hope. He got him out of the time-prison. He even spoke so well of Kuleens. *He can't be a Kshin pawn.*

They heard the sound of machine-gun fire at a distance, and all three of them ran outside.

IO
DOWNFALL

ozeek stood on the door of the Kuleen office, firing at three thousand rpm through his six-barreled electrically-driven rotatory machine gun. His eyes filled with blood-thirsty rage and his teeth visible in a rapacious smile.

Possessing the body of a Rory-clone, he shelled incessantly. The bullets were shredding anything and everything in their path. Several Kuleens hiding beneath the desks and behind the cubicle walls got wounded as bullets grazed their skins and pierced their bodies. A few of them who were brave enough to stand up and return fire lost their lives instantly.

Beth, Pete, and Tej, who were at the very back, had taken cover behind a desk. Tej felt weak in his gut. He had been betrayed once again. By a time-demon, at that. His confidence in his own judgment was shattered—and then the guilt followed. Mozeek had played him.

Mozeek fired for a full ninety seconds, after which he stopped and took a few steps inside. He then started to reload his weapon.

"Is that Mozeek's current vessel?" Beth whispered

to Tej, who nodded. "This is a class-A secured location. And we're compromised," Beth murmured to herself.

"We led them here." Pete was unable to meet Beth's gaze. "They must have been on to us the whole time. Following our every movement. That rescue, it did feel so easy at the time, but I didn't give it another thought. The car A.I., which usually never changes its course, did that. The signs were all there. I kept ignoring them." Pete shut his eyes.

Tej, too, was going through the events of the past few hours. He had inadvertently led Mozeek to a secure Kuleen location.

One of the Kuleens hidden behind a cubicle gathered courage and got up as Mozeek was busy loading his massive gun. He was about to fire his pistol when a voice thundered through the whole office hall.

"Do not attempt to resist. We don't want to lay down more bodies than we already have." A woman emerged behind Mozeek and walked to the front. She was Jarna, dressed in a red leather zipped jacket, tight red trousers, and long black gumboots. Her hair was neatly tied at the back, and she carried two shotguns, one in each of her hands, pointed to the front. She wore an official city police uniform, as she possessed a local police captain.

The Kuleen who had gotten up a few seconds back threw his pistol, sat down on his knees, and put his hands behind his head.

"Good choice," Jarna smirked at him.

"Why don't I shoot another few thousand rounds in here? Then no one will ever get up." Mozeek raised his gun again. His dormant bloodlust was revitalized.

"Enough. We have sent our message."

"Don't you give me orders, Jarna. I work directly for

Nefe, not for you. I could have taken down this Kuleen hideout alone. I never wanted you to come with me."

"But Nefe did. She knew that your chances of acting recklessly are fairly high. In any case, Nefe's orders were for the most possible live arrests. We need to know what these dogs are planning."

"Ah, I miss those days of 600 BC. Human sacrifice was so fucking easy back then. I used to color a whole river red. These days, you have rules and courts and whatnot." Mozeek lowered his gun, with a look of disappointment on his face.

"Why don't you time-travel back to that era and be the King Mozakira of Abreen again? Or possess his son this time, if the King's old body can't support your soul. It's so easy for you time-crawlers to possess. I envy you."

"Nah, I'm bored of that primitive age. I love this world. But this urge of taking lives is forever lingering."

"You are not taking any more lives today." Beth walked towards them. "I am the in-charge of this facility." Pete tried to stop her, but he knew she would give her life to save her people. She continued. "You can arrest me, but may I know the charges first?"

Beth walked up to Jarna and looked at her in the eye. She then read the nameplate on Jarna's uniform, which said 'Michelle Ramsey.'

"Michelle Ramsey, the unfortunate police-woman now possessed by a Kshin."

Jarna clasped Beth by her hair and whispered in her ear, "Michelle's life is over, Bethany. You should be worried about yourself. Ask your people to cooperate with the arrests, or no one leaves here alive."

"Do whatever you want. We are not afraid of monsters like you. Sooner or later, humans will find a way to end your tyrannical dynasty. You may be a few thousand, but we are billions."

"Billions of sheep, ruled by thousands of tigers. Sheep never revolt; they only follow. Arrest them. Leave none!" Jarna shouted.

A hundred men armed in full military gear entered the office. They started pulling Kuleens out from beneath the desks and behind the cubicles. Two of the Kuleens who tried to resist were shot on the spot and served as an example to others.

A few soldiers collected documents, hard drives, and computers, and bagged them.

"And go find that time-demon, Tej. He too comes with us!" Jarna screamed.

"Don't think he will linger. He'll have taken flight already." Mozeek popped his gum.

"We'll see. Nefe has shown a special interest in him."

At the very back, Tej and Pete were still hidden. Soldiers hadn't reached there yet. Tej's guilt knew no bounds. "I am sorry, Mr. Morales. I led these monsters to your doorstep. Mozeek rescued me from a time-prison, and then later, Kuntala the time-reader also acquired his name. I was pulled into their story full of lies."

"You don't need to apologize. You trusted him in the same way I trusted you. A man would blindly trust someone who pulls him out of a life-or-death situation. Those bastards first baited your time-reader friend by feeding her Mozeek's name. Then they put you in a situation where he could do a favor to you. They used both you and your trusting nature to get to us. That's it."

"Isn't there an exit we can use?"

"No—these facilities are designed to have only one exit, and we guard that exit with all our might. Many exits offer many entry points for enemies."

"What should we do? How can I help?"

"You can be of great help, buddy." Pete clasped Tej by his shoulders and looked into his eyes. "I can't escape, but you can. Leave this body."

"I would never do that. I'll be with you until the end."

"Hear me out, Tej. Your capture here won't help our cause. But you can still help Kuleen cells in other locations. Give me a moment."

Pete closed his eyes and concentrated. Tej tried to say something but Pete raised his index finger, signaling him to stay quiet. He opened his eyes after a few seconds.

"I have relayed a message to my twin brother, Jake. He works with the New York Kuleen Cell. He has a body ready for you to take over. Your destination is Sugian's Bakery and Catering services in a Suburb outside NYC. The bakery is only a front. It's actually a hospital which cares for Kuleen operatives wounded on the field. They also have some machine-designed clone bodies ready for you to take over."

They heard the soldier boots approaching them.

"Mr. Morales, I can't leave you! They will kill you!"

"No, they won't. They'll continue my interrogation. Go now—come back for me later."

The soldiers were approaching the place where they sat hidden.

"But …"

"Go now, Tej!" Pete screamed, which attracted the soldiers' attention.

They came running and pointed their guns at Pete and Tej. "Freeze! Hands where I can see them! Now!"

"You were too late." Pete turned around, about to reprimand Tej, but his host lay dead. Pete smiled.

Tej woke up in a large freezing room. He was among the five identical naked bodies on five cement slabs. Each body was covered with a sheet of white cloth. This room reminded him of the "Chamber of Time Travel" where Rigu had kept the bodies of Kumbh and Vetri.

The door opened, and Jake entered. He wore a white shirt, black jeans, and a white coat. His face shared a lot of similarities with Pete's, but he had tears in his eyes. "What happened? Have they …" Jake's throat choked.

"No. I mean, I don't know. I escaped before they reached us. Pete said they wouldn't kill him—they would only arrest and interrogate."

"Yeah, let's hope for the best. That's the best we can do." Jake wiped his tears. "My brother praised you a lot. He sent me a very short message, but he said you were a good soul. And as I see, he was right."

Tej realized Jake was looking at his forehead in wonder. Tej wiped his forehead with his hand. "Is there something up here?"

"No, I was studying your aura."

"So, you're an empath too?"

"All Kuleens are; some, more powerful than the others. Let's get you some clothes." Jake started to walk out of the room.

Tej also got up. "Kuleens can also talk inside their brains with each other?"

"No, not all of us. Kuleens who are twins usually can. We are connected mentally. I and Pete could talk seamlessly." Jake walked out of the room, Tej followed him outside, stumbling, wrapped in a white sheet.

An hour later, Tej and Jake were inside another Kuleen facility. Jake had driven his car through several maze-like roads and reached a small coffee shop. They again went into the broken restroom, going through the "mirror door," and then took an elevator to a deep basement office. This facility was very similar to the one where Pete had taken Tej.

Tej was seated in a waiting room, and he could see Jake arguing with a woman. The woman was Miranda, the leader of the New York Facility. Miranda had gray-white hair and sharp facial features, and she wore a maroon formal shirt and long grey plaid skirt. Tej could only see them but hear nothing. He tried to lip-read them.

The NYC cell was planning a major operation on the eve of the solar eclipse the next day. They planned to hit three Kshin targets of importance in NYC. Each of their three attack teams, T-Chi, T-Gamma, and T-Zeta had one Kuleen and one time-demon working together. Miranda was already tense because of this massive undertaking. Jake bringing Tej into the facility without her prior approval was another headache she had to deal with.

"He just leads Kshins to the SFO facility, and you want me to trust this man?" Miranda was livid. "And not only that, you want me to send him on a mission for which we have been preparing for months? As my next-in-command, I expected you to work with more responsibility, Jake."

"He was manipulated by Kshins. Many of us have been at some point. But we are all here working for our cause. Why can he not?"

"We're all humans, but he is a time-demon."

"Oh, so that's the problem. That's why he cannot be trusted. What about the time-demons already working for us?" Jake was furious. He knew his brother Pete was rarely wrong about people, and he stood by Pete's decision. Pete would never have sent Tej to them if he did not wholeheartedly believe in him.

Miranda was looking for words. "Those time-demons who work with us have gone through a thorough vetting process. But this one has not. How can you be so sure about him?"

"First, Pete trusted him. And you know Pete—he isn't wrong when it comes to people. And second, Tej has a very different aura."

"So what?"

"I have never seen such a green aura, Miranda."

"Well, we have all kinds."

"No, I never have. None of the documents penned down by old empaths mentioned an aura like this. Humans have a light blue aura; Kshins' is a very faint light fuchsia. Time-demons are a mixture of light green and aquamarine. I have never seen this shade of green. Almost neon."

"Your point, Jake?"

"He *is* different."

"So we should blindly trust everyone who walks in here with this aura? Those are our objective scientific criteria now."

Jake wanted to argue further but relented. Miranda had an over-arching responsibility to make sure the facility was safeguarded from dangers outside and within. He also realized that the mission next day was keeping her on the edge. "All right. You know what, Miranda? The mission doesn't start until a few hours. Why don't we vet him? The vetting process takes two hours max. You need a time-demon for Team Zeta, right?"

"Yeah, we do." Miranda chewed her lip and looked at Tej sitting inside the room. Tej managed a faint smile.

"We have been together twenty years, Miranda. I would never let you down. This man here is another victim of the Kshins' atrocities. Nefe attacked his village and tortured his folk. He is not just another time-demon on our payroll. He is not someone who merely agrees with our cause. He's a man who has something strong against Kshins. Give him a chance."

"All right, Jake, you drive a hard bargain. But if this goes south, it's on you," Miranda relented. Jake smiled. She asked Jake to make the necessary preparations.

Tej was asked to attend three consecutive sessions. Each session was thirty minutes long, with three different Kuleen interviewers. They asked him various questions about his life: his past, his motivations, and some very personal details. Tej answered as truthfully as he could. One thing was common in each of the interviews: the Kuleens often paused in the middle of their questioning and notes to look at Tej's forehead.

After these interviews, he underwent a thirty minute-long brain scan. As he lay on a table, a technician fitted a circular metallic apparatus with complex circuitry on his head. He was again asked a series of questions while an operator pressed some keys and took notes.

When the process ended, Tej was placed in another waiting room. Having gone through the vetting process, Tej was feeling good. If the Kuleens decided not to include him as a part of their team after this vetting, he would understand, but he hoped they would trust and include him. He still felt guilty about leading Kshins to the Kuleen hideout.

With that, each inch of his body filled with hate for Mozeek. After Rigasur, he should have been more careful with another time-demon. His own race was full of treacherous bastards who knew no morals. He longed to right this wrong by siding with them and serving with them. There was a faint hope he would get a chance to strike Nefe. He had no idea the universe was listening.

After ten minutes, Jake entered his room carrying a few chocolate bars. "Here you go. Eat this."

Tej tore the white wrapper back and started nibbling on the dark brown chocolate bar. "Oh God, the taste is horrible," Tej exclaimed, the pieces of chocolate still in his mouth. "Can I get some real food? Although I am not at all hungry—do clone bodies feel hunger?"

Jake laughed. "No, they don't. The one you're in is a synthetically designed clone body of a particular type. These don't have the same intricate and complex digestive systems as we humans have. These can only ingest a simple mixture of proteins and vitamins. The food designers were kind enough to package it in the form of a chocolate bar which clones could eat with ease."

"Oh, God. Which means this is my only food? How many of these I have to eat?"

"Five."

"Five every day?"

"No," Jake chuckled. "Five every year. One bar will last roughly seventy days."

Tej took a sigh of relief.

"Okay, Tej, coming back to the good news. You have passed the test—you are a vetted member of Kuleen group." Jake shook hands with Tej. "And there's more. Tomorrow will be a total solar eclipse. We are planning a strike mission. And by a stroke of destiny, we have one time-demon position open in one of our teams. Would you want to be a part of it?"

Tej felt a sense of elation going through him but controlled his emotions. Jake smiled.

"No need to say anything, Tej. I can see the rush of positivity through you."

"You gave me what I wanted the most, Mr. Morales. I will not let you down. In the fight against Kshins, I stand alongside Kuleens unto death."

"Great. Our team will love your enthusiasm. Now follow me."

Jake followed Tej through a corridor, from which they took an elevator to another floor. They walked for two minutes until they reached a big brown door which said, "Conference Room 53-XC."

Jake halted at the door and turned around to look Tej in his eyes. "Tej. Not everyone here is as excited about you as I am. Many have their reservations. And I am not saying you must sell yourself, but ..."

"Don't worry, Mr. Morales. I will speak from my heart, and I will speak the truth. That's the best arrow I have in my quiver."

"Very well."

Jake opened those big doors, and they entered the conference room. The room was completely set up to handle and monitor a full war-zone. At the opposite wall, three screens ten feet high and three feet wide towered next to each other. Each of the screens was displaying a different building. Texts reading "T-Chi," "T-Gamma," and "T-Zeta" were displayed at the top and bottom on each of the screens.

Between the door through which they entered and the screens at the other end was a fifteen-foot oval table. Several people sat around this table talking in hushed tones. Sheets of paper, pens, water bottles, computers, and other electronic equipment were strewn across the table. All the men and women in the room were in their late thirties and early forties and wore formal dresses. Tej noticed Miranda also sitting at the far end of the table near the screens. All their gazes fixated at Tej.

"So he is the one whom we're considering to be my partner." One of the Kuleens, Jiten, stood up. Jiten was assigned as a drone-operator to Team Zeta. "There is no chance we can get Zovial back?" Jiten referenced the time-demon previously assigned to team up with him for Team-Zeta's mission plan.

Miranda nodded in negation. "Zovial sent a message saying he is not 'available.' At best, he has chickened out. At worst, he's joined forces with Kshins. I can't say for sure at this moment. Intelligence is trying to track him."

"So then, that jeopardizes our mission, right?"

"No, it doesn't. He does not know anything about the mission. We top brass have played it close to our chests. The field operatives will be briefed only today, one day before the mission."

"But he knows we are planning something big. So if he's with the Kshins, they'll know it too." Jiten scratched his beard, as he did when he was nervous.

Miranda maintained a calm demeanor. "Doesn't matter. Kshins always know that we are planning something all the time."

"I don't know, Miranda. I recommend that we abort." Jiten sat down, looking dejected.

This was another setback for Miranda. Their intelligence and strategists had spent several weeks tailing three key Kshin targets. They had studied their movements, patterns, habits, security details, and formulated a watertight plan to infiltrate Kshin security and assassinate the target. They would extract the attack-team with minimal risk to their lives.

"You cannot give up right now. Tomorrow is the total solar eclipse. Kshins will be powerless. Without their telekinetics, they would be very weak. What are you afraid of?"

"I am not afraid." Jiten looked at Miranda with an indignant frown on his face. He had been a Kuleen fighter for a long time. "But I am no fool either. Executing a perfect plan is one thing, and following a flawed plan is another. Yes, strategies do go haywire as soon as we enter the field. But here, I see last-minute changes even before we start. I and others in this room, we have risked our lives many times. Every time, meticulous and intricate planning was the only thing that saved us. Now one of our time-demon operatives backs out last-minute, and we bring in someone very new?"

"Hello, everyone, can I say something?" Tej spoke for the first time. He now had the whole room's attention. He looked at Jake, who signaled him to go on.

"I am sure everyone here has been tormented by Kshins in some way or the other. I won't compare my story to yours. And I know it's tough for you to trust me because I am an outsider. Fair enough. But there is one emotion, one passion I share with each person in this room—getting the world freed from the grip of these alien tyrants." Tej didn't realize he'd banged the table really hard. "And I assure you, I will do everything in my power to fight them with my last breath. If you choose me to be a part of your fight, I will be honored. You can use me as a weapon in this righteous cause. But if not, I will understand, and I will continue my individual attempts to hurt Kshins regardless."

There was a short-lived silence in the room. Everyone could hear each other breathe. Tej's passionate words had mellowed several folks in the room.

"Appreciate the fiery speech." Jiten broke the silence. "But why is no one talking about the incident at SFO facility involving him?"

"Tej's been vetted," Jake interjected.

"The vetting process isn't foolproof. We have seen true negatives. Plus, with the SFO office compromised, I don't know where all this information has spread. I am sorry, Miranda. I will sit this one out." Jiten got up and walked out of the conference room.

Miranda sat with a straight face, but inside of her, she knew that everyone in the room felt weak in their guts. With Jiten gone, Team Zeta was incomplete—and this team had the most critical target.

"I'll go," Jake said. Everyone in the room looked at him with surprise.

Miranda looked up. "No, Jake."

"Why? You need a drone-operator for this team. Jiten is out. I volunteer myself. I am omega-certified to control five hundred drones at once. My drone flying experience includes thirteen hundred hours without expert supervision. Not as good as Jiten, but I fit the bill."

"Jake, it's not about experience. Your brother was captured and is now missing in action. Without a psychiatric evaluation for you, I don't think we should ..."

"No. No more of these processes and evaluations.

I and Tej here have both suffered losses of our loved ones at hands of these tyrants. We both are raring for revenge. And I trust Tej as a partner. We should go together. What's the worst that will happen? I will die. I am not worried about that. But if I can help take even one Kshin down, I will have done my duty as a Kuleen."

Miranda saw no other option but to agree. The other choice was to abort the mission for Team Zeta—but that would have been a major setback since they wanted to hit all three Kshin targets at the same time.

11
BLEED THEM BY A THOUSAND CUTS

The meeting ended, and one of the Kuleens took Tej to a room with a small comfortable bed. Jake came to wish him goodnight and assured him that they'd see each other tomorrow.

Tej tried to sleep, but his thoughts kept drifting to the torturous experiences from the Infernex. Kumbh throwing his mother down the cliff. Being captured in a dark box full of creepy-crawlers still sent shivers down his spine. He thought of time-traveling to the next morning but decided against it. After a few minutes, he dozed off.

The next morning, Tej and Jake sat in another room and were handed over three documents. Two strategists sat with them and explained the whole plan.

Three targets had been chosen for assassination. The first was Elna Govendera. A famous South African politician in the race to become the Minister of Exports, she planned to use her political clout to manage a massive human trafficking supply chain from Asia to the Americas.

The second was Wang Kurd, an American of Chinese origin. The ex-mafia man had been chosen to lead and operate a secret facility on the Chinese mainland. The third was Vedika Sharma, the CEO of Vedvance Corporation in the United States.

As per Kuleen intelligence, all three humans were possessed by powerful Kshins. Tej was assigned to the team responsible for assassinating Vedika Sharma, possessed by Nefe—a name with which Tej was familiar.

The total solar eclipse was predicted to occur at 8:14 PM EST, 25th December, the same day. At the time of their meeting, the clocks read 8:30 AM. Which meant they had around 12 hours to prepare for the mission.

The eclipse would last for 110 seconds, roughly two minutes starting 8:14 PM. But the one hour window from 7:44 to 8:44 was considered the golden period by strategists. This was the time when Kshin powers would be at their weakest and their bodies most vulnerable to attack.

Each attack team was to infiltrate the defenses for their respective targets and attack them during this golden period. This tactical part of the plan was kept flexible from a timing perspective. But each attack was preceded by a distraction event. The choice of weapon for the attack was the Zason-bombs or Z-bombs as Pete called them. They had the capability of dematerializing anything caught in their vortex.

"Each team will have its own tactical plan," Jake explained Tej. "You and I will off Nefe, while two other teams go after other two targets. Since this is a high-risk event we are keeping the human involvement to the least. I'll take a heli-convertible car along with three hundred missile drones. Before you attack, I'll create a distraction at the periphery of Vedika's mansion in the suburbs. Whereas you will possess a human on the inside and lead the attack on her."

"Wait for a second, I will possess a human? A live one? I can't do that. That's against the only principle of time travel I have."

"Desperate times call for desperate measures, Tej. In these times, we need to sacrifice personal principles for the larger good." Jake paused. He wanted Tej onboard with the plan but did not want to impose the plan on him.

"Let's do one thing. I will show you where exactly this Kshin is holed up. You study the situation yourself. If you can come up with an alternate plan which does not involve possession, I will run it up by Miranda."

Jake picked up a spherical baseball-like device and kept it on the table. He gestured with his hand, and the device started throwing out a 3D projection. The projection showed a big multi-floored mansion in the middle of a massive empty land. Grey but decorated walls surrounded a neatly designed architecture with European-style windows.

"This is Nefe's newly constructed mansion. She got it built soon after she possessed Vedika. Tomorrow being an eclipse day, she will stay at this mansion under very heavy guard. The property is spread across five acres of land, with the mansion building at the center. The boundary wall is being guarded by a small army of two hundred armed men and fifty robotic attack-dogs. Inside the mansion, we estimate another fifty commandos.

They would be less armed but are all proficient in Chinese martial arts and knives.

"And this is not all. Nefe is also holding Vedika's daughter, Jess, and plans to use her as a human shield. When Nefe killed Vedika's wife Rubina, we all wondered why she kept Jess alive. This was the reason."

"Hmm. A very tight security ring. Kshins are petrified of the solar eclipse days. Aren't they?" Tej was thinking about all possible combinations.

"Yes. Given this tight security, there is no way any human can reach her without being killed at least ten times. But you, you can possess anyone inside that building. Do the job and get out," Jake concluded and sat down on a chair.

It was up to Tej now. He was at a loss for words. Given what he had just seen, there was no other way than for him to follow Jake's plan. Including time-demons in their plan had been a master-stroke from the Kuleens.

"I can go in, Jake, but how will these Z-bombs go in?" Tej realized he called him Jake, and not Mr. Morales. He felt a deep connection with him. Jake, too, had lost loved ones to Kshins, just as he did.

"We have a plan for that, too. Nefe will spend most of her day in the innermost room of the building, which is a huge bedroom and study. There will be one Chinese commando outside her bedroom door the whole day. We have obtained the name of the guard who will be assigned this duty that day. His name is Li Xiu."

Jake pressed a button on the projection device, and a face and some details came onto the screen. "Is this information enough for you to locate him?"

"That's enough, but you haven't answered my question. Where are the Z-bombs? How will you get them to me?"

"Coming to that. Two days ago, one of our Kuleen operatives, Mark, engaged in a fist-fight with Li Xiu in a bar. It came across as a normal drunken bar-fight. But during that scuffle, Mark managed to dislodge all the three left-side molars from Mr. Li Xiu's mouth."

"Wow, this operative of yours took on a well-trained martial artist?"

"Yeah, but Mark's in the hospital with three broken ribs, one damaged eye, and severe blood loss." An expression of sadness took over Jake's face, and he closed his eyes. He could feel the pain Mark went through. "Anyhow, he'll live. Now, after this fight, Mr. Xiu visited a dental facility for tooth surgery. There, he was fitted with three new titanium teeth. Latest technology. Except that two out of those three were not titanium teeth, but were our Z-bombs, coated with titanium and made to look like teeth. That dental facility has been owned and operated by Kuleens for months."

"So, this Xiu guy is moving around with two bombs inside his mouth. Unbelievable," Tej chuckled.

Jake laughed. "The scientists who crafted these bombs tell us they are safe in there. Unless he tries to uproot them himself and check. And after you possess him …"

"I would actually need to uproot my teeth." Tej winced at the mere thought of it.

"Yes. Tap on the last two molars. A sharp pull and they should come out. There is a bit of pain involved."

"Pain? Story of my life. When do I possess him?"

"The total solar eclipse starts at 8:14 PM …"

"Wait, the eclipse is happening at night? It's not an eclipse then, right?"

"It doesn't matter if it's night-time at our geo-location, Tej. A huge astronomical body, the Moon, is coming right between the Sun and Earth. That's the actual event which impacts Kshins all around the world. It suppresses their powers, regardless of their geo-location. It doesn't matter if the eclipse is visible from that location or not. It should be happening somewhere in the world; that is enough."

"Okay." Tej made a mental note to not try to wrap his head around the technicality behind how eclipses affected Kshins. "Continue, please."

"I will create a diversion at exactly 08:12. Anytime within the next two minutes, the mansion will be buzzing with a red alarm. That is when I will send a radio message to you, and you have to possess this man Li. How much time do you need for possession?"

"Less than a second. I think all time-demons take about that long."

"Isn't that convenient?" Jake winked. "Kshins take days, even months before they can establish control over a new body. You are way faster. I've worked with time-demons for the past few years, but let me tell you, every new possession fascinates me."

"I'm not particularly proud of this power." Tej was flustered. "But why do I go in just before the eclipse? Why don't I take that body earlier and do some recon inside?"

"Because Kshins are meticulous bastards. They have made all the arrangements to welcome you time-demons, too. In all major Kshin buildings, safe-houses and facilities, there are three kinds of alarms: blue, yellow, and red. The blue alarm is a minor alarm. It goes off if a normal human breaches the premises. Yellow goes off when a time-demon is sighted. And red, the most lethal one, is triggered when the place is under an attack by robots, drones, or any kind of machines."

"Wait a second. How would they know a time-demon has entered the place?"

"They have detectors which pick up the time-demon's radiation signature. So as soon as you possess that body, the yellow alarm will go off. Which is why we are planning a diversion using drones. A drone attack will trigger the red alarm, and once the red alarm goes off, no other alarm goes off—so you will go in undetected."

Tej found it amusing that Kshins viewed attacks by automatons as more dangerous than those by time-demons. "I have another question, Jake. Not sure if it's relevant?"

"Go on, shoot."

"Kshins taking over positions of military and political influence is understandable. But why did Nefe possess a tech company CEO? What does she gain out of it?"

"Technology is the dual-edged sword of our times. Whoever controls technology controls the world. Which is why Nefe, one of the most powerful Kshins known, is handling the corruption of Vedvance Inc. herself. Rubina Vance and Vedika Sharma were two honest, smart entrepreneurs who built Vedvance from the ground up. They wanted to achieve man-machine singularity for the benefit of mankind using a device called the Concordia V1."

"I have heard that name before." Tej knew this was the same device which Kumbh wanted to use to kill billions.

"You would have. The company and its products are fairly popular. Their pre-order lists are huge. But ever since Nefe has taken control of the company, it's going in the opposite direction. They have modified Concordia to a version called the VX. Using this device, they will plug human brains into virtual reality prisons and torture them. Nefe is using this tech company to further her powers and propaganda. With that, they are building a mysterious technology in stealth mode—something so dark and powerful that it will make them near invincible."

"What tech is that?"

"We don't know yet. Our spies will find out sooner than later. But the next total solar eclipse falls on May 11, 2059. If we miss today's eclipse, our next window to attack these alien bastards is several months away from now. At the rate Kshins are moving with Vedvance, we don't have that much time. We cannot wait for specifics of what their plans are. It's now or never for us to take down these prominent Kshin targets and cause serious damage to their plans."

"We kill Nefe and two other powerful Kshins. Then what? What about others?"

"One battle at a time, Tej. We cannot defeat such a formidable enemy with a single strike. We will bleed them out with a thousand cuts."

After a session with Jake, Tej was also a part of several other sessions. Trainers repeated the same information, schematics and plan a few times. Those re-trainings bored Tej, but a detailed session on the usage of Z-bombs sparked his interest. He found it remarkable that humans of the future had developed a weapon which could take down an advanced alien race such as Kshins.

At 4:30 PM, Jake left for the airfield from which he was going to start his operation. He hugged Tej before he left and wished him luck.

At 7:00 PM a support specialist Debbie seated Tej in a calm room. She asked if Tej needed some scented candles or any special ambiance to help him concentrate, but he refused. Debbie told him that some time-demons they worked with had expressed such weird requirements. One of them wanted to be fully submerged in water before he could time-travel. Another one wanted a jungle-like environment. Tej asked for a glass of water and sat down on a sofa.

At around 7:45 PM, Jake had taken a flight from a secret airbase and was traveling towards Vedika's mansion. He was in a small black heli-convertible car with two rotors on top and was cruising at a fast velocity. A set of three hundred drones followed his flying car in a triangular formation. Each drone was fitted with a mechanical-trigger enabled fully-automatic machine gun.

Disobeying the flying vehicle traffic rules, Jake had not switched on any headlights for his car or drones. He was totally relying on the car's automated navigation system. Given his current speed and wind direction, he anticipated reaching the mansion periphery right around 8:10 PM.

Inside the mansion, Vedika sat on a bed, reading something, and Naaz was combing Jess's hair. Jess was playing a game on a screen projected on her arm. Li Xiu stood outside the door with a pistol placed in a holster tied to his belt.

"Mom, why did we come here? I miss my school and

my friends."

"Oh God, this thing's started again," Nefe murmured under her breath.

"Madam, can I take her to her room?" Naaz spoke in a feeble tone. She had once been close to Vedika, but with the changes in her behavior recently, Naaz was now very terrified of her.

"She stays here until midnight today, in my room. I told you that."

"I was saying she may disturb you …"

"Give her two pills of Voxine Peracyclate. She'll sleep." Nefe turned over a page in her ebook-reader.

"But that dosage is too strong, even for an adult."

"Then find some other way to keep her quiet. I don't care."

At exactly 8:12, they heard a muffled explosion from outside. Nefe immediately got up and tried to hear in silence. Outside the room, Li Xiu drew his revolver and started contacting the main gate security.

The periphery of the mansion property was fortified with twenty-foot tall walls in all directions, constructed with steel and reinforced concrete. There was one twenty-five foot high gate on the northern side. Jake and the drones approached the mansion from the northwest. He maintained a height of fifteen feet above the ground, staying as silent as he could, waiting for the clock to strike 8:12.

At 8:12, Jake started off. He threw a small bomb on the gate and then started heavy shelling. He did not enter the periphery on purpose and stayed outside. He knew that within those walls were hidden frequency jamming devices that could mess with his car's electronics. He had to stay outside and create this distraction for Tej.

Within ten seconds of Jake's initial fire, fifty men gathered behind the gate with their floating bullet shields. They returned fire, but Jake's three-hundred-drone onslaught was so massive that they had to duck to take cover. The head of security seated inside the building asked for the anti-flying-object gun to be brought out from underneath the ground. This was a drone attack but he was evaluating if he should press the red alarm button or not.

Jake waited for building security to trigger the red alarm.

Back in the Kuleen facility, Tej sat on his sofa, waiting for Jake to call. The clock now read 8:13:25 PM and Tej's heartbeat was rising.

8:13:26, 27, 28

Why did Jake not call? Had the mission gone sideways?

30, 31, 32

Only thirty seconds left. At 08:14, the eclipse would start.

34, 35, 36

Jake's voice crackled on the small ear-plug device in Tej's left ear. "Go, Tej, go. They've trigged the red alarm."

Tej closed his eyes and started concentrating on Li Xiu and the location.

Jake knew his part was over. He turned his car around and sped away. Around fifty of the three hundred drones followed him. The rest remained in their place, continuously firing.

41 ,42, 43

Tej was gone. His clone body slipped from the sofa, lifeless.

He opened his eyes and regained his senses. He was in Li Xiu's body and had a gun in his hand. He tapped on his wrist, and the skin illuminated to show the digital clock. 08:13:44. Only sixteen seconds before the solar eclipse started. Inserting his index finger into the back of his mouth, he pressed and tapped on the last two molars. He applied some pressure, and they dislodged from the root.

He experienced sharp pain and blood in his mouth. Using a handkerchief from his pocket, he cleaned the two shining molars. These were the Z-bombs. The end of his jaw still radiated with throbbing pain, but he had to go on.

The clock now read 08:13:55. He turned around and looked at the door behind him. It was locked, and a pitch-black finger-print reader stood in place of the lock. He swiped his finger on the reader, which read his print and turned green. The door clicked open, and he rushed inside with his gun pointed forward.

Inside, he saw two women. He recognized one as Vedika and pointed his gun to her. Vedika pointed a gun at him and screamed, "Li why are you inside?"

Tej kept silent and looked around. He saw little Jess hiding behind Vedika, peeping at him.

"Why are you here, Li?" Vedika shouted again and tightened her grip on the gun.

Tej knew he had less than two minutes to get the girl away from Vedika. "Enough of your shenanigans, Nefe. Let the kid go."

"What? You get out of here right now, or I'll shoot."

Tej brought his gun down and put it back in his holster. In the heat of the moment, he didn't want to shoot the girl or the other woman. Vedika kept aiming her gun at him. Tej took one titanium molar in each hand and pressed them together, as taught in the training. The

Z-bombs were now activated. He knew he had ten seconds before he would need to release them. But the kid still stood behind Vedika.

"Run, kid, run!" Tej screamed at Jess.

Vedika shot Tej in his right shoulder, and blood spurted out. Tej cringed in pain but stood his ground. Afraid of the gunshot, Jess ran from behind Vedika and towards Naaz. Naaz clasped the kid in her arms and dived behind a cupboard.

Seeing the kid leave Vedika, Tej hurled the Z-bombs towards her and dropped to the ground. Vedika fired several shots. But the bombs had started spiraling all around her at a rapid pace, following a spherical pattern with a three-meter radius. She was now caught in the Zason-vortex, which was sucking all the matter within its radius. Her feet were no longer touching the ground as she was slowly lifted in the air. She tried to escape, but couldn't. The revolving intensity of the bombs kept increasing for a few seconds. There was a huge lightning spark, and the vortex disappeared, along with Vedika.

Tej got up with difficulty and looked at his wrist clock. The time read 08:16:07. He walked towards Naaz and Jess.

"Please don't kill us!" Naaz pleaded as she held Jess close.

"I am not here to hurt you. Are you two all right?"

Naaz nodded.

"Will you take care of this girl?"

Naaz nodded again. Tej lay down on the ground. His shoulder hurt like hell. "And take this man to the hospital," he murmured and closed his eyes. His mission was successful. It was time for him to go back.

He opened his eyes. He was back at the Kuleen facility, inside the clone body. As a reflex, he instantly pressed at his right shoulder with his left hand, but there was no wound. He felt a short-lived ghost pain. But after he stretched his right arm a few times and moved his shoulder, he felt nothing.

"Jake, are you there?" He pressed the little device in his year and spoke.

"Yeah man, Tej, I'm here. How did it go? Did we nail that bitch?" Jake's voice sounded distorted.

"Yes, we did."

"What? Say again. The connection isn't clear."

"We did it, Jake. She's gone!" Tej raised his voice. After a very long time, he was smiling.

"Woohooo!" Jake almost screamed in Tej's ear. "I'm coming back, buddy. See you in a few." The radio disconnected.

Everything happened so fast. He went in, bombed a Kshin, and came out, all within a span of three minutes. He was now beginning to realize the magnitude of what he'd pulled off. But this had required months of intelligence gathering, planning and getting each part of the plan bang-on right. He'd only reaped the fruit of a very meticulous plan laid out by Kuleens.

Half an hour later, Miranda and Jake came in with several other Kuleens to congratulate Tej. Jake was still wearing his drone-pilot uniform, and came right up and hugged Tej. He told Tej that other two missions were also successful, without any other casualties. These were by far the most successful simultaneous operations conducted by them against Kshins.

They took Tej to the central hall of the facility, where hundreds of Kuleens had gathered. Everyone was in a celebratory mood because of the major win. People were hugging each other. Several people came and shook hands with Tej. Speeches were given, champagnes were opened, and chocolates were distributed. Tej found a sense of simplicity in their celebrations.

Jake grasped Tej by his shoulders and shook him. "I am going to dance the whole night away, Tej, and you are going to dance too." He was in seventh heaven.

"Dance? Is there a party?" Tej smiled.

"Hell yes. We Kuleens work hard, and we party harder. We will clean up all these cubicles and stuff, and this hall right here will become a dance floor. Miranda is going to set up a retro early-2000s kind of a disco ambiance. Tomorrow is a new day for another fight. But tonight, we can enjoy ourselves. And I bet you won't have heard the awesome songs Muzingaa plays."

"Muzingaa? Some DJ?"

"Nope, my friend. DJs are so 2039. Muzingaa is the music selection A.I., which senses the party mood and plays songs accordingly. Load it onto your music console. It pumps you up with one hit after another. You will love it."

"With all due respect, Jake, I'll have to turn this offer down. I'd like to go back to my village and check up on my folks."

Jake's happy expression turned into a nervous smile. "Tej, you were part of a major win. We would love to have you relax among us." He paused. "But if you really want to go, I would understand."

"Sorry, Jake, I need to do this. I left my village folks in distress."

"You don't need to say sorry. Go ahead, go back to your loved ones. But the way you travel, I don't know if we can ever stay in touch."

"I'll be there when you need me." Tej hugged Jake and took leave.

He went ahead to the same waiting room and laid down on the sofa. Manika had advised him against ever coming back to the same moment. A small hit and miss could mean he went back before the moment he commenced his journey, and lead to a chain of paradoxes. He targeted a specific time in 3057 BC, eight hours past the moment he started.

12
END
OF EVERYTHING

ej woke up and noticed Manika sitting next to him. Roughly eight hours had passed in this time-slice since he was gone. He got up and hugged her. "Oh, Manika, we did it! We took down that Kshin. The one who killed Kuntala, the one who is tormenting my village people! She is dead."

"I have good news too, Tej. People in your village are getting better. I just did a time-read. Your father, your brother, and others, they have woken up. They show no disease symptoms."

Tej jumped with joy. His usual boyish grin was back. "I need to go to Sarp-Nagar. Right now." He chuckled like a kid.

"You just came back from a tedious journey, Tej? Why don't you take a rest?"

"I have had enough rest. I will leave right away. Will you come with me?"

"Well, I don't know anyone in your village. What will I do there?"

"What will you do here?" Tej was careful not to sound too elated, but he really wanted her to come with him.

Manika paused. "You are right. There is nothing left."

He could sense the dourness in her voice and a grim expression taking over her face. "Come on, cheer up. We won a huge battle, and you were a part of it. Kuntala's sacrifice was not in vain. There were indeed some hiccups along the way, but yes, we cut off the head of that serpent."

"I know—I did not see a lot of it because the quantum-veil kept blocking my visions, but that Mozeek guy turned out to be a traitor. I should have time-read him before sending you along the way."

"We both witnessed what happened to Kuntala. You were in no space to do a time-read. Anyhow, there is a lot to talk about. We will do that on the way."

Manika packed a few clothes, and after a few minutes, Tej and Manika started for Sarp-Nagar.

The setting in the Kuleen facility had transformed into a party. Blue background lights, rotating disco lights on the roof; an open bar was generously serving drinks. All people, young and old, were losing themselves on the dance floor.

Jake and Miranda sat together on a sofa on the side and drinking from plastic cups. After shaking a leg for a few minutes, they had chosen their cozy corner to spend the rest of the evening.

"I miss drinking fine wine from those stylish glasses." Miranda took a sip.

"That's not difficult. I can take you to any pub you

want." Jake moved near her, and his body was touching hers. She didn't mind.

"That's impossible, and you know that. We two must be at the top of the Kshin hit-list. More so after today."

"No, Mir. Please stop worrying about tomorrow, just for a second."

"I'm terrified." Miranda looked him in the eye, clutching the cup with both hands. "I'm afraid that we have just kicked a hornet's nest. We have finally poked the sleeping beast in the eye. I don't know what will happen tomorrow."

Jake put his glass down on the table and cupped Miranda's face with his hands. "Whatever happens, we will face it together. We will fight it together. And to be honest, I feel just the opposite. I feel like, for the first time, we have wounded the Kshins in a way that we never had before. For the first time, they will feel the real fear in their hearts."

Miranda managed to smile, but inside, she was petrified.

A loud bang in the hall caught their attention. Jake and Miranda looked at each other and stiffened. Jake got up and drew his gun. He looked in the direction of the sound. There was a commotion. One man who had too much to drink had fallen on a big sound-speaker and had caused it to break. He was being taken away to the restroom.

One of the men spoke on the microphone, "It's nothing, guys. We are setting up the music again. Keep the party alive, people."

"It was … it was nothing," Jake stammered. He kept his gun back and sat down. He was a bit embarrassed because of the way he'd reacted.

Miranda was looking at him with a funny expression on her face.

"What?" He asked.

"Nothing."

"What the fuck, Mir? Why you looking at me like that?"

"Look at your face." Miranda burst into laughter and rolled over.

"What? Why are you laughing?"

"You are terrified on the inside. Aren't you?" She tried to control her giggles.

No, I'm not. There's nothing wrong in being prepared for the worst." Jake picked up his glass again.

Miranda was still tittering.

"Well, at least I made you laugh. I'll drink to that." He gulped the whole glass in one go.

Tej and Manika had reached Sarp-Nagar, where things were getting back to normal. People who'd been unconscious with a severe fever had now woken up and were returning home. Tej's foster father and brother had also returned.

After meeting his family and introducing Manika to them, Tej went to visit Manu Kumar. Manu was delighted to see him and hugged him tightly. At first, he chided Tej for going away for so long, but Tej managed to cajole him.

Nefe's army had earlier ransacked several houses, broken farming equipment, and wounded some animals, too. With the help of several other young men in the village, Tej started repairing the damage and rebuilding the village. He knew that the Kshins were far from being eliminated, but by getting rid of Nefe, his work was done. The Kshins were a Kuleen problem, and as Jake said, they would die a slow death one day. He could now go back to living in peace.

It was half-past midnight, and even after four hours of boozing and dancing, the Kuleen party hadn't come to an end. The older folks were now sitting on the sofas on the sides, while the younger ones kept the party alive.

Miranda was sleeping with her head in Jake's lap. He was smoking a cigar and sipping an occasional beer. During the day, she was his boss, but during the after hours, they were something else. He couldn't say she was his girlfriend. He couldn't name that relationship. But they were close—he knew that much.

A few more beers later, Jake was drowsy. He was struggling to keep his eyes open when he saw a small kid standing on the entrance of the hall. He rubbed his eyes and checked again—the kid was gone.

"How is that possible? This party is strictly eighteen-plus." He laughed at himself. "Come on, Miranda, we gotta get to bed. Not that I am saying you have to sleep with me, but we need to sleep in our own beds. Miranda, you listening?"

She didn't move—she was fast asleep.

There was a loud bang again, but this time, Jake laughed it off. "Yeah, you bozos can break all the equipment. You break it, you pay for it!" he screamed loudly to the crowd, and closed his eyes.

There was another loud bang, and this time, a woman screamed. Music stopped. Jack sneaked himself from under Miranda's head and got up. "Wake up, woman," he whispered and drew his gun. He tried to walk steady but was too drowsy.

He saw the girl again, standing at the entrance of the hall. She was around five or six years old. He rubbed his eyes again and finally recognized her. She was Jess Sharma, Vedika's daughter. She wore a light pink frock and matching shoes. She also carried a small doll.

"What the hell are you doing here, kid?" Jake murmured and moved in her direction.

Behind Jess stood several men aiming their semi-automatic weapons at the crowd. Several Kuleens had also drawn their guns, but most of them were inebriated, and not in a position to take aim.

"How did you all get in here?" Jake knew that Miranda never took chances with the security. There was a ring of hundred security personnel around this Kuleen faculty who'd been ordered to stay sober and stay guard as others partied.

"I told your security to go home, and they did," Jess spoke in a soft voice with a calm face and tilted her head to one side. "Although they had to be persuaded."

"Who the hell are you?" Jake pointed his gun at Jess, sensing something was wrong with the kid. The men behind Jess took an aim at Jake. Several other Kuleens came and stood by Jake's side with their guns pointed forward.

"There are a lot of guns pointed at each other here, guys. Why don't we all calm down?" Jess again spoke in a soft voice.

Jake noticed a small red scar on her cheek. "You are Nefe, aren't you?" He balked. "You swapped bodies from Vedika to Jessica before Tej hit you. You kept Jessica close to you because you were slowly possessing her."

"Wow. No shit, Sherlock. Your powers of deductive reasoning are amazing. Did this scar give me up?" Nefe laughed. "And nice to know that Tej was the one who hit me. I'll deal with that pigeon later."

Jake felt guilty for blurting out Tej's name. Nefe being here meant death for all the Kuleens present in this room, but he'd inadvertently dragged Tej back into the conflict. He went on the offensive. "You bitch. You didn't even spare this innocent kid?"

"You shouldn't swear in front of kids, Jake. Bad manners."

"What do you want?"

"I came to thank you, actually. Three of us Kshins were in a race for the position of *The Supreme*. I was leading the race, to be honest, yet the approval ratings of the other two within the Kshin community weren't bad either. But your Kuleen warriors came to my rescue. You took out two of my strongest opponents in one clean stroke." Jess bowed a little.

Miranda emerged from behind the crowd and joined Jake, pointing her gun at Jess.

"So, you are the leader of these dogs." Jess now had a serious expression on her face. She pointed a finger at Miranda. "You killed my favorite lieutenant five years back, so you will have to pay. You dipshits don't know how much time and effort it takes to cultivate a good subordinate. He'd been with me for two hundred years." Jess clenched her teeth.

Miranda knew her death was imminent, but she was not mincing any words. "And what about the lives the humans and Kuleens have lost at your hands? Don't they matter?"

"NO!" Jess screamed. The whole hall shook a little. Bottles and glasses on the table burst; mirrors on the walls cracked.

"You humans and Kuleens are like cattle and poultry to us. On this planet, only Kshin lives matter. Everyone else is expendable. It's better your race learns this soon. Be our slaves, or go to your graves."

That jibe hurt every Kuleen in the room. That was the essence of their fight. The alien invaders who had silently taken over Earth held no respect for the original inhabitants of the planet.

Jess controlled her anger and smiled again. "However angry I am, I won't dirty my hands with your blood. These men will take good care of you all." She started to walk out of the hall, and the armed men behind her gave way for her to leave. She reached the door of the hall, stopped, and turned around.

"But I don't want my men to get hurt, so I'll take all your toys with me." Jess curled up her index finger, and all the guns and knives the Kuleens had were snatched from their hands by an invisible force. The weapons flew out of the hall as if they were riding an unseen conveyer belt. The Kuleens were totally unarmed.

"None of them leaves here alive." Jess walked out and the doors closed behind her. Sounds of rapid bullet fire and human screams filled the entire party hall.

Back at the village, Manu Kumar had again developed a high fever, and Tej was sitting by his side. He was half asleep and was speaking incoherently in his sleep. Tej was dapping Manu's head with a damp cloth to keep his forehead from warming up a lot when Manika entered the room.

"This fever shows the same symptoms as before, Mani." Tej was worried.

Manika's face bore a foreboding expression. "I have bad news. Many other people in the village are reporting the same symptoms again. The fever is coming back. Their skin is turning light green, with red blisters all over the body. Three old people who were already very weak are on their deathbeds."

"This should not have happened. I killed Nefe. All this should have gone." Tej stood up. "I need to go back. The Kuleens are the only ones who can help us. They are waging a great war against Kshins. They must have some cure."

"Wait—don't go blind this time. Let me time-read."

"Read Jake Morales. He is a Kuleen fighter. Focus on December 25th, 2057. No … no, they must be partying. Focus on December 26th, the morning."

Manika closed her eyes. Tej could see her eyeballs moving. A motley of expressions ran across her face in a sequence, as if she was living each moment she saw. She smiled for a few instants, but gradually, her expressions turned sad. A tear rolled down her cheek.

Tej gulped. *She's time-reading Kuleens. I left them in a festive spirit. What could make her cry?*

"They are dead. I could see this man Jake and several others around him lying in a pool of blood. Each body has been shattered with hundreds of bullet holes."

"How is this possible?" Tej's throat was heavy. "Go a few hours back. See what happened."

"I tried. I got the same blank visions."

"Kshins! They were there." Tej said nervously to himself. "But who could it be? I killed Nefe myself. It's impossible."

Manika could barely control her tears. She had rarely seen so much gore in a time-vision. "I saw symbols written on the wall in blood. Seems like one of the Kuleens tried to give a message before he or she died. But the symbols look like English letters. I don't completely understand that language, at least the written part of it."

"I do. Can you draw those symbols for me?" Tej fumbled through the room and found a piece of paper and charcoal, which he handed to Manika.

Manika closed her eyes and focused on the symbols.

Tej read those symbols. "n e f … Nefe." He jammed his fists in his forehead. Manika placed her hand on his shoulder.

"We have lost everything, Manika. We're defeated." Tej sat down on the ground. He took deep breaths as he sobbed, and tears erupted from his eyes. "She is alive. She butchered all of them. Kshins are indeed invincible."

"No, Tej. Have hope." Manika knew her words sounded as hollow as her hope, but she couldn't bear to see Tej breaking down in front of her. "We will figure something out."

"What will we figure out, Manika?" Tej snapped and got up. "What? My people are dying of a strange disease we know nothing about. Kuleens, the only hope there could be against these aliens, are dead. Their most effective weapon is rendered futile. We have lost, Manika. We have lost."

"Tej … are you there?" Manu Kumar opened his eyes. The skin on his face, arms and legs was turning light green, and small red blisters were visible.

Tej sat down on his knees near Manu's bed and caressed his forehead. "Manu, I am here. Are you feeling better?"

"No. I'm not. I feel my time is over. I can see *Yamraaj*. I can see him riding on his monstrous black bull. He is laughing loudly and charging towards me with a thorny whip in his hand."

"Manu is hallucinating." Manika had tears in her eyes.

"Tej, can you call my parents, please? I want to see them for the last time." Manu gave a faint smile.

"Don't speak like that. Nothing would happen to you. I am with you." Tej took Manu's hand in his hand and tightly grasped it. "I will call your parents." Tej got up and started walking towards the other room, but Manika held his arm.

"What?"

"Both of them are down with a high fever, too." Manika looked away. "I checked them a few minutes ago. Their pulses are low."

Tej stopped and saw Manu looking at him in anticipation. "My parents, are they here, Tej? You told them I was unwell, right? Mother loves me a lot. She can't see me in pain."

Tej controlled his tears. Manika was already crying as silently as she could, her lips covered with her hand. Tej again got down near Manu. "I ... I have sent them the news, Manu. They are on their way. Stay strong."

"It's all right, Tej. You are near me. I am happy." Manu tried to smile. "I have only loved one person in life other than my parents. That person is you. My mentor, my friend, my love."

"I love you too, Manu. I love you more than anything." Tej's eyes were red, and his throat was heavy.

"Can I get some water? I am very thirsty."

"Yes, yes." Tej wiped his tears and quickly filled a glass of water from a jug. "Here you go." Tej kept his hand behind Manu's head and tilted the glass to his lips, but Manu did not drink. "Come on, Manu, you were thirsty. Drink some water."

Manu had stopped responding. His body was motionless. His eyes were open, staring into oblivion.

Tej clenched his teeth in anger. He grasped Manu's hand in both his hands and burst into tears. His best friend, the love of his life, had left him and there was nothing he could do.

Manika ran outside. She could not watch more death today.

Within the next two days, several people in the village lost their lives to the deadly disease. Very few, who were still healthy, ran away from the village. The news that Sarp-Nagar was cursed by the witch had already spread. Tej's foster parents and his brother were among the dead.

The village funeral grounds had no more space for burning the dead bodies; the dead were now being burnt in batches. They couldn't even find a priest to do the last rites for the departed, as the village priest was dead, too, and no nearby village was ready to help a cursed community.

At sunset, Tej stood at the gate of the funeral land and looked at hundreds of pyres burning in front of him: a monument to his unimaginable loss and colossal defeat.

13
LAREM

A month had passed, and the number of deaths per day slowly came down. Most of the community had perished—only around one-fifth survived. Everyone who was forcibly made to ingest the green liquid by Nefe's men had died. Those who were not in the village at that time or those who went into hiding were the only ones remaining.

Tej made all efforts he could, but he was helpless in face of death. Nefe's men had also burned down several food storage houses and butchered the cattle.

Tej traveled to King Kirtivarman's court to seek help. Kirtivarman was a minor king, and Sarp-Nagar fell under his jurisdiction. Tej took the village headman's fourteen-year-old son Jai with him. Jai was also unaffected by the green disease, as he'd been outside the village at the time Nefe raided it.

Tej and Jai were examined by the palace doctors for disease symptoms. After that, they were taken before the presence of the King. Since Jai's father was dead, Tej introduced Jai as the new village headman.

Fearing an epidemic, the king was inclined to burn

down the village, along with the inhabitants. Tej convinced him against it. Tej assured the king that if he donated enough food-grain to the village, the villagers would have no reason to go out to seek food. That would further prevent the spread of the disease. He also told the king that a poisonous plant and not a witch's curse had caused the disease and deaths, so there was no cause of further worry. To prove that, he gave his own example—explaining that he did not consume the dishes made with that plant, and hence, he survived. When he was asked if he was a position of authority in the village, he clarified that he was a representative for Jai.

Tej returned to the village with five bullock-carts full of food grain and five healthy cows. He also started to rebuild the village and re-start the farms with the help of remaining youth.

He was already a beloved son of his village, but his efforts to restore the community made him a hero. Jai even considered him his elder brother.

Though nothing could take the place of the departed, the settlement was slowly coming back to life again.

One fine day, Tej and Manika visited the Lord Shiva temple at the center of the village. It was a very old temple with several cracks in its walls and pillars. Dried leaves from a nearby tree had filled the temple compound. Two small earthen lamps flickered near the Lord Shiva statue.

Tej just sat and stared at the deity. A thousand thoughts crossed his mind. His life of the past few days, which seemed like years, flashed before his eyes.

Manika got up and picked a broomstick lying nearby. She started sweeping the temple floor.

Tej sat quietly with his back resting against a pillar. "Mani, have you heard about the lore of Goddess Trikaal

Devi?" he spoke nonchalantly.

"Yes. Heard a lot in the ancient lore, and also learned about her from my visions of the future." Manika kept cleaning the floor in a nonchalant manner.

"Visions of the future?" Tej sat up.

"Yes, two quantum physicists, Adriana Johansson and Kavitha Kavyaluri, extensively studied time-demons. In long-drawn research from the years 2032 to 2046, they actually alienated the unique radiation given out by time-demons. Using a sophisticated material-dating technique, they concluded that this radiation was increasing at a slow rate."

"That's right," Tej interjected. "Jake also told me that Kshins use some kind of radiation signature to track time-demons. But how does this relate to Trikaal Devi?"

"If you would only let me complete my time-vision, perhaps all your questions will be answered." Manika looked at him with feigned anger.

"I am sorry. Please continue."

"Adriana and Kavitha published a paper in February 2047 called 'Search for the Last Reminder'. The paper could not win them the Nobel Prize for Physics that year, but it caught the attention of the scientific community and time travel enthusiasts. These two scientists built an algorithm which took the radiation readings and ran a reverse time-series analysis. This algorithm predicted that at the time of the Big Bang, the world had forty-two and a half time-crawlers."

"Crawlers? Even Kshins call us time-crawlers." *So that's where this word comes from.*

"Kshins may have picked up that name from this study itself because that was the first time anyone used this word. Adriana and Kavitha, being scientists, could not have used a colloquial and mythology-inspired term such as *demon* in a research paper, so they used the word 'crawler' for entities who could crawl through time. But their initial algorithm conclusion didn't make much sense. That half in the forty-two and a half could not be explained. They checked and re-checked their calculations, yet that half always remained. How can a half time-crawler exist?"

Manika got down and started collecting the leaves in her saree. "They realized that half can only be a result of a time crawler who doesn't just crawl through time but exists in each time-slice. The sum of an infinite arithmetic series that starts on one fourth and halves with every passing second would result in a half. They called that half time-crawler the Last Reminder, shortened to Larem."

"Larem, a time traveler who exists in all time-slices?" Tej exclaimed. He had ignored every scientific fact Manika had thrown at him and picked up only this one word.

"Yes. It sounded practically impossible but was the result of their years of research. Many scientists checked their models and results. Many even questioned the concept of time-crawlers. But facts and experimental data were irrefutable. The radiation signature was present, and the algorithm's predictions were impeccable."

Tej sat listening, like a kid engrossed in a fairytale.

"Later, some theologians and time travel geeks took that research paper and came up with their own hypothesis. Since the time-demon lore also says that Goddess Trikaal Devi exists in all time slices, the popular theory was that she is the same as Larem: a divine entity who sees everything, knows everything, and is present everywhere. She is deep-rooted in the passage of time itself.

"Oh, that's the connection. Larem is Trikaal Devi. They both are the same."

"Yes, that's the prevalent thought. Though the sad part is that no one except time demons can ever see her."

"Why is that?"

"Because only time-crawlers can enter time in a way that it's not a dimension."

"You know what I think, Mani? This is all crap. Kumbh said something similar before I took him out. If gods and goddesses existed, they would not have let this happen to innocent souls."

Manika kept quiet and heaped the leaves together on one side. Tej rested against the pillar and closed his eyes. He felt tired and sleepy. "Hey, Mani?"

"Yes."

"The temple priest is dead, right?" His eyes were still closed.

"Yes."

"Then who lit those two lamps kept near Lord Shiva?"

"Don't know. Some villager."

"Nah, who's left in the village? Everyone is either dead or sick or has fled the place."

"I lit those lamps."

Tej heard a different voice and woke up. An old lady draped in a saffron saree was walking towards him with a metal plate in her hands. The plate had some fruits and sweets. Tej got up and bowed his head a little out of respect. The lady smiled. She was in the late fifties, but her hair was dark black. Her face showed signs of old age, but no wrinkles. She had a bright red *tilak* on her forehead.

"Who are you, Devi?"

"My name is *Advaita*. I am the new priestess here."

Tej bowed down and touched her feet out of respect, eagerly looking at the plate of fruits she was carrying. The plate also carried some rose petals usually served to the lord during the daily worship. Advaita smiled and handed over a rose-petal to Tej.

"Can I get some of the fruits?" Tej asked her. "I am sure that these are the *prasad* offered to the lord."

"But I heard you saying you don't believe in God." Advaita brought her eyebrows together and looked at him.

"I … didn't mean …" Tej was at a loss of words.

Advaita smiled. "Anyhow, the fruits and sweets are for the village kids. They need them the most."

Tej nodded and stepped aside. Advaita walked towards the temple entrance. Tej noticed that Manika was nowhere to be seen.

"Umm, Devi, did you see my friend Manika?"

"No, you were sleeping here alone when I came." Advaita kept walking.

Something within him compelled him to keep the conversation going. "Do you believe in God?" Tej asked loudly.

Advaita stopped and turned around. "You are looking for answers, aren't you?"

"Yes, I am."

"There was someone whom you looked up to for answers. Who was he?"

Tej frowned. *What was this lady trying to say?*

"Yes, there was someone. A snake who came in the guise of a guru, but deceived me. Used me as a pawn."

"Let me ask you another question. You were bitten by a snake once. Why could it not harm you?"

"The poison in my body saved me. Why are you talking in riddles? Say what you have to say?"

"Poison cuts poison."

"What?" The lady was not making any sense to Tej.

"Beware of the snake behind you," she warned.

Tej turned back and saw a snake right behind him, with his hood spread out. The snake leaped forward and bit Tej's foot.

He cried out in pain and woke up. He had been dreaming, and his forehead was drenched with sweat. He saw Manika was still cleaning the floor.

"Mani, I had a dream."

"Okay?"

"In dreams, our subconscious actively works to solve problems which we cannot figure out when we are awake."

"So, you are some kind of a brain-doctor, now?"

"I don't know where I got that theory from. I possessed a few folks in the future—perhaps from one of them. Anyhow, I know who can help us."

"Who?"

"Rigasur!"

"That's your solution?" Manika was furious. "You want to go seek help from a demon?"

"Hear me out. Nefe is a schemer, an evil one. And Rigasur is the same, an evil schemer, and a pretty good one at that."

"Yes, and Rigasur worked for the Kshins. That's one detail you are conveniently ignoring. And what about the deceptive game he played with us for years?"

Tej realized this thought was a far-fetched one. "You are right. What was I thinking?" He closed his eyes again. *That lady Advaita, she looked so real.* Her face floated in front of his eyes.

An hour later, Tej was trying to unlock the door of his house, but the key was stuck in the lock. Manika stood to the side, waiting. Their visit to the temple hadn't given them the spiritual relief they sought.

She looked around. The village bore a post-apocalyptic look: empty streets and playgrounds, deserted farm equipment, the occasional barking of stray dogs and vultures circling the sky.

Manika noticed someone at a distance. A hefty man was running towards them with his full might.

"Tej, who is this man?"

"What, Mani?" Tej was still trying to turn the key into the lock. The man was approaching fast.

"Tej, turn around, he's coming!" Manika screamed.

Tej turned around, but the man jumped in the air and kicked Tej in the chest. The kick was so powerful that Tej and that man tore through the wooden door behind him, and landed inside the house. Manika ran inside after them. The man had now picked up Tej by his neck and smashed him against a house wall. He was pushing on Tej's neck with his arm and the full force of his body, gagging him.

"Mangat, what … are … you … doing?" Tej recognized him as Mangat, the famous village wrestler.

"The man spoke in a hoarse voice. "Why did you send her after me?"

"Who … whom did I send?" Tej was shaking vigorously to get free, but couldn't. Mangat's eyes were full of rage.

Manika closed her eyes for a second and opened them. "He is Rigasur." She took a step back.

Rigasur continued gagging Tej. Manika looked around, picked up a wooden stick, and struck Mangat on the back with all of her force. The stick broke into several pieces.

Rigasur turned around in anger and let go of Tej, who fell down on the ground, coughing.

"You bitch, you are definitely involved in this!" He promenaded towards her.

"Involved in what?" she stammered, walking backward.

Tej got up and ran inside the adjoining room. Manika fell on a cot kept behind her. "Please don't kill me!" she pleaded.

"I think I should. I always had a soft corner for you time-readers. No more. Whoever bothers me goes straight to Hell."

Rigasur was about to attack Manika when Tej jumped on him from behind and swiftly wrapped a metal wire around his neck. Rigasur struggled to get free, but Tej rode on his back, tightening the wire.

"Now, I don't want to kill this man, Rigasur. Don't make me," Tej spoke in his ear. "Will you calm down and talk?"

Rigasur kept trying to free himself. He was smothered, and his face was turning red.

"Will you calm down?" Tej shouted.

Rigasur nodded. Tej loosened the grip and alighted from his back. Rigasur removed the wire from his neck and sat on the ground, gasping for air. He sat with his head down. Tej sat next to Manika on the bed. She was still jittery.

Rigasur looked at Tej. "What did you say to her?"

"Say to whom? You are not making any sense."

"To Trikaal Devi, Larem, whatever you call her?"

Tej and Manika looked at each other.

"You have lost your senses, Rigasur. Trikaal Devi is a bit of folklore, and Larem is a scientific hypothesis. Nothing else."

"Now you will teach *me*? One of the oldest Demons of Time?" Rigasur smirked.

"The so-called oldest Demon of Time, who was a mere attack dog for Kshins," Manika taunted. She'd cultivated far deeper hatred for Rigasur than Tej ever could.

Rigasur wanted to let out a terse response but held his tongue. He spoke after a few seconds, "Yes, I served the Kshins. As if you don't know how powerful Kshins are. Have you ever seen Nefe? Her powers are endless, and her cruelty knows no bounds. What was I supposed to do? Revolt against her and end up like Kumbh? Kumbh was the number-one enemy on her list. Look what happened to him."

"Enough of the past, Rigasur. Talk about the present. Why are you here? And why did you attack me?"

"I spent three decades of my life staying in these primitive times and creating this university of time-readers. I laid down the most perfect plan and captured Kumbh. I superseded Mozeek and was on my way to becoming the closest time-demon aide of Nefe. But then, at the very end of it, you bit me and trapped me in that vessel. My years of hard work washed down the drain. Mozeek won Nefe's trust, and I was sidelined like a piece of junk. Nefe doesn't like losers."

"If you are talking about our past interactions, Rigasur, we have several scars of our own." Tej was agitated.

Rigasur was acting as if he was an innocent victim in this whole situation.

"I know. I deceived you, you tricked me, we're sorted. I am way past all of that, kid. I was, in fact, spending some cooling-off time in the 2060s, taking my much-awaited long hibernation. But then, a few minutes ago, Trikaal Devi visited me and she asked me to help you. And by the way, 'ask' is a rather soft word I am using here. Her tone was more of dictation."

"Did she visit you in a dream?"

"Well, that doesn't matter, Tej. What matters is that I was finally getting out of this Kshin, Kuleen, Time-Demon war triangle. I had retired to a rather isolated island in the Pacific, where I planned to spend at least the next decade in peace. I was basking in the sun on a beach when she tapped my shoulder, dragging me back into this mess. You tell me why she did that?"

Tej shrugged. "I … I don't know why she would ask you to help me."

"Why, then? She rarely partakes in these worldly matters." Rigasur was half-talking to himself.

"You also met her, Tej," Manika spoke in a low voice. "Tell him about your dream."

Rigasur looked at Tej in anticipation.

Tej narrated his dream.

Rigasur had a sullen expression on his face. "She wants me to help you fight Kshins?"

"Appears so."

"Why is she so benevolent to you?"

"Why wouldn't she be? And why are you so terrified of her?"

"You don't know her, kid. She's virtually everywhere. Her existence is woven in the threads of time. She's faster than the speed of atomic rotation, swifter than the speed of thought. She's the most powerful time-traveler the world has ever seen. She once was so angry, she put all the time-demons to sleep for a thousand years. I have always evaded being in her presence. So when she visited me this time, I thought it was the end of me." Rigasur was again half-talking to himself.

Manika and Tej were both surprised and amused to see him in a state of mortal fear. They always reckoned him, a powerful time-demon, to be a calculated villain— but at that moment, he looked like a small child afraid of a bully.

"Well, when she referred to you, she said poison cuts poison.' If I were you, I would take that as a compliment." Tej smiled.

"Is it a joke to you, buddy?" Rigasur got up in anger.

"So Larem wants you to help me, but it seems like you are refusing? I can try summoning her again. And I'll tell her that instead of helping me, you actually attacked me." Tej relaxed against a wall smiling.

Rigasur was furious but remained tight-lipped. He started walking back and forth in the room contemplating. He stopped decisively. "All right, I will help you. But that's the last you are seeing of me."

"I wasn't planning on a long-term relationship either. It hurts me more to team up with a monster such as you."

Rigasur closed his eyes and clenched his teeth. He took a deep breath calming himself. "All right. Let's meet on the 8th of January 2069. That's when the Kshins will start executing their final plan."

"What plan?"

"Sorry, I don't have detailed information about how

they are going to screw up with this world. I just know they're up to something big. I need to get in touch with some of my resources. If we need to take on Kshins, we need help from the best of the best. Though …" Rigasur paused, and an expression of dread floated on his face. Tej and Manika waited for him to finish.

"Though knowing Kshins up close, I am fully sure we will lose this fight." It was clear Rigasur was tied between upsetting Larem by not helping Tej versus facing the wrath of Kshins by doing so.

"How did you get up after I bit you?" Tej was curious.

"I'd built an antidote to your poison long ago. I took it every day when you were in my vicinity. I woke up after a week and left that vessel." Rigasur was about to leave the body again when Tej stopped him.

"Where did you possess this body?"

"From the wrestling ground."

"Please leave it back there. I am not going to carry this hefty wrestler back to his place."

"Arghhh!" Rigasur opened the door and walked out.

"Where do I find you in 2069?" Tej asked.

"Ask your time-reader girlfriend." Rigasur walked out.

"She's not my girlfriend," Tej shouted, but Rigasur was gone. "Does it look like we are in a relationship, Mani?"

"Shut up!"

14
WORLD'S LARGEST POULTRY FARM

8th January 2069

World population: **10.50 Billion**, Concordia
VX pre-orders: **3.15 Million**, Adoption: **0.03%**

crowd of five hundred media members gathered at the Mondenira Building hall in downtown Manhattan. Rigasur and Tej were present there, possessing two journalists sitting next to each other.

At exactly 09:00 AM, Jessica Sharma, the 17-years-old CEO of Vedvance Corporation possessed by Nefe, started her press conference. "A very happy 2069 to everyone."

Many in the crowd echoed her back.

"My parents, Mrs. Vedika Sharma and Mrs. Rubina Vance, laid the foundation of this company more than a decade ago. Back in 2057, we were very close to building this product. But due to some unfortunate circumstances, I lost both my mothers in a very brief span of time. I was only six years old at the time." Jessica paused, took a sip of water and wiped a tear from her eye. Many in the crowd reacted with sympathy.

"Nefe is such a great actor," Rigasur whispered. Tej kept silent.

"No one can fill the void they left in my life. But I was fortunate enough to be surrounded by an amazing board of directors and company executives. They helped me continue building what my mothers started. Their untimely demise did push us back several years. Being the incredible company we are, we turned around and pushed ourselves really hard.

"Today, as I remember them, I am not sad. I am happy that we are able to give this world a gift which will benefit mankind for thousands of years. Today, we are at a crossroads of history. Ladies and gentlemen, I present to you all the most awaited tech product of 2068. The stabilized version of man and A.I. singularity—the Concordia VX!" Jessica spoke the last words louder and stood up clapping.

A fifteen-foot curtain behind her started opening, and the crowd offered a round of applause. Loud rock music started to play. The curtain revealed a giant screen featuring the words "CONCORDIA VX." The screen displayed a small chip-like device with six spider arms. Several lines of text and labels trailed the limbs.

Rigasur again whispered in Tej's year, "This press conference is a sham. The owners of major media houses, internet magazines, news channels, and even dark-net-chatrooms have been bought, coaxed, or possessed by Kshins. All this drama is for the gullible masses, who will now line up to get this device into their bodies without asking any questions. It will be a fucking rage."

After a few seconds, Nefe again took on the microphone and started a presentation.

"This device, Concordia VX, is the 10th version we have built over the years. This silicon-based device is three nanometers in length and two nanometers in breadth, and the technical specifications are state-of-the-art. Twenty thousand PFLOPS speed, more than 99.99 percent accuracy. Your decisions won't just be faster, they will be blitz-fast." Jessica took a two-second pause, allowing the information to sink in. The crowd burst into a round of applause once again, which continued for a few seconds and then died down.

"I will now take questions."

Several media people raised their hands. Nefe pointed to a journalist, who got up and started speaking. "Thanks, Ms. Sharma. Peter Mckhoy from Tech Evenings Manhattan. The news in tech circles is that there is a surgery involved in getting this device into your body. It's reported that once the device goes in, it jams itself onto the spine using the six spider legs."

Nefe laughed. "The way you put it sounds very evil. But let me clarify. Concordia VX can be simply injected at the back of the neck. No surgery is required. The device floats into the bloodstream and attaches itself to the back of the spine using these arms. You got that part right. These arms act both as a glue as well as a transmitter.

"From there on, the device will send and receive signals to the brain. This bridge will give the human brain complete access to machine-level intelligence. This will allow a human to enhance his or her intelligence, decision-making, and reactionary instincts. Your neurological processes will be enhanced ten-times over those of a normal human being."

Nefe paused. Her voice went softer as if urging. "This singularity between man and machine is an unparalleled feat of technology. My only request is that you all welcome it with open hands, and not with fear. Please don't let baseless rumors prevent you from embracing a path-breaking technology. The device has been tested on one million test subjects, and the results have been nothing but phenomenal."

Nefe then chose another journalist, and he got up and spoke. "Over the past few months, you have gathered several million pre-orders for Concordia VX. Is that correct?"

"Three million, a hundred and fifty thousand, two hundred and forty-three, to be exact. As a base of the whole world's population our adoption is 0.03 percent," Jessica completed with a smile.

"Yes, so over three million pre-orders. Which means these many people have already had the device injected. When do you plan to activate these devices?"

"Within a few minutes, we will remotely activate all the pre-orders today. Anyone who orders going forward will be activated within three hours of being injected."

Another journalist, Neena, stood up and asked out of turn, "There are rumors that you are going to use these devices to control the masses. Is that true?"

Nefe frowned for a second, then calmed herself. "I'm sorry, I didn't even choose you to ask your question. But now that you have, I would say I do not answer to baseless allegations such as these. Representatives of the general public are most welcome to visit our facilities and audit our practices. Except for Concordia's proprietary software and algorithm, which we keep close to our chest, we are a pretty open company. And we are not coercing acceptance of the devices. Everyone is welcome to make a choice over whether to get injected or not."

"But the control of all these devices is in your own hands." Neena was not mincing words.

"No, that's completely false." A look of indignation floated on Nefe's face. "Please don't spread these unfounded rumors—not in this prestigious forum."

Neena stood her ground. "Deny it all you want. Your lies will come out one day."

"I apologize in advance, but I will have to ask security to remove you from these premises. We are entering a brave new world, and we have no space for fearmongers such as you. You spread baseless rumors and mislead the masses with unsubstantiated falsities." Nefe signaled to two burly security guards at the entrance of the room, who walked up to Neena and dragged her outside. Neena's mic was disabled, but she kept shouting.

"Please be respectful to her." Nefe smiled. She then addressed the reporters. "Who else here sees me as an evil techno-entrepreneur with secret plans of world domination?" Several in the crowd laughed and applauded.

"This reporter, is she a Kuleen?" Tej whispered in Rigasur's ear.

"There's a slight possibility." Rigasur took a deep breath. "Kuleens have been targeted and murdered by the Kshins over the past few years. Their genocide escalated, especially after the attack of 2057, which made Nefe the uncrowned queen of the Kshins."

"This reporter, I assume she'll be dead soon?"

"Yeah, gone. Wiped from the face of the earth, as if

she never existed."

Thereafter, Nefe took no more questions. She walked through another presentation which showed how Concordia worked. She also launched three million Concordia devices, counting down before activating them. The last announcement was that Vedvance engineering team would send several updates and bug fixes over the following few months. The remote updates promised to make the Concordia VX more integrated with human consciousness.

"That is all for today, friends. I'll now welcome you all to a high tea at our Concordia themed Sky-park. Heli-Shuttles will be waiting outside. Please have your badges displayed at all times," Nefe ended, to continuous applause from the crowd which lasted a whole minute. Rigasur and Tej slipped out.

Two hours later, they both sat at a coffee shop. Tej was talking about what all he learned at Kuleen facilities.

"So, whatever "big" the Kshins are planning, I am guessing that ties into this Concordia VX." Tej took a sip of his mint-flavored chai-latte.

"Yes. Concordia is a linking mechanism. Kshins are going to spread this technology like a virus among the masses. If you remember, Kumbh wanted to bring about an apocalypse on earth. His plan was to alter this device to send electrical signals to human brains and fry them en masse."

"Yes, by possessing that hacker. I'm forgetting her name." Tej rubbed his forehead trying hard to recall the name.

"Karlesha. But that's not happening now. Kumbh is out of the equation."

Tej sat tight in an alert pose. The interesting part was coming out. Rigasur was finally showing his cards. "So, the Kshins are going to wipe out humanity now?"

"No. Even worse. As per my sources, Kshins will use these devices to convert this world into a poultry farm."

"A poultry farm? But who are the poultry here?" Tej finished his coffee and relaxed in his chair. With Rigasur on his side, he felt more peaceful.

"Humans. They will be cultivated for their emotions. Billions will be tortured every second. Their emotions will be filtered and collected for the consumption of Kshins."

"That's exactly what Pete Morales told me. To be honest, this eating-of-thoughts theory is beyond my understanding."

Rigasur eyed Tej with a penetrating gaze. "You have been inside of Infernex. Right?"

"Yes, I have." Tej shivered at the mere mention of the word.

"Infernex 2.0 was just a pilot project on a small scale, with a few hundred thousand people. Kshins have now built a much powerful virtual reality, an upgraded version called Infernex 3.0. This software can connect and torture billions of people at once. Brand new massive servers, blitzkrieg Wi-Fi connections. It would be a mega VR slaughterhouse. Kshins will wait in stealth mode till Concordia VX adoption reaches a critical mass. And then one day, with one stroke of a key, they will push every Concordia user into Infernex. They will start storing their emotions into a capacitor. This storage will feed the whole Kshin race for thousands of years to come."

"How can anyone store emotions? They are not tangible."

"For Kshins, they are. Emotions are their food. Most of the wars, conquest, and mass-slaughter waged in the last five thousand years have been the Kshins' doing. Every major war or conquest was a mega-feast for them. Oodles of pain, anger, frustration, and fear to be devoured."

"Oh, come on. These wars and conquests were because of time-demons or greedy humans fighting with each other."

"No doubt time-demons were the actors. But behind the scenes, the fuel of the fire was provided by the Kshins. Many time-demons were their pawns—like I was. Those who didn't dance to their tunes were removed. The Kshins' gory imprint is evident in all major events leaving carnage."

Tej went silent. The truth was simply too hard to digest. These aliens not only planned to rule the world, but they also wanted to plunge it into an abyss so dark, it would be difficult for humanity to crawl back.

"You know a lot about them, don't you?" Tej's question was half-taunt.

Rigasur averted Tej's gaze. "I worked for them for centuries, kid. Learned a thing or two. Now let's go. We need to find a time-reader in this era. And we're going to meet the best of the best." He got up.

"What's the use? Time-reader can't see Kshins, and even when someone tries to peep through their veil, they never come back." Tej still got goosebumps remembering Kuntala. "Kuntala lost her life trying to time-read them."

Rigasur grimaced at the mention of Kuntala. "Yes,

Kuntala, Manika—those were readers from three thousand BC. The guy we are going to meet now belongs to the modern age. He uses chemicals and machines to enhance his time-reads. Kshins can't see him or sense him."

Tej got up. The humanoid robot waiter came to their table with a payment machine. Rigasur swiped his wrist and started to walk out.

Tej followed him. "What's his name?"

"No one knows, and I never asked. He calls himself 'Historical Scientist,' though. I call him Histor."

Rigasur and Tej stepped outside in the street. Rigasur tapped his wrist and spoke, "Taxi, please." A yellow-colored sky-taxi came down and landed at a pod near them. The small yellow box resembled a mini helicopter, with two seats. On top, it was powered by two big rotors on the front and one at the back. Its landing skids also had a mini staircase for passengers to board and alight with ease. The number 1729 was imprinted on the front glass, the doors, and even the landing skids. Tej and Rigasur sat in the seats and tied the belts.

"Welcome to Beetel and Morgan's taxi service, Mr. Mamnoor. You are passengers of Taxi number 1729. Where do you wish to travel to today?" The taxi AI recognized Rigasur by his host's name.

"Sanguan Mental Health Facility, please."

"Absolutely, sir. As a rule, I must update you that your destination is in Kentucky, and is across state borders. You will have to pay an extra air-fare because we will use inter-state air-routes. You can refer to the detailed fare chart in our app. Is that charge acceptable to you?"

"Yes let's go ahead." Rigasur smiled.

The taxi doors were locked, the rotors started churning, and they lifted off. The taxi slowly rose until it joined a series of vehicles flying in pre-designated air-paths, few feet above them.

Sanguan Mental Health Facility, Kentucky

Histor was standing in the hallway, talking to a doctor. A man in his late forties with a slightly heavy build and a fat belly, Histor had thick white hair, light stubble, and wore a blue uniform. With a jolly expression on his face, his eyes and gestures conveyed that he was blind. Doctor Amol Patel, who was the senior visiting psychiatrist at Sanguan, was a lean man in his late thirties. He sported a thick mustache and had sharp facial features. Dr. Patel seemed to be in a hurry to leave, but Histor held him up in a conversation.

"Wait, Dr. Patel, you didn't answer me. Can I talk to you about my visions? I promise you'll love hearing what I have to say." Likeably, he even patted the doctor on the shoulder.

"No, you cannot." Dr. Patel adjusted his spectacles. "Have you been consistent in taking your medication? Please take your pills, or I'll have the nurses give them to you by force."

He was always nervous while talking to Histor. Histor's medical checkups proved beyond a doubt that he was blind, but Dr. Patel had a strong feeling he was not. This feeling usually landed outside his perfect rational explanation of how the world worked—and all he could do was brush it off.

"Don't worry, I'll take my medication." He paused

but spoke before the doctor could even think of leaving. "As I told Jokie, no-one understands us time-readers. But being a man of science, I thought you would understand me."

"Please don't start with this time-reading thingy again. I thought you were getting better, and that talking to other inmates would help you recover. But I was wrong. These conversations are reinforcing your delusions. I'll have to put a stop to them." Dr. Patel looked even more worried now, but he had a meeting to go to, so he turned around and started walking.

"You think I'm insane, you think my words don't make any sense. But do you know what the famous philosopher, Francioso Tez Natazinho, said in the year 4011? He said, 'Those who dance are considered insane by those who can't hear the music.' You can't hear the music, Doc. Histor can." Histor laughed.

"Oh, please." Dr. Patel turned back. He hated it when people misquoted other people. Histor had stepped right on his pet peeve. "This is not a quote by some Natazinho in 4011, but a quote by that philosopher Nietzsche sometime in the 1800s."

"Yeah, him too. He was a time crawler. He quoted this in both time-slices he frequented."

The doctor almost facepalmed. Being a visiting doctor in a mental health facility, he had seen and learned to tolerate all kinds, but somehow, Histor always got on his nerves. "Forget it. Two visitors are coming in to meet you in around fifteen minutes. They are journalists who are doing some story on patients with mental health issues. Behave yourself in their presence, or there will be repercussions."

"I know them. They're here to talk about my visions." Histor walked closer to the doctor and spoke in a hushed tone. "They are time crawlers who are plotting a war against the secret forces that run this world." Histor paused, and his last sentence was almost inaudible. "Don't tell anyone Histor told you this."

The doctor shook his head in frustration and walked away. He signaled an attendant, Natalie, to take Histor to the visitation room.

Natalie grabbed Histor's arm, but Histor looked at her in anger. "Do you think I'm blind? Yes, I am. But I am a time-reader, girl. I can see the present. I can see everything around me."

"Sir I am trying to help …"

"You go help others. Histor helps himself."

Natalie looked at Histor in amazement as he walked towards the visiting room without any help. She'd seen patients with vision impairment walk without support, but he moved and turned as a sighted person would. She still accompanied him.

She swiped her badge, seated Histor in the visiting room, and closed the door on her way out. The visiting room was an austere space with gray-colored walls, gray table, and gray chairs. Histor sat at the table, smiling, his fingers tapping the table as is if he was listening to a song and humming along.

Fifteen minutes later, two journalists entered the room and sat in front of him. They were Rigasur and Tej, still possessing the journalists. Histor kept tapping the table.

"We are here, Histor …"

Rigasur tried to speak, but Histor shushed him.

"Shhh, I am watching Jack-a-belle Morgan's concert live. Man, punk rock will never die." Histor gazed into oblivion, smiling. His fingers still tapped the table as he half-sang a song.

"See, Histor? I am sorry for Cape Town." Rigasur had a guilty expression on his face.

"Please shut up, Rig. I didn't agree to this meeting because of you. I agreed to meet you because of the poor guy you brought along with you. So why don't you keep your lips sealed tight?"

Tej coughed and interrupted, "Sir, actually …"

"You are Tej. Aren't you?" Histor looked at Tej, his finger stopped tapping. "First, give me a hug, buddy." Histor got up and spread his arms. Tej felt awkward, but got up and hugged the old man. Histor tightly held him for a few seconds, then let go and sat back. Tej also sat.

"What brings you here? And before you speak, I would suggest you, Rig, to keep absolutely quiet."

"Look Histor, what happened in Cape Town was a mistake. My mistake, and I own it," Rigasur spoke again.

Histor got up and screamed, "Attendant!" He then looked at Tej, "See, if you want my help, ask this guy to sit quietly, or I am outta here."

Tej eyed Rigasur in anger, who offered a weird expression.

"Sir, he won't speak, I assure you. You and I will have a conversation. But we need your help. I need your help. Please."

Histor sat down. His face bore a momentary serious look. "What do you want?" Then he again burst into a smile.

Tej urged, "You know what I want. I want to end Nefe, at any cost. She has taken everything away from me. I want her gone from this world."

Histor kept quiet for a few seconds contemplating.

"You met Larem recently. What did she say?"

"I am still in two minds about that whole experience. I still think it was just a dream."

"Nah, she was Larem, a hundred percent. I can't see her—no time-reader can. But I recognize a bright spark on the timeline when I see one." Histor banged the table in excitement. "Tell me, tell me, come on. I've been dying to ask you."

Tej chewed his lower lip, "Sir, she was cryptic about it, but my deduction is that she asked me to work with Rigasur."

Histor's smile vanished, and he looked at Rigasur with disdain. "Wonder why would she ask you to get in bed with a snake?"

Rigasur wanted to say something but stopped.

Histor took a deep breath. "All right, buddy, I will help you, because this world has had enough of Nefe and her evil minions. I have faith in you. While others pee their pants in Nefe's presence," Histor eyed Rigasur with contempt, "only you, Tej, have the courage to face her."

"And how do you know that?" Rigasur snarked.

Histor ignored him completely and addressed Tej. "You tried to off her once, didn't you?"

"I tried, but it didn't work. I ended up killing an innocent person. I am not even sure how that happened." Tej sat with his head down. The guilt of killing Vedika always lurked at the back of his mind.

"She switched hosts just before you hit her. She possessed the daughter. Anyhow, your friend Kuleens were all hunted and butchered. What's your plan?"

"That's why we came to you!" Rigasur blurted.

"You can't keep quiet, can you?" Tej scolded him.

"Can't you see myself and Mr. Histor are talking?"

Histor chuckled. "Boy knows how to deal with you."

Tej continued using honorifics, noticing the elation on Histor's face every time he addressed him like that. Blinded in the future without a time reader, Histor was their only source of information. "Sir, we know that you are special. Unlike any other time-reader, you can see the Kshins."

"I can. Whenever these doctors give me electro-therapy, my powers are enhanced. The electricity running through my body enhances my time-reading abilities increase multifold. I am able to tear through the quantum veil Kshins wrap around themselves. I see them, and they can't see me."

Tej and Rigasur shared a quick glance. "When is your next therapy scheduled, sir?"

"I had it last night. And I saw something."

"What?"

"Kshins' physical bodies. They are on Earth now." Histor grinned. Rigasur sat attentively. This was news to him, too.

"Physical bodies? I don't understand, sir. I thought Kshins had let go of their physical bodies ages ago."

"That's only a partial story, son. Only some of the Kshins did that. The rest of them were put into a long hibernation. Thousands of Kshins were packed in heat-controlled boxes and put on a spaceship. Only a very small crew comprised of Nefe and few other key Kshin military officers drove that ship.

"They arrived at our solar system sometime around 5000 BC. That ship stayed near our Sun for around two thousand years. They wanted to wait for the earth's population to increase so that they could consume all these emotions and gain power. But since their resources were depleting, the ship's crew started leaving their bodies and possessing humans on Earth. That happened around 3000 BC, which is why you saw Nefe around that time."

"Even I know these historical facts, Histor. What's new in this?" Rigasur again spoke, but this time, Histor didn't mind.

"What you don't know, Rig, you pompous fool, is that their spaceship is completely destroyed now."

"So where are their physical bodies?"

"Inside an artificial Sun." Histor sat back and let Tej and Rigasur grasp that for a moment.

15
HISTOR

"I'm not able to follow you, sir. You are saying that Kshins have physical bodies. But they are kept inside what?" Tej had never heard the term "artificial sun."

"In the year 2059, a group of Chinese scientists did some successful experiments on nuclear fusion. They were able to create a small replica of our sun. It's a sphere one km in diameter and is stored in a secret facility on a deserted island in the South China Sea. They created this with good intentions, as an experiment to understand our sun better. But Kshins saw an opportunity. They took over the people in key positions and created a cold cavity inside this artificial sun. They now call it SuryaX, named after their home-star, Suryaksh."

"With SuryaX they re-created the conditions which suited their home-star's conditions," Rigasur completed.

Tej sat silent. A thousand thoughts crossed his mind. *This was big. All the Kshins were now on earth. This had to be a part of their grand plan.*

Histor took a deep breath and put his arms on the table. All the mirth on his face had disappeared. The muscles on his forehead were tense. He was not done talking.

He looked Tej in the eye. "Up until now, Kuleens, and time-demons have always targeted individual Kshins. There have been hits and misses. But my question is very simple—why hit the offshoots when you should be hitting their lair? Why not hit this island, destroy this artificial Sun and free us of all Kshins in one single shot? See, their consciousnesses can roam free for only one reason: they used machines to generate the replicas of their consciousnesses, which means that they are still tied to their physical bodies. So, if their physical bodies are gone, they will be gone too."

Rigasur's scheming brain was already considering multiple plans of action.

Tej spoke, "That artificial sun should be powered by some power-source. What if we can hit that power source?"

"Our brother Rig here was a long-time bitch for the Kshins. He would know everything about this artificial sun," Histor jabbed, but Rigasur didn't mind. What Histor revealed to them had changed things.

Tej looked at Rigasur with suspicion.

Rigasur spluttered, "Look, I know about that project. But I didn't know about Kshin bodies being in there. The only fact I know is that SuryaX is self-sustaining. It has been pre-loaded with a lot of fuel and can continue for ages. It doesn't need an external power to sustain itself. We were always told that this was a Kshin project to create an infinite power source. No one talked about Kshin bodies stored in there."

"We can bomb it. There are a thousand things we can do." Tej looked at both Rigasur and Histor.

It's not going to be that easy." Rigasur smirked.

"There would be naysayers, yes." Histor gazed Rigasur with scorn, then addressed Tej, "But I see it as the only way. Will this SuryaX be fortified from all directions? Yes. Will Kshins defend this SuryaX with all their might? Yes. But Tej, even if you have to fight the biggest battle of your life, would you not rather fight this one? Would you not hit them where it hurts them the most?"

"It makes all the sense, Mr. Histor, sir. Tell me the full details about this island. You have seen it all."

"I have a better idea, Tej. Why don't you possess me for a micro-second? Copy all this information."

"Are you insane?" Rigasur was livid. "Time-demons are prohibited from ever possessing a time reader. This rule was put in place for good reason!"

"What the fuck, Rig? When have you time-demons played by rules?"

Rigasur frowned. He cautioned Tej. "Don't do this, kid. Histor will have multiple versions of time-visions inside of him. You will have no way of knowing which visions are right and which are variations that never happened. Your memories will be nothing but a corrupt hard-disk. Quite a few time-demons have lost themselves trying to possess a time-reader."

"Shut up Rig. Don't scare the kid." Histor was furious. "Tej, I am a patient with retrograde amnesia. I had a major car accident five years back. I have no memories of my life before that. The quantity of my memories is not much different from that of a five-year-old time-reader. And what Mr. Rig here doesn't know that time-visions only have multiple versions if there are actions involved in that. My readings of this island and artificial sun are factual time-visions of the present. So there are no multiple versions. It's static information."

"But what's the fucking need!" Rigasur banged the table. "You give us the details, we walk out of here."

"You are not going anywhere, you idiot." Histor looked into the oblivion. "Nefe's left hand Miran has entered this facility and is moving towards us as we speak. She's possessed the area sheriff. You two thought you could possess journalists, slip in and out of Nefe's press conference, and she wouldn't know. You have been followed. She will get here, arrest us, and take us to some unidentified location. Do it, Tej. Do it now and get out of here."

"Don't do it, Tej. It's a big risk. We will figure out some way."

"She's almost at the end of the hallway, Tej."

Tej was speechless. He didn't know what to do. He was torn between two ridiculously difficult choices. On one side was the solution to everything, which had the potential to destroy the Kshins. On the other side was a risk of losing himself. Could he trust Histor completely? He wasn't sure. Trust Rigasur? Not his first choice.

An idea struck him. "Why don't I possess someone else and visit you two hours ago? We will have more time then."

Histor facepalmed himself. Rigasur almost laughed.

"You didn't tell him about time-webs, Rig? What kind of Guru were you?"

"Tej, you can't go back two hours ago in the same time-slice. And I can't explain to you why right now because it's very complicated."

"We are too late. She's right outside the door." Histor got up.

There was a knock on the door. Tej swiftly moved and touched his forehead to Histor's forehead and closed his eyes. Histor had a smile on his face. For a moment, his eyes went pink, then returned to their natural color.

"Open up, or I'm breaking this door." They heard a loud caution.

"We need to leave!" Rigasur screamed.

"All right, where to?" Tej said, still feeling disoriented.

"Rendezvous point," Rigasur said and left the body. The journalist fell on the ground, unconscious. A moment later, Tej left as well.

The door broke open with a bang, and a lady police sheriff walked in with two deputies. Histor sat in his chair, smiling, tapping the table with his fingers. Two journalists were sitting on the ground, clueless as if they had woken up from a deep sleep.

"What happened in here?" Miran came close to Histor, but he kept smiling and tapping the table.

"You know what, arrest all three of them and let's take them back to the station."

The doctor-in-charge came running. "What happened, Sheriff? Why this sudden visit?"

"I am Sheriff Amanda Rodgers. We got information that this inmate of yours and these two journalists were planning a terrorist attack."

"What? He's Histor, a blind man with mental health issues. How can he be involved?"

"All a façade, doctor. These people are experts at taking fake identities."

The doctor found the sudden entry and accusation strange. "Can I see a warrant, Officer?"

Miran turned towards him. "I'm getting the sense that you're involved, too."

"What, are you accusing me without any evidence? Let me call my lawyer." The doctor started dialing his phone.

Miran motioned for her deputies to wait outside.

The doctor had just started speaking to his lawyer when his phone automatically disconnected. He realized the sheriff was looking at him and smiling. "Why are you looking at me like that?"

"You humans. Inquisitive. Curious. Always want to put yourself in dangerous situations."

"What do you mean, Sheriff?"

Miran lifted her hand in the air and jerked her wrist. The doctor's neck snapped, and he fell like a cut-tree.

She turned around and addressed Histor, "Now I'm getting you in for a cold-blooded murder."

"Oh man, the alternative rock will never die." Histor was now nodding his head as if listening to music.

"Drop it, fucker. You have no idea who I am!"

Histor stopped tapping and got up. He bought his face close to Miran's and whispered, "Is that so, Miran?"

"How do you …" Miran's eyes widened.

Histor showed his teeth in a wide grin. Miran grabbed him by the collar and pushed him out.

Tej sat in a meditative pose in a small room. Rigasur sat on a recliner next to him, smoking. They were both inside the bodies of two empty clones. Like Mozeek, Rigasur also had a secret stash of clone bodies in their backup rendezvous location.

"No use meditating, Tej. Against my sound advice, you have loaded a lot of corrupt memories in your brain. The repercussions could be huge." He let out a ring of smoke.

Tej's face bore a serene look, which bothered Rigasur. He opened his eyes. "Ever since I started exercising my powers, I thought of time travel as the only power I had. But when my primitive brain figured out that you were not what you appeared to be, I realized possession is a tremendous power, too. You learn so much from your host's brain."

Rigasur let out a sardonic sound. "Well, you do learn a lot from your host, but you get all the garbage stuff, too. You can't just pick and choose. Histor would have seen a vision a hundred times. All those versions are inside your brain. Which one is true?"

"Nope, that's where you're wrong. I *can* pick and choose. I am reading his brain dump like a book."

"But how?"

"You know the first host you sent me to? Shambhu the shepherd? I made the same mistake with him. I read through his brain all at once. Got overwhelmed. Fell into a seizure."

"Yeah, I know."

"That didn't happen when I took on Ravi Kumar Cheri. I learned to let it come to me slowly. One at a time."

Rigasur was visibly impressed. Tej had been a time-demon for only a few days and he was already an advanced user of his powers. "What do you see in there?"

"Mozeek."

"Mozeek?"

"Yes. I see that son of a bitch everywhere. He is pretty high-up in Nefe's organization. If she trusts one person as much as her Kshin generals, it's Mozeek. He protects them, he runs their operations during solar eclipses, he compliments their powers. If there are any chinks in

Kshin armor, Mozeek fills them."

Rigasur had a look of disappointment on his face. "I know all this already. I used to be Nefe's right hand. Now with me gone, Mozeek had to just climb a couple of rungs and take my spot. I thought you were looking for the island where we get to take down that artificial sun and all the Kshins in one shot."

"We'll get to that, Rigasur. But first, Mozeek needs to go. Otherwise, he'll just undermine any offensives we take."

"I would love to nail that bastard. I can search for a few time-prisons."

"Nope, time-prisons can always be broken out of. I am looking for a few permanent solutions."

"Killing a time-demon? Bold!"

"Nothing a Zason-bomb can't do."

"Z-bomb? Interesting!" Rigasur sat next to Tej.

"Let's go dig some old Kuleen stash-houses."

"Hold your horses. Nefe would have seized or destroyed all of them when they conducted the Kuleen genocide. But even if you manage to find the Z-bombs, killing a jackal like Mozeek is extremely difficult. He mostly lurks in shadows, rarely ventures out in open spaces. And if you are on his tail, before you know he will be several steps ahead of you."

"Wow, you admire him so much." Tej jibed.

"Ha, admire him? I hate him more than you ever could. He was the one who freed Kumbh in the first place and peed on my three-decade-long plan, just to take my place with Nefe. But let's be practical here." Rigasur got up, opened a bottle of scotch, and poured some in a glass.

Tej paused. "You're not yourself, are you? You are not

the Rigasur I knew. Are you getting old?"

Rigasur kept quiet for a few moments. "No, it's not my age. It's the motivation. I don't want to be a part of this. If Larem hadn't asked, I would never have agreed to this."

"But why?"

"Because I don't come out of this alive." Rigasur gulped the drink in one go.

"How do you know?"

"Histor told me. When Nefe was tearing your village apart, I woke up and slipped out. I traveled to this time and met Histor. He told me what Mozeek had done, and that Nefe no longer needs me. I was filled with rage and thirst for revenge. But Histor told me that if I go after Nefe …"

"You will end up dead?"

"Yes."

"But if you know exactly how you die, we can avoid situations where your life is in peril."

"I have time-traveled for a long while, Tej. I know several different paths still lead to the same outcomes. A man misses a car accident but dies of a heart attack five minutes later. The routes are different, but the results are the same. Time is attracted to the future like a fluid by gravity. It reaches where it must, regardless of the conduit it takes. If I'm in this, I am dead."

"But Histor could be wrong. Time-readers predictions have a level of inaccuracy."

"You met the man. He can even time-vision Kshins. He's the best of time-reader of this era. At least, the best I know. He is rarely wrong." Rigasur poured himself a large peg this time. "These fucking clone bodies don't even get drunk. Their fucking brains."

Tej now understood why Rigasur acted so strangely. He had a fear of mortality. Tej had led a normal human life for so long. He always understood the inevitability of death. But Rigasur, being a time-demon, had always considered himself immortal. Now he was getting into something which could lead to his demise.

Tej got up and looked Rigasur in the eye. "You once told me that you need my head in the game. Without me performing at my best, we couldn't have taken down Kumbh. Could we?"

"No. We couldn't have."

"It's the same here. If your head isn't in this game, then we are on the path to defeat. If that is the case, we may as well go and surrender on Nefe's front gate. Isn't that right, Rig?" Tej emphasized the last word.

"Rig? I like the sound of that." Rigasur smiled. He accepted his own advice. "You're right. If I am going down, I may as well go down all guns blazing. Tell me, where should we begin with Mozeek?"

"You're a schemer. Think of something." Tej could see a flash of positivity in Rigasur's eyes. He knew that alone, neither of them stood a chance against the Kshins, but together, there was a faint possibility.

"All right. You have Histor's brain dump. Search for Mozeek, especially on days when he's out in the open or unguarded."

Tej closed his eyes, tilting his head for a few seconds as if trying to find something.

Rigasur looked at him intently. A time demon reading visions, even pre-stored ones, was nothing short of a miracle to him.

"I have a date for you. 25th of October 2069. He will be out in the open."

"Why would he be out in open that day?"

"Not sure. I see him standing in a large open ground. Walking among a crowd of thousands of people."

"25th of October it is. Tell me more." Rigasur's brain had started chalking out a plan.

Nefe sat in a capacious bathtub in her posh Manhattan apartment, immersed in a scented bubble bath. She was enjoying the youthful vigor of Jessica's young body and the comforts bought by her immense wealth. The luxurious bathroom had a spacious shower space, several basins, and cupboards. On one of the corners was a separate dedicated dressing area. An attendant was giving her manicure as she smoked a cigar.

She heard a beep emanating from her left arm. It was an intercom call from her housekeeping head downstairs.

"What now? … Pick up," she voice-commanded the chip embedded in her wrist. A video of her housekeeper's head blinked on her arm.

"Ma'am, Mr. Andrele is here to see you. He says he has an appointment with you."

"Oh, is it 9 PM already? Send him to the wash-area."

"Ma'am?"

"You heard me." Nefe jerked her wrist lightly, and the call was disconnected.

A few seconds later, there was a knock on the door, and Andrele's voice was heard.

"Come in," Nefe casually said, and gestured the attendant to stop massaging her fingers.

Andrele coughed and entered the bathroom, embarrassed. The twenty-five-year-old man had voluminous curly hair and wore nerdy glasses. He was dressed in a light blue shirt, dark blue trousers, and a matching blue tie.

Jessica was still dipped inside the tub up to her neck. "Andrele, my friend, how are you?"

"I … I'm good, ma'am. I could have given you the report tomorrow morning in the office. There was no hurry from my end."

"But I am in a hurry. Show me."

Andrele handed over a sheet of paper to Jessica. The page had a diagram with text below. The diagram moved, the text constantly updating itself.

"How many of them do we have now?" She returned the paper to him.

"Seventeen thousand, ma'am. All have been evaluated as class-one time-readers."

"Seventeen thousand class-ones. Brilliant job, Andrele." Jessica clapped and raised a glass of wine. "Without your algorithms, we would not have been able to sift gold from iron."

"But ma'am, they have been plugged into Infernex, and I think we're keeping them in inhumane conditions."

"You don't approve, Andrele?"

Andrele gulped. "No—I didn't mean to be offensive. I meant that I could have written machine learning algorithms which would have tracked time-crawler movement with ease. Why do we need to rely on these people? Computers can do a better job."

Jessica got up from the tub and stepped out. Her attended swiftly got up and offered her the bathing gown, but she refused. Andrele tried to look away, but could not un-see water rolling off her soap-covered naked body glistening in the ceiling lights.

Jessica came close to him and grabbed his collar. "Andrele, you are my principal AI engineer. So when I say that I trust you and your algorithms, you believe me, don't you?" Andrele nodded, sweating.

She continued, "Your computers can track time-crawlers in real-time. But they can't predict the future as accurately as these gifted individuals do. I know we are being harsh on them—I feel you there. But we need to track and capture the terrorists who intend to cause harm to our company, to me. Don't you agree?"

"Yes … yes, ma'am," Andrele stammered. He was aware of Jessica's short temper, though all he could see in her eyes was lust.

"Vedvance is about to become the topmost tech company of the world. Fresh Concordia Orders are coming in by the thousands each hour." Jessica's hand was sliding on Andrele's chest, onto his stomach, and moving further down as she whispered in his ear. "Just give me four more years, and I promise you, we will rule the world. And when we are at the top, I see you as my closest partner. Not only in business—but in my bed, too." Her hand touched his crotch, and his heart skipped a beat.

She stayed there for a second, then asked the attendant to help her with her gown. Andrele stayed there, silent, both terrified and aroused.

"If you don't want to be a part of this success, then you are free to leave any day. It would be tough to find a replacement." Jessica paused. "Tough, but not impossible." She winked and left the bathroom.

16
RAAVAN ANNIHILATED

25th October, 2069

World population: **10.51 Billion**, Concordia
VX activation: **520 Million**, Adoption: **5%**

rongalley desert area was an expansive stretch of land three hundred kilometers away from NYC. This desert spread across three hundred acres. During its prime, it had once been a lush farm, but with time, it had slowly morphed into an infertile land. The area was full of quicksand and marshy spots, but most of the land in the middle was empty, barren space with no establishments or factories.

17:30 hours: the occasion was Vijayadashmi, or Dussehra, a popular festival among Hindus. A day celebrated as the victory of Lord *Ram* over the Demon King *Raavan*. On this day, Hindus erected huge effigies of ancient demon-king Raavan, his brother *Kumbhkarn*, his son *Meghnad*, and put them on fire. The effigies were usually filled up with powerful fireworks.

The Hindu population in the United States had celebrated it every year. It was a gala event. Thousands flocked to the venue to witness the spectacle. They also looked forward to relishing Indian delicacies sold at thousands of stalls. Since a mega-fireworks show was part of the ritual this festival was not allowed inside city boundaries. Wrongalley desert area was an ideal spot for hosting it.

This day was no different. A two hundred foot-high and a fifteen-foot-thick effigy of Raavan was erected at the center. On its left side were similar, though smaller, figurines of Kumbhkarn and Meghnad. The effigies were made of paper, plaster, and cardboard. They were stuffed with fireworks in the torso, arms, and head. Their caricatured faces were made up with big eyelashes, long curly mustaches, and wide-grinning teeth. Their design gave them a terrorizing, demonic look, while their attire included black, red, and green flashy colors.

Around the effigies, a crowd of hundred and fifty thousand people had gathered in a circular arrangement. People were chanting slogans in name of Lord Ram, Lord Hanuman, and other Hindu deities.

Mozeek stood quiet in the crowd, possessing the body of a muscular Rory-clone. He loved such crowds because these were perfect abduction grounds. Kshin-experiments such as Infernex needed lots of live human subjects every month. Mozeek routinely supplied humans by raiding such large-scale events.

As per his usual modus operandi, he had placed trigger-based smoke bombs at strategic places in the crowd. His idea was to spread panic, confusion, and cause a stampede. He would use the chaos to kidnap several people. His men would then transport them out of the venue before the smoke cleared out.

The burning of effigies was scheduled at 8:01 PM local time and he planned to trigger smoke bombs a minute after. That would give a false impression that some fireworks from the effigies spilled over into the crowd causing the smoke. Only later would authorities come to know that those were well-planted smoke bombs.

Mozeek was doing last-minute checks on a small hand-held device when his gaze settled on a moving ticker message. The ticker was running on the mega-announcement board on one side. As he read those words, his eyes turned red with anger, and his nostrils flared. He tore through the crowd and moved towards the flea market. The market was full of hundreds of booths selling food, clothing, and other merchandise, which slowed him down. Rigasur's plan had started to work.

Tej and Rigasur stood near stall number 1742, sipping piping-hot masala tea. Rigasur was inside the body of an old carpenter. Tej possessed a thirty-five-year-old woman who died two hours ago. He still had issues possessing live hosts, whereas Rigasur had had no such qualms.

Rigasur was monitoring booth number 1729 from a distance, the booth which was critical to his plan.

Booth 1729 was twice the size of other normal stalls at the venue. There was a small stage set inside the booth towards the end. Several dummy trees and stuffed animal props decorated the dais. Five theatre actors were standing on the stage, rehearsing their lines, getting ready to start a live performance.

A small crowd had gathered near the booth, waiting for the performance to start. A few people were talking to the director of this play performance. The booth had a small billboard, which read, "The Shameful Defeat of

Mozakira." This was also the name of the play they were planning to perform.

"Are you sure he will come?" Tej took a deep sip of the tea.

"If he is here, he won't be able to stop himself. I have pressed the right buttons. We need to hold our breaths and wait."

"And these bozos you hired to act on your script? They don't seem up to par."

"Bozos? They are the most expensive troupe in Paris. It took five hundred grand in Euros, plus travel expenses to the US. They have been practicing for this performance for a few weeks now. I hope they do justice to my script and portray how the mighty king Mozakira was defeated by a puny farmer back in 647 BC." Rigasur chuckled. He was really enjoying this, which gave Tej hope that he was sure of his success. But having seen Mozeek in action, Tej was not without doubts.

"I don't think this is insulting enough to irk Mozeek."

"Nah, it's more than enough. He is a pompous son of a bitch. He takes pride in the fact that he mercilessly ruled the city of Abreen for decades, where he massacred thousands for fun. Human hunting, religious sacrifices, and pedophilia in name of necromancy were some of his favorite regal hobbies. He continued unabated until one day, Nefe hired him to establish her empire. He was never defeated in reality—but in my script, he was. This is bound to prick him in the right spot."

Tej took another deep sip. "But there are hundreds of booths here. He won't even notice."

"That's why I have paid fifty grand and bought advertising space for our booth on this events announcement board. They will be displaying our advertisement using a ticker, once in every ten minutes. Look, there it is."

Rigasur pointed to the advertisement board at a distance. "Witness the Shameful Defeat of King Mozakira: A One-act Play. The live performance begins shortly at Booth 1729."

"Wow. That's hard to miss!" Tej exclaimed.

They didn't have to wait long. A muscular man wearing a dark military uniform was walking towards Booth 1729—he was Mozeek. Rigasur froze and elbowed Tej. Both of them watched as Mozeek sauntered toward the booth in anger.

Stopping two meters away from the booth, he took out the same hand-held cell-phone-like device. He stretched his arm forward and moved it as if scanning the space around the Booth.

"What's he doing?" Tej whispered.

"He's scanning the booth, looking for Time-Demon signatures." Rigasur bit his lower lip. "He ain't gonna find it, because they are all humans." It was all unfolding as he planned.

Mozeek kept the device back in his pocket and spoke, "Hey you, who's in charge here?"

The director of the play, Robinet Montreuil, stepped forward. He was a thirty-seven-year-old man, though his frail body structure, thick eyeglasses, and a big beard made him look older. He wore loose denim trousers, a yellow shirt, a blue casual sweater, and rugged slippers.

"Yes Monsieur, Robinet here. You can call me Robby. I am the director of this play." Robby brought forward his right arm, offering to shake hands with Mozeek, but he stood unmoved. Robby retracted his arm and stood straight. Mozeek's bulky structure intimidated him.

"You've written it all wrong, Rabby." Mozeek was

clearly furious.

"Robby—my name is Robby."

"Whatever. Mozakira was a great king who remained undefeated. You can't go around saying shit about him."

"Well, Monsieur …" Robby adjusted his specs, "I don't know that. As per the script I have received, this Mozakira fellow was badly defeated. He was even dragged behind a horse for fifty kilometers until he died. Received a pretty bad beating for a king, if you ask me."

"Enough!" Mozeek screamed. He walked towards Robby, who took a couple of steps back.

"I want this stall closed. And then you are going to tell me who gave you this script."

"Don't worry, good sir. A group of expert archeologists and historians have meticulously studied the remains and tablets from the 600-500 BC. This script was a result of their extensive research." Robby was now sweating. He took out a handkerchief from his pocket and wiped his forehead.

Mozeek held Robby by the collar and lifted him above the ground. "Who gave you the damn script?"

Actors inside the booth started jumping off the stage and running out. Robby was pleading, "Monsieur, please, put me down, please. If you have any critiques on our performances or our content, you can get in touch with our promoter. Or you can even leave your feedback on our website. Please put me down."

"To hell with your performance!" Mozeek threw Robby inside the booth. Robby's body flew several feet in the air and crashed onto the stage.

Mozeek entered the booth and started demolishing props, billboards and other objects with his muscular arms. Robby got up and ran out as fast as he could.

"The booth is clear of humans now, Tej. Go. Go!" Rigasur whispered in urgency, and Tej ran. He knew what to do. He had a small spherical balloon filled with a viscous black liquid.

As Mozeek was busy breaking the wooden stage, Tej jumped on him from the back and smashed the balloon against his head. Mozeek cringed in pain and swung his arm. Tej ducked and missed Mozeek's blow. He turned back to run out of the booth, but Mozeek grabbed him from the behind. He tightened his left arm around Tej's neck, lifted him, and walked out of the booth. A lot of onlookers were standing at a distance, watching the spectacle.

The viscous liquid had now spread itself on Mozeek's head and was dripping onto his forehead, ears, and neck. The liquid was slowly solidifying.

While holding Tej by his left arm, Mozeek pulled out the scanner device from his pocket. He pressed a few buttons; the scanner beeped, and the screen showed a signature. Mozeek smiled. "So, Mr. Tej. You finally not only showed up but made a foolish attempt to attack me. What is this liquid weapon you have used on me?"

"It's not a weapon, Mozeek. It's super-charged electrostatic gel. You are imprisoned up there." Rigasur was standing in front of Mozeek with two Z-bombs in his hands.

Mozeek saw a different signature on his scanner and grinned. "Hey Rig, long time no see? You want to trap me in this body. You think this gel will not let me leave this host?" Mozeek was still maintaining a tight grip on Tej.

"You know, you're trapped. Be ready to die. Tej, leave this body." Rigasur was about to hurl the Z-bombs but stopped. He noticed that a fancy handcuff studded with small levers and gadgets was wrapped around Tej's wrist. Mozeek's left wrist also had a similar gadget. Rigasur froze. This device was a consciousness synchronizer.

Mozeek chewed his words. "Tej, you should have left this vessel when you had time. Now our consciousnesses are locked together. I tied both of us soon after he burst this gel balloon on my head."

Rigasur and Tej both recognized the handcuff. It was similar to the one Tej saw Mozeek use earlier when they'd escaped from the coffee shop. Rigasur, too, was familiar with this tech.

"Go on, throw those bombs on me, Rig. If I go, your beloved disciple Tej goes, too." A nasty smile floated on Mozeek's lips.

Tej was gagged because of the tight grip on his neck but mustered all his courage to scream. "Do it, Rigasur. I am ready to go with him."

Rigasur was thinking fast. He could hear sirens in the background. They were either human police, or Mozeek had called for reinforcements. Either way, they were more trouble.

Mozeek had also pulled out a sharp knife from his back pocket and tried to cut through the gel. Rigasur knew Mozeek would even cut through his host's skin and scalp to get rid of the gel cover.

"Do it, Rig!" Tej screamed again, struggling from Mozeek's grasp.

"Yeah, Rig, do it. Throw your pet into non-existence."

Rigasur pressed the Z-bombs and hurled them towards Mozeek. In the split second, he also drew his gun and fired two precise shots at the handcuff. The handcuffs were shattered, but within two seconds, the

Z-bombs rapidly spiraled around them in a spherical pattern.

The Zason vortex engulphed Mozeek and Tej and sucked their bodies in. Mozeek tried hard to escape. He was even able to push his arm out of the spherical bubble but was pulled back in. After five seconds, both of them disappeared.

Rigasur sat down on the ground and clasped his head in his hands. Mozeek was gone, but he'd lost Tej, too. The police came, arrested him, and escorted him out of the venue. The whole crowd cheered as a decorated flying car carrying actors dressed as Lord Ram, Laxman, and Lord Hanuman flew near the effigies. The actor dressed as Ram shot three flaming arrows from his bow and lit the three effigies on fire. This embarked a mega fireworks show, triggering a huge uproar from the mob.

Rigasur had a final glance at the spectacle before he was thrust at the back of a police truck. The crowd was unaware that on the sidelines of the event, Rigasur, too had annihilated a Raavan that day. He too brought evil to dust, but with that, a good soul was lost as well.

He could leave his vessel anytime, but couldn't. He had tears in his eyes. He wanted to mourn Tej. The police truck drove out of the venue amidst the colorful fireworks which now decorated the sky.

Back at Rigasur's safe-house, one of the clones opened his eyes. Rigasur was back inside the clone. He'd left his host somewhere on the way when police were taking him to the precinct. He went to the bar, poured a large peg for himself, and gulped it in one go. He poured another one.

"Would you not pour one for me?" Rigasur heard a voice and turned around to see another clone sitting on the bed, staring at him.

Rigasur felt a strange relief he hadn't experienced in a long time. "Tej? You son of a bitch. You scared me. You did escape?"

"Yes, I did. As soon as you blew off those handcuffs." Tej smiled, snatched the glass from Rigasur, and drank it. "You weren't mourning me, were you?"

"Nah, I was happy you were gone. You're a bigger pain in the ass for me than Kshins are." Rigasur poured another glass for himself. He did have a lot of blood on his hands but he knew he would have had a hard time living with Tej's death on him. He now realized that Tej wasn't just another entity in his world he didn't give two hoots about. He was something—someone close to a friend.

"Congratulations. Mozeek is gone." Tej struck his glass to Rigasur's. "The plan was very well executed."

"I didn't plan for that handcuff thing, though. But all's well that ends well."

"Now what?"

"Now we lay low for a few days. Make sure Mozeek is actually gone. Meanwhile, you search Histor's memories for that island where that artificial sun is housed. That's our final battleground."

17
TIME VISION
FACTORY

At 18:30 on the 25th of October, 2069, a caravan of armored cars with bodyguards entered an abandoned factory area. Four bright halogen lights illuminated the factory compound.

Nefe, possessing Jessica Sharma, got out of her car and started walking towards the entrance of a warehouse. She was followed by her company's CFO, Misha Berklof, possessed by Jarna. Both the ladies wore business casual, as they were coming in from a corporate high tea event.

Twenty armed men followed them. These men, called Tharr, were trained Muay-Thai warriors. They were a part of Nefe's personal security. She had recruited them eight years back, shortly after possessing Jessica's body.

They walked towards a huge warehouse building in front of them. Fifty men guarded the gates. They went through a small metal door and entered the warehouse. The door shut behind them. The compound was thousands of feet in length and breadth, and at least a hundred feet high. The walls were made of metal sheets.

Powerful neon lights fixed on the ceiling illuminated the whole space. This compound, once a large warehouse, was now transformed into a massive detention center.

They stood for a moment and looked at thousands of cages in front of them. Cages were arranged in a neat rectangular pattern with alleyways, lighting, and numbering. Each cage, built of hardened polymer, was five feet by five feet, ten feet high, and housed exactly one human.

Inside each cage was a time-reader lying on a cushioned recliner chair. Their hands and legs were tied to the chair, and their head was fitted with a helmet made of complex circuitry. A few wires from within the circuitry were going into their necks, down to their spine. Each of them had been inoculated with the Concordia VX hardware. Using this setup, their brain was plugged into the software Infernex 3.0.

Andrele welcomed Nefe and Jarna and asked them to follow him. Andrele led them to a large monitoring station with several computers. The monitoring station was bedecked with TV-screens, keyboards and similar paraphernalia. Above those monitors, a gigantic TV screen twenty-four feet long and twelve feet high was set up. Two men and one woman sat at the monitoring station, Andrele's engineering assistants. They stood at attention as they saw Jessica and others approaching.

"The arrangements look solid, Andrele." Nefe took off her glasses and eyed the setup. "How many time-readers, you say?"

"Seventeen thousand, three hundred and forty-five."

"How did you manage to get so many of them?"

"Through our CCTV database, I identified occurrences of people having visions and marked them as potential subjects. Then I cross-referenced them with hospital records and removed cases where such visions were observed only after an accident. I then provided all the information to Mrs. Berklof." Andrele signaled towards Jarna, who smiled and acknowledged. "Her on-ground team picked those subjects and brought them here." Andrele was still not comfortable with using the word "kidnapped."

"Great teamwork, both of you." Nefe clasped her hands together. "And now you are saying that you can see what they see? So you can see their time-visions?"

"Not yet, but yes, we are working on it. Another set of machine-learning algorithms I wrote are going through their brains and training themselves to see what they see. We are projecting images on their retina and recording how the neuro-receptors near their occipital lobe are re-acting. This will train our algorithms. Then later, when we record any activity in their brains, we can reverse-predict the image they are seeing using machine learning."

"Brilliant, Andrele. Brilliant. I didn't understand half of it, but if you say it works, I'll take your word for it."

Jarna was still not convinced. "So, how will that work in an ideal state, Andrele?"

"We will ask them a question. In their subconscious state, their minds will not resist answering it. For example, we can ask them, 'Show me Manhattan Square four days later.' Their time-visions will navigate to that time and place, and they all will see those visions."

"Oh, so that is why we have this giant screen. We will see seventeen thousand visions here?" Jarna was sarcastic. Nefe was smiling.

"No, no ma'am," Andrele spluttered. "The computer will study all those visions and will stitch them together. It will check each vision pixel by pixel, and wherever it sees a majority vision piece, it will choose that. If more than half are seeing the same vision, the computer will choose that as the best vision. On this screen, you will see only one most probable vision."

"I doubt it will work," Jarna cautioned Nefe.

"Let's remove all doubts. Let's test it. Andrele, ask them a question right away." Jessica sat on a chair nearby.

"It's not ready yet. We still need to run—"

"Do it!"

"Okay. What's the question?"

"Show me where I was yesterday night at 9 PM."

"Come on. Time readers won't be able to see you." Jarna winked.

Nefe's face expression was stern. "Let's try."

"Type in the question. Use completely clear verbiage," Andrele commanded one of his assistants. The assistant typed in the question and pressed enter.

Andrele turned back and explained. "We need to ask very specific questions to the time-readers. Otherwise, our queries will confuse them. So here, we typed, 'Where was Jessica Sharma, the CEO of Vedvance Corporation, on October 24th, 2069?"

The huge screen started flickering with a series of visions. The screen got flooded with chunks of thousands of images, which were coming together as one as if pieces of a jigsaw puzzle were getting arranged. Finally, a picture came through, which was Jessica's mansion in the outskirts of the city.

Jarna laughed. "Were you at your mansion yesterday night, Jessica?"

"No, I was not. I was aboard a chartered flight."

"What a gigantic waste of time. Your machine doesn't work, buddy." Jarna laughed. She wanted to say more, but she got a phone call and she excused herself to answer it.

"Mrs. Sharma, ma'am, the machine is not ready yet. We need a few more weeks to learn their brain patterns," Andrele tried to explain to Jessica.

Jarna returned back with a sullen face. She got down and whispered in Nefe's ear. "Mozeek is gone. Z-bombs. Tej is the suspect."

Jessica's face glared with anger, but she swallowed her ire. Mozeek's death meant a huge loss for their operation. "Andrele, how much more time until this is ready?"

"Two to three weeks more?" Andrele stuttered.

"Three days," Nefe ordered and got up.

"But ma'am, that is not possible! There is still so much for the algorithms to learn." Andrele rebelled. Jessica was asking for the impossible.

Nefe promenaded towards him. "You listen to me, you, science roach. Time-crawlers killed a prominent member of my team today. If this machine was ready on time, that could have been foreseen and prevented. Now you have all the resources in the world at your fingertips. Machines, computers, animals, humans, dead or alive— whatever you want. You and your team don't eat, sleep, or shit for next seventy-two hours. I don't care. I need this done in three days. Period."

Andrele nodded. Nefe and Jarna walked out of the facility. Nefe signaled for her men to bring over her car.

"Jarna, you stay here and oversee these humans. Ask Miran to get more information on Mozeek and add one more circle to my security layer. Until this machine is ready we still need to rely on existing intelligence network. Find Tej." Nefe ordered as she sat in her armored car. Jarna nodded, and Nefe's caravan of cars sped away.

She got on a call with Miran.

The next morning at 08:00 AM, Tej prepared some tea for himself. Rigasur was still in his bed. Tej went and shook him, but the clone's body was stiff. Rigasur had ventured out.

For a couple of hours, Tej did not know what to do. His mind was full of questions and anxieties. He was still not confident Mozeek was gone. Trying to focus on finding that artificial island was also not working. That vision was buried somewhere deep in the memory-dump from Histor. Still, he pushed himself and kept on sifting through the memories. He finally found a bunch of visions at around 10:30 AM, when Rigasur's clone host showed movement.

"You are back. Where were you?" Tej opened his eyes. He got up and sat near Rigasur as he woke up.

"I went on to get the news. Possessed a good Samaritan who was surfing the internet. The venue was a wretched internet cafe on a narrow street in a small town."

"And the news is?"

"Zilch. Nada. There was a ton of coverage on Vijayadashami celebrations by the Hindu community in various states. A few news articles also covered the Wrongalley desert area event, along with pictures and footages. But no news of any people disappearing into thin air. As expected, Kshins have suppressed this news. But then something interesting happened. As I surfed the web, I mistakenly typed 'Wrongalley.' I should have done a general search."

"Why is that a mistake?"

"Within five minutes, there was a police car at the spot, and two officers started questioning me."

"What?"

"Tells you a lot about the power, the reach, and the speed of Kshin intelligence networks. How fast they can act in even remotest of the places. I did one keyword search, and something in their system alerted them. And within five minutes, there were cops at the spot with orders to detain and question my host. Imagine what they have done to the main cities."

"What happened then?"

"Nothing. I bolted out of that host."

"What would happen to that man?" Tej had a worried look in his eyes.

"Nothing much. They would let him off." Rigasur knew Tej deeply cared about other people, so he trivialized it.

"Or they would torture him till the end of time?" Tej confronted him.

"That's on them, son. Not on me."

"Why do you need to ruin people's lives to access basic internet? Why don't we have a computer in here?"

"Don't even think about it. A computer can never come in here. I bought in supplies which will last five years in this secret bunker, and have sealed this from all sides with cement. The only way in and out of here is through our possession. The clone bodies don't need air to breathe, so we are good."

Tej sat sulking for a few minutes as Rigasur poured himself some tea and lit a cigar.

"What about all this smoke—will that not fill up in this restricted space?"

"Well, the walls have pollution-absorbent paint. They suck up all these smoke particles. Forget about this. Did you concentrate on Histor's memories?"

"Yes, I did. There are twenty-seven visions of that artificial sun, SuryaX, in there. Some visions show the location of that facility at an island in the South China Sea. Some show the facility to be somewhere in the desert of Nevada. I am confused."

"That's confusing. That can only happen if they created this Sun at one place and later shifted the location." Rigasur thought for a few seconds. "Do you have dates of these visions?"

"No, sir, they're not neatly cataloged in here," Tej retorted sardonically. Reading the time-visions again and again was becoming cumbersome. They looked like his own memories, but he was aware they weren't. It was so difficult to not lose himself in that mesh of false remembrances.

"Hmm. How many visions of the Chinese island, and how many of Nevada?" Rigasur took a sip of the tea.

"I'll have to count that." Tej closed his eyes. "Fourteen of the island and thirteen of Nevada."

"See, that's why Histor said the island. He took the majority vision as the right one. That's how time-readers work. But we need to check both the places out. We need access to powerful satellite imagery. But let's locate them on a map first."

Rigasur fumbled through a cupboard and brought out a rolled sheet of paper. As he flattened that sheet of paper, Tej realized it was not paper, but a foldable electronic tablet. The gadget was seventeen inches long and ten inches wide.

"You said no electronic items were allowed in here."

"I said no computers and internet in here. This tablet's facility to connect to any Wi-Fi or internet systems is disabled. This is an encyclopedia with billions of facts pre-stored on it—including details about our galaxy, our planet, continents, and our history." Rigasur clicked a few buttons, and a world map opened on the screen. "Now, point out both these locations on the map."

Tej looked at the map and touched it in two places. A black arrow appeared at both places, along with geo-coordinates of both locations. Rigasur saved it as an image.

"All right, Tej. I have memorized both these coordinates. I will go find out more."

"Okay, we can divide it up. You can research the island. I will get more info on Nevada location."

"You are not going anywhere."

"Why? I won't just sit here and do nothing. Why are you not involving me?"

"We need to lay low."

"But you aren't lying low. You were almost caught today."

"Yes, and when *I* can get caught, you can imagine your odds," Rigasur emphasized the *I* part. "We can't fall in their trap and jeopardize this."

"So I sit here and do nothing?"

"No, you can do a lot of good work. You have this tremendous encyclopedia with you. You find different ways of how we can destroy this sun. I find out the location, you find out the way, we fix a date, and we make a strategy around it."

"Oh, come on, you are going out in the field and I am stuck with a desk job?"

Rigasur was now getting frustrated. He remembered how he had to answer many of Tej's inane questions earlier, too. He was an inquisitive soul. "Look. You yourself said I am the best schemer around."

"I didn't say the best."

"Whatever. So believe me when I say this is the right thing to do."

Tej relented. He had seen Rigasur execute a perfect plan on Mozeek. He trusted him more than ever. Rigasur went out again, and Tej set to search stuff on the tablet.

A few hours later, Rigasur returned and found Tej playing games on the tablet.

"Wow, kid? I am running around in the heat all day long, and you are here enjoying yourself?"

"I searched for all possible ways, and there is nothing workable we can do. We can pump the sun with more matter. That way, the gravitational pull overcomes its interior nuclear fusion, which leads to its eventual collapse. This process may lead to a huge explosion, and our planet may not survive. Besides, in this encyclopedia, all mentions of stars collapsing are for bodies of astronomical sizes. I don't know if they apply to an artificial sun of this small size."

"So we can't destroy the sun. Game over, then."

"No, we can't find any way to destroy the sun, yet. What about you—found something?"

"Not yet. I have let out the birds in the air. My sources would get back to me by tomorrow. Kshins are laying a very tight grid search out there. Taking out Mozeek has put them on high alert. We have to tread carefully."

"We need more info on this SuryaX, too."

"Kuleens will know about it."

"But Rig, you said that Kuleens are all dead." Tej paused. "Only if we can go back in time before they were killed …"

"It's nearly impossible. You already existed in that time-slice. You left that time-slice on the 26th of December, 2057. So if you go to an instant before that, it can lead to time webs and paradoxes. And after that date, Kshins cracked down on Kuleens for the next three months. That was another period of high alert for Kshins. So going into that time block is suicidal too."

"There should be some other period before the year 2057 where we can go and interact with them."

"No, Tej. Forget about you traveling back in time and interacting with Kuleens."

"But why?"

Rigasur closed his eyes, trying to control his temper. "Okay, tell me, which Kuleens did you meet?"

"Several of them. Pete Morales, his brother Jake, and their facility in-charge, Brenda. Maybe her name was Bethany. I was also introduced to a few senior Kuleens during a meeting."

"Yes—so let us say you now go to the year 2053 and meet Kuleens. If you interact with any of those Kuleens you named in the year 2053, they would form a new memory of you, which will stay with them till 2057. But that was not the case earlier. When you met them in 2057, earlier, they were meeting you for the first time."

"So?"

Rigasur almost pulled his hair. "So that's a paradox. You are forcing the timeline to update itself. Time travelers have to avoid these timeline changes, or the future will drastically change. You won't even realize how the world changed. We can't afford that, buddy."

Tej grew silent. He remembered how his wife and his daughter were taken away from him because of his travel to the future—when he was not even intending to change a timeline.

"Although, there is another very convoluted way in which you can contact Kuleens." Rigasur scratched his head. "But that way will make sure that our actions don't alter the timeline."

"Okay. I am listening."

"Who is the Kuleen you think can help us here?"

"Pete Morales, the first Kuleen I met. He was leading some sort of program where quantum physicists developed these Z-bombs. He would know for sure."

"He is dead, but you can summon his consciousness."

"How can I summon a consciousness? I only learned a demon invocation spell, Rig. I am not a full-fledged necromancer." Tej chuckled.

"But Rudrakshini is."

Tej stiffened to gauge if Rigasur was joking. "Rudrak-shini?"

"Yes. You need to pay her a visit again."

Tej shuddered at the thought of meeting Rudrakshini, the veteran necromancer. But he realized this would work. "I do remember the date in the year 3362 which I traveled to last time. She conducts a reanimation ceremony daily. I can go the very next day."

"No, let's not keep the dates too close. If you miss the destination even a little, you may end up going earlier than that date. Go to any moment after two weeks."

18
NOCTOUS

The year was 3362 BC. Rudrakshini was performing a re-animation ceremony in her lair. Rudrakshini was a woman in her eighties with a wrinkled face, shining white hair, and sharp eyes. She wore a long black robe and a necklace made of human bones and a goat skull. A long *tilak* of animal blood was smeared on her forehead.

The lair was a huge ceremonial hall carved out of a large red rock. The hall had thousands of candles burning along the sides of the walls, illuminating the whole space.

As she chanted mantras, her eyes were half-open, yet her eyeballs not visible. Only the white space in her eye sockets was seen.

Three muscular men carrying large drums were slowly beating them. They matched the rhythm of her incantation. Words sputtered out of her blackened, puffed lips as she held a human skull in her left hand. Her right hand danced through the air as if calling someone. Every once in a while, she slightly swayed to her sides.

Two hundred men and women looked on in awe as the dead body lying in front of them shook a little. Rudrakshini increased the pace of her incantation, and her voice grew more hoarse. Drummers upped the intensity of their beats. Crowd gasped.

Rudrakshini brought her incantation to a high point and halted with a jerk. Drummers froze. The crowd was quiet, too. The whole hall came to pin-drop silence.

"What happened?" she murmured to herself. "This body should have been united with the soul. Janardan, are you there?" she asked the corpse lying in front of her.

Janardan the blacksmith had died a day before and Rudrakshini was trying to re-animate him. Seeing no movement in the corpse she kept the skull in her hand on one side. She then clasped her hands into fists and thumped the chest of the corpse with her full force. The corpse reanimated, and Janardan woke up with a deep breath. He was now breathing. The drummers started beating drums at their full intensity. The crowd cheered the name of Rudrakshini. Many in the mob hugged each other and cried. They were Janardan's family.

Janardan's wife Lakhya came running and wanted to hug him. But Rudrakshini made a loud noise, "Huhn," and shook her head. She signaled Lakhya to go back, which she promptly did. No one dared questioned Rudrakshini Devi.

Rudrakshini then asked everyone to be quiet. The hall again came to silence. Janardan sat on the cement block and looked at Rudrakshini, an expression of fear and guilt on his face.

"You are not Janardan, are you?"

"Mother, it's me. Tej."

"I knew it. You have done it once again, you imbecile!" Rudrakshini thundered. Tej got up and tried to touch her feet, but she stepped back.

"Get out, everyone!" she shouted at the top of her voice. The whole hall cleared out within seconds. It was only her and Tej.

Rudrakshini started to walk in the room back and forth. Her breathing was heavy, and she talked to herself. "Liar, deceiver, cheater."

Tej gulped. She wasn't very happy with his re-visit. "Mother …"

"Don't you dare speak," she cautioned. She walked to him and brought her face close to his. Tej stepped back and almost fell.

"Do you have any idea what I promised to these people? I promised to unite them with their loved one for one day. Now, thanks to you slipping into this body, that is not possible."

"My apologies, Mother …"

"Quiet! Don't call me Mother! I know what you are going to do next. You will start with another sob story. The world is in danger, and you need my help to save it. You emotionally blackmailed me last time. This time, you stand no chance."

Tej again got up and touched her feet. This time, he didn't let go for a few seconds. Rudrakshini slowly calmed down. Tej's humility was tough to ignore.

"Go, on. Say it." Rudrakshini sat down on a jute chair nearby and closed her eyes.

Tej described the whole ordeal with Kshins: his travel to the future, meeting Mozeek and Kuleens and where he was right now.

"Hold on, kid. This time-demon Rigasur, he deceived you last time. And now what I am hearing is you are working with him. Another time-demon, Mozeek, also fooled you into believing that he was on your side, whereas he was fighting alongside these aliens."

"Yes, Mother."

"So your problems can be halved if you start exercising better judgment in people, especially your own species."

"I do, Mother. In both these cases, they were the ones who saved my life. How should one not trust someone who does that for you?"

"Fine. What do you want from me now?"

"I want to reanimate a soul. Pete Morales. He knows about weapons which can destroy these alien tyrants."

"All right, Tej, I will help you."

"You will?" Tej was elated. He never expected that Rudrakshini would agree so easily.

"Yes, I will. But this time, my help will not be for free. There is something I want in return."

"Okay, Mother. Please tell me how I can be of service."

"Not now. You are on a path towards a goal. I will not distract you from that. Fight your war, win over your enemies. If you survive this, I will ask for the price of my help."

"I will be ready, Mother." Tej bowed his head and clasped his hands together as a salute to her.

"All right, then. I need to find a fresh corpse and prepare for another re-animation. You will have to wait for a few hours."

"I understand."

Rudrakshini walked out of her lair, and Tej sat down in meditative pose. He didn't want to waste any time, so he started reading more into Histor's memories, opening doors which were thus far still closed.

28th October 2069 | Andrele's Time-vision facility

Under heavy duress, Andrele had finally managed to complete his time-vision machine. Nefe, Jarna, and Miran were sitting on chairs looking at the giant screen. The screen was showing a faded color, poor quality video of Rudrakshini's lair. She was doing the soul invocation ceremony with the seven women. Tej was seen standing at a distance. They didn't know who was who. The video was hazy in some places and was constantly flickering.

Jarna was giving Andrele a tough time, as usual. "I don't understand this, Andrele. We asked you to find Tej. Why are we seeing this pre-historic necromancy ceremony? Who is this ugly looking old woman? Who is this man standing near them?"

"I don't know, ma'am. We inputted this question, 'Where is Tej, the time demon?' We asked this question to them several times, and every time, we got this video footage. I have used several filters to clean up the video, but this is the best we can get."

"I told you this won't work," Jarna addressed Nefe in a taunting tone. She was unable to fathom why Nefe was wasting so much time chasing this ambitious project. In their pursuit of Tej, they had ended up creating something which they did not understand.

"You don't approve of this method?" Nefe smiled.

"I … I didn't mean …" Jarna stammered. Nefe's question was a double-edged sword. "See, what do we have in front of us? These time readers are feeding us some bull-crap. Where is Tej here?"

Nefe stood up from her chair and walked to the screen.

"This is brilliant, Jarna. Do you realize, we are seeing exactly what these time-readers are seeing? Andrele here has created a time-viewing machine. That alone should earn him a Nobel prize in Computer Science or some shit like that. Have you thought of a name for this time viewing machine?"

"It's technically not a machine in a physical sense." Andrele corrected. It's part of an A.I. which we have been developing to interpret time visions."

"Oh, shut up. These things should always be named properly. I hereby call this *Tamas-Shakti*. The power of darkness. A darkness which is about to fall on this world very soon."

"This A.I. is remarkable," Jarna calmed down, "but what's the use? What are we looking at, here? Instead, should we not double down on our intelligence network?"

"Hah." Nefe let out a sarcastic sound. "Our intelligence network works very well when it comes to finding a human. But for time-crawlers, our intelligence guys can't do jack-shit. Tej attacked me right inside my house. Almost killed me. Have we caught him? It's been years."

Jarna kept quiet. Nefe was right. Their covert spy network had zero leads on any of the top time-crawlers on their hit list.

Nefe paused, thinking and chewing her lower lip.

"What if one of the people we are seeing on this screen is, in fact, Tej? He is a time-crawler; changes bodies like clothes. We can't recognize him through physical appearance." She eyed Andrele. "Why don't we have audio here, only the video? Do time readers only see visions, they don't hear sounds?"

"No, ma'am, they do hear sounds. But our machine

only interprets the brain-waves related to vision. Sound is much more complicated."

"Then how would we know what place is this, or what exactly is happening here?" Nefe tapped Andrele's cheek.

Andrele thought for a moment while he rubbed his forehead. "I have an idea."

"There you are. I love this guy." Nefe walked back to her seat and sunk into it. "We are all ears."

"I can run this video through the lip-sync neural network algorithm and get the words they are speaking. And if they aren't speaking English, I can put a greedy language translation algorithm on top of that. We will get something optimal. But we won't know how accurate that would be."

"Something is better than nothing. How much time do you need?"

"Two hours."

3362 BC | Rudrakshini's Lair

A loud clang noise woke Tej up from his meditation. He saw seven women dressed in black sarees. Each of them banged a metal plate with a thick metal baton. Tej clasped his ears at the irksome noise they were making.

The women surrounded the cement block on which a body wrapped in a white cloth was placed. Rudrakshini wasn't present. Tej got up and tried asking the women what was happening and where Rudrakshini was, but they gave no answer. They kept clanking the plates in a rhythm as if they were in a trance.

"Enough!" Rudrakshini shouted as she entered her lair. The seven women came to a standstill. Tej wanted to speak, but Rudrakshini's forehead was wrinkled, and her eyes were wide open. He couldn't tell if she was angry or in pain. He kept quiet.

Rudrakshini began her elaborate ceremony, which lasted a few minutes. She chanted several mantras and drew several symbols on the corpse's body using a red liquid. Tej suspected it to be someone's blood. He hated being present during a necromancy ceremony, but for this one, he had to be there. He asked for it.

After the first set of incantations were over, Rudrakshini picked up a human skull. She began an even more vigorous chant. This time, the seven women joined her, too. They swayed from side to side. This continued for another few minutes. Then Rudrakshini gave Tej an uncanny glance.

"What happened, Mother?" Tej wiped the sweat off his brow.

"You are standing too close, son. Take five steps back. We are too close to invoking the soul. Since you are also inside a borrowed body, we may end up summoning you."

Tej gulped and took six steps back. He wanted to be extra cautious.

"Good. Now, what's that man's name?"

"Pete … Pete Morales."

"Hmm. Did he die a painful death?"

"I don't know, Mother. They were all killed. But he died in the future, so I don't know if we can even call him here."

"After death, a soul passes into another realm. That realm is beyond time. Tell me something more about him. His father's name, his siblings' name; where did he live? That will help me narrow down to the soul."

Tej told her about his brother Jake, where he lived,

and a few other details he knew. He then stood stiff as Rudrakshini started her chant again. This time, she included Pete Morales' name in her incantations. She also chanted details about his brother and his home.

After reading a few mantras, she threw the skull on one side and punched the corpse in the chest with her full force. The corpse sat up with a deep breath and started crying, saying something incoherent as if pleading to someone.

Tej was taken aback. The man was alive. Was he Pete Morales or someone else? It wasn't clear.

Rudrakshini gestured for the seven women to go out and asked Tej to come close. Tej ambled towards the cement block and stood near it, opposite to Rudrakshini. He whispered, "Why is he crying and pleading, Mother?"

"A sad death. He saw his loved ones tortured or murdered before he was killed. Those memories are coming back to him. A soul carries compressed memories, which stay dormant in the soul realm. In that realm, the soul vibrates at a different frequency. When we invoke a soul, its frequencies again resonate back with our world. Then those last pre-death memories are invigorated. Give it a few seconds. He will calm down."

The man sitting on the cement block stopped crying and sat with his head down. Rudrakshini signaled for Tej to talk to him.

"Pete? Are you there?"

The man looked up. His eyes were wet. As soon as he saw Tej, a weak smile floated on his lips. He hugged Tej and burst into tears again. "Tej, is that you? My man?"

"Yes, it's me. I am here, Pete." Tej hugged him and comforted him by patting his back. He gave a confused glance to Rudrakshini and whispered, "Mother. I am not in my own body. How did Pete know it's me?"

"A soul can sense another soul. His senses are not limited to the wits of this mortal body. He can see you for what you are. I will let you two talk now. When you are done getting your information, ask him to lie down and close his eyes. He will slowly drift back into the soul realm."

Rudrakshini went away.

Pete stopped crying. Tej pressed his shoulders. "Enough, my friend. You have suffered a lot. It's my mistake that we brought you back for you to suffer through those memories again."

"They murdered everyone, Tej. They massacred everyone. Those butchers."

"I know they did. They destroyed my village, too. Took away my family, friends, everyone from me. And now I am going after them."

"No, don't, please. Don't. They are ruthless. They will kill you."

"I have nothing to lose. It's the final battle I will fight. Now listen to me carefully." Tej paused. "We are working to get the location of a secret facility where the bodies of all Kshins are stored. We can take down their whole race at once."

Pete wiped his tears. "No, you can't. Only eliminating the bodies won't be the end of them. Their body and consciousness both need to go."

"Yes, and we planned to use Z-bombs, but they have a very small blast radius. It can kill only one Kshin at once. You need to give me some other solution. Some other way to hit them. That's why I had to bring you back."

Pete had calmed down. He sat blank for a few moments. Tej stood quiet, praying Pete gives him something, and he did. "Z-bombs can do that. But you need bigger ones, with a larger blast radius."

Tej grinned. "That's why I am here. Tell me more."

28th October 2069 | Andrele's Time-vision facility

Nefe and Jarna sat on comfortable sofas in an air-conditioned cabin. They read a transcript on an electronic tablet, a translation of spoken words Andrele could get from the video.

"What is this crap, Andrele? This text reads like some cryptic English poem. And then from another realm comes a different radio. What is this?" Jarna wanted to smother Andrele for wasting their time.

Andrele's handkerchief was drenched with sweat. It could not absorb more of the liquid appearing on his forehead. He mustered the courage, "The language they are speaking is unknown. It seems like an ancient dialect of Sanskrit. But the words are different. Some words have varied meanings, so the algorithms can only provide an approximation."

Nefe gave a menacing smile. She too was on the brink of losing her patience. "Did we get their names?"

"Yes. That man sitting on the side, his name is Tej. We got that from the lip-sync software. But the lady's name was not obtained from the video, because no one in the video speaks her name. Tej addresses her as 'Mother', so perhaps she is Tej's mother. Then I asked another question to the time-readers, and they showed me another vision. In that, her name was inscribed on a book written by her at that time. That book was written in Sanskrit, and the author's name is Rudrakshini."

"Is that it?"

"There is one more weird detail, which I don't know you are interested in or not. The corpse on which necromancy was being performed, his name is Pete Morales."

Nefe and Jarna froze and glanced at each other. They were familiar with this name. He was the team leader for the team of quantum physicists who developed the first stable Z-bombs.

Andrele continued, "It struck me as odd, as this name kind of did not fit the antiquated situation. I rechecked the lip-sync code logs for maligned translations but there were none."

"Great job, Andrele." Nefe got up and grasped Andrele by his shoulders. "This is perhaps the biggest breakthrough you could have provided us. Can we get the geographical and temporal details of this time-vision? Where and when?"

"I can try asking more specific questions to time-readers. But getting specific facts and data is usually difficult, as interpretations are involved."

"Do whatever it takes. We are very close to nailing this bastard down."

"Yes, ma'am." Andrele rushed outside.

"Jarna, we killed this Pete Morales, right?"

"Yes, we did. Mozeek shot him in the head, before my eyes."

"And we collected all the secret stashes of Z-bombs too?"

"Yes, we did. Which is why there have been no Z-bomb incidents in the past twelve years, except ..."

"Except for the recent one with Mozeek. The time-demons chose to come to 2069. They hit Mozeek first. And now Tej is trying to invoke Morales' spirit via necromancy. Why? What's his plot against us?"

"We need time to figure this one out."

"No, we have to move fast. Is there any Kshin leader in and around 3000 BC at this point?"

"No, Nefe, everyone has been called back to 2060s. We have also closed down the worm-hole bridge. All the Kshins are in 2069, and I won't advise re-establishing the bridge and us going there. Especially so close to the eventuality."

"Then it's time we bring Noctous in the picture."

"Noctous?" Jarna's eyes were filled with surprise that slowly morphed into dread. "Are we so desperate that we need to unleash Noctous?"

"Yes!" Nefe's face bore the cold expression which Jarna knew very well. It was the look of absolute decisiveness.

"Nefe, with all due respect, I would strongly suggest reconsidering."

"I have made my decision."

"You do realize that after Noctous destroys Tej, he may come for us." Beads of sweat were appearing on Jarna's brow. There were very few things in the world which frightened her, and Noctous was one of them.

But Nefe was not ready to budge. "I know how to deal with Noctous. He is the known devil here. But Tej needs to be quashed now. After Andrele gets the time and place of this vision, I want Noctous released. We are back to the critical path for the eventuality. I can't take any chances with these time-crawlers."

Rudrakshini's Lair

Tej had finished his conversation with Pete and put him to sleep. The corpse showed movement for a few seconds, after which it went cold. Pete had gone back to where he came from.

Tej waited for Rudrakshini to come back so that he could pay his respects and take leave. He sat near the cement block and again started to meditate when he again sensed movement in the corpse. He quickly got up and checked. The corpse opened his eyes and grabbed Tej's hand. "We need to run, Tej. We need to run right now."

19
BOUNTY

ej could somehow sense that the consciousness now in this body was not Pete. "What?
Who are you? You're not Pete. He's gone."

"Tej, it's Rig."

Tej was furious. "Rig? Why did you come here?"

"Nefe has gone desperate. She has freed Nakht from
the time-prison. And I am not sure how, but Nakht is
coming after you. Here."

"Wait, hold on. What the hell is this Nakht?"

"*Nakht-pishach* in Sanskrit, *Noctous* in Latin; he has
many names. He is a psychotic, deranged time-demon
who knows no reason."

"I thought all time-demons were psychotic." Tej was
unable to understand the gravity in Rigasur's tone.

"Not a time for jokes. You don't know this beast. We
need to get back to 2069 right now."

"If an evil entity is coming after me, I can't leave
Rudrakshini Devi alone."

Rig got off the cement block. "She better run too.
Nakht is pure death. He can possess hundreds, even

thousands of bodies at once. Bring down the whole cities." He walked to the door and peeped outside. "He could possess the same host as you and repress your consciousness forever. He is not someone you can reason with. We don't have time for this debate. This is not our battle. It's now or never. If we stay, Nakht will devour us."

Tej saw mortal fear in Rig's eyes.

Morghipur village was a small settlement ten miles away from Rudrakshini's Lair. A woman, Revati, was cooking lunch for her family when she heard a loud bang. The main door of the house was ajar. She ran outside and saw her husband walking toward the broken pathway at a fast pace. At a distance, the pathway joined the main road that ran through the village.

She ran after him and stopped him. He turned back, and his face appalled her. His eyes were bloodshot, his face was pale white, and his mouth was frothing. She couldn't say a word. He resumed his brisk walk, and after taking a few steps, he started running. She saw several men from the village running. They all ran in one direction—on the road that led to the path outside the village, to where Rudrakshini lived.

Back at Rudrakshini's lair, Rigasur and Tej's argument was ongoing.

"All right Tej. Suit yourself. I am leaving." Rigasur lay down on the cement block and closed his eyes.

"Wait a second!" Rudrakshini cautioned, as she entered her lair. She was now carrying a sword. Her sword was drenched in blood, and her face had bloodstains as if she was returning from a battle. Three of her brawny disciples followed her inside.

Rigasur opened his eyes and got up from the cement block. "Please accept my greetings, Rudrakshini Devi."

"This man is not that person Pete, I reckon." Rudrakshini scoffed.

"Yes, Pete is gone. This man is …"

"My name is Rigasur, Devi." Rigasur stood respectfully and bowed a little.

"Oh, you are the perfidious bastard who stained the name of gurus by claiming to be one. And then deceiving his own disciples." Rudrakshini took a cloth and started cleaning her sword.

"I …" Rigasur was taken aback by the abrasive verbal attack.

"I don't have time for your explanations." Rudrakshini signaled him to stay quiet. "Tej, who the hell has followed you here? In several nearby villages, people are turning into some kind of vampires in trances. These strange creatures are collecting outside my lair. Some attacked me and my disciples at our prayer grounds. They tasted the end of my sword."

"May I speak, with your permission, Devi?" Rigasur interjected. "I know exactly what this is."

"Go ahead, speak."

Rigasur told Rudrakshini about Nakht and who'd unleashed it. Rudrakshini heard him.

"So, a time-demon is chasing another time-demon, and a third one came to bail him out," Rudrakshini roared. "Have you demons ever thought how many innocent men, women, and children are caught in the crossfires of your conflicts? While you escape at the first hint of trouble, the poor humans are left reeling with the loss of lives."

After a brief, uncomfortable pause, Tej spoke. "I am with you in this fight, Mother. I am not going anywhere. Rig was just leaving, but I will stay."

"No, I can fight my own battles, Tej. You have a whole another war to win. I can deal with this Nakht."

Rigasur coughed a little and interrupted again, "With all due respect, Rudrakshini Devi, Nakht will keep possessing people around you. He will turn your own armies against you. You don't know who you are dealing with."

"Perhaps this Nakht doesn't know whom he is dealing with." Rudrakshini threw the sword on the side and took out an old book from a shelf on the nearby wall. Dusting the book off, she said, "I don't intend to fight this battle in the field. I am going to start a hell-damnation spell. That will throw all the demonic entities in a hundred-mile radius into a dark abyss. You two better get out right now, or you too will be caught in the wake of this spell." She paused and looked at Tej. "You, remember your promise."

"I will, Mother." Tej bowed and touched Rudrakshini's feet. She placed her hand on his head and blessed him.

Rigasur and Tej both looked at each other, and the very next moment, their bodies dropped to the ground.

"They're fast," Rudrakshini murmured. She ordered her disciples, "Get every disciple possible and stand guard at the door. No one comes in until the spell is complete."

Within a few minutes, the battle formation was set. Rudrakshini's thirty disciples stood outside with bared swords in their hands. They were fine warriors, but seeing hundreds of blood-thirsty zombies gathering in front of them sent jitters down their spines.

Inside the lair, Rudrakshini quickly lit a small sacred fire and initiated a rapid mantra incantation. She knew time was running out. The speed with which Nakht was possessing the souls was frightening. She was reading the last mantra of the spell when all her guards came inside.

"I asked you to stay outside!" she screamed and continued her chant. They did not respond. Their eyes were bloodshot, and their mouths were frothing. Rudrakshini was sitting at a six-foot distance from the door where the guards stood.

For the first time in her eighty years, she felt a cold chill down her spine. Nakht had taken her by surprise, and now he was standing right at the door of her lair. She touched the skull necklace around her neck. Till that necklace was off, Nakht could not possess her.

All the guards spoke together. Their voices were harsh and shrilling, "Rudrakshini, I have no conflict with you. Give me Tej and I will be gone."

Rudrakshini completed her chant, took a knife and sliced her palm. She dropped her blood in the fire.

All the guards charged towards her.

She picked up a fist full of green bhasm powder and said, "Nakht, now you go to hell." She threw the powder in the fire with her full force, and the fire raged to the top of the roof. All her guards fell down unconscious. Outside the lair, all the zombies started dropping to the ground.

Rudrakshini took a deep breath of relief. The spell had been successful. She had averted imminent death for herself and hundreds of others. Nakht was thrown into the deepest recesses of a dark realm.

Year 2069 | Rigasur's safe-house

Tej and Rigasur were back in his safe-house. Tej was still recuperating from the whole ordeal. He laid down on a bed and closed his eyes. Possessing a clone body was not easy for him. It took him longer than usual to feel he was back in one. As per Rigasur, the clone brain-structures were not as complex as human brain structures and were not appropriate for long term time-demon possession.

After two hours, both of them got to talking. Rigasur was curious about the information Pete Morales gave to Tej, but Tej only felt anger and guilt.

"So, did you get to meet Pete? Do we have something against Kshins, or should we call off our crusade?"

Tej murmured to himself, "We should not have left Rudrakshini alone there."

"Oh, come on. That lady is a tigress. The mere mention of Nakht sends a shiver down people's spine. But that woman, I saw no fear in her eyes. Can we stop digressing and focus on our fight?"

"How the hell did Nefe know where and in which time-slice I was?" Tej was frantic. "All our plans will be rendered futile if Nefe is getting all the details of our whereabouts."

"She knows because …"

"Are you passing on this information to her?" Tej looked in Rigasur's eyes.

There was a silence in the room. Rigasur clenched his teeth. "Did you just accuse me, kid?"

"Looks like I did." Tej was firm.

"I am the one who came to Rudrakshini's lair to warn you. When time-demons hear of Nakht, they run in the opposite direction. But I came for you. And you are doubting *me*?"

"Given your treacherous past, it's not a far-fetched thought."

"Wow. I am putting myself at stake to fight your battles for you. I go out there to get *you* some intel. Because of *you*, I am perhaps one of the top names on Kshins' hit list right now. And you are doubting *me*? I have heard enough of this word, 'treacherous.' Going forward, you will give me the respect a veteran time-demon such as myself commands, or you go fight these Kshins on your own. I doubt you will last even one day out there." Rigasur got up and poured himself some scotch.

Tej also calmed down. He knew antagonizing Rigasur was the last thing he wanted, but seeds of doubt were germinating inside him. "Let me remind you that you are not helping me out of goodness of your heart." His tone was calm but assertive. "You dread the wrath of Larem."

"No shit." Rigasur gulped the whole thing in one go. "I have been drawn back into a conflict from which I had retired years ago."

"The question is still open, Rig. How does she know? And I need to know the answer before I take one more step."

"I know how Nefe is tracking our steps. That's the last piece of intel I got. But I can tell you all about it after you stop accusing me."

"Go ahead."

"Nefe created an organization of time-readers, as I did. But she used more sophisticated means. She abducted several thousand time-readers, linked their consciousnesses to Infernex, and started milking their abilities using software algorithms. In a way, she built a time-viewing machine. But I have taken care of it."

"How?"

Rigasur smiled. He loved telling people about how his magnificent schemes were about to unravel. "Nefe's chief computer scientist is a guy named Andrele. I have put a ten million dollar bounty on his head. Poor guy will be dead before sunset. With him gone, her so-called time-vision project would be doomed."

"Why are we killing an innocent human? You could have had him kidnapped."

"Innocent? Come on." Rigasur hated this aspect of Tej's personality: his unending love for human life. "The information Andrele provided to Nefe resulted in Nakht attacking you in 3362 BC. Can you imagine how many people possessed by Nakht are being murdered there by Rudrakshini and her disciple army? This 'innocent human' may not have wielded a weapon to butcher those men, but his hands are stained with their blood nonetheless."

"Why don't I possess him and have him drive down the whole program into a hole?"

"You can't. Every human close to Nefe has been injected with Concordia VX device. Her security detail, her doctors, lawyers, even her masseuse. And not only her, but all major Kshins have also had humans in their inner circle inoculated with this device. Whoever has the device attached to their spine cannot be possessed by time-demons. This device keeps sending a very mild electric current through the subjects' brains. Keeping us off."

"Kshins have taken extreme measures."

"Yes, your attack on Nefe in 2057 is the reason behind these measures. The Kshins are watertight on all fronts. Whatever we do going forth, we need to do from a distance. They can smell us from a mile away."

"So, there is no other way. Andrele has to be out."

"Yes. If Andrele keeps making his time-vision machine stronger, we are doomed for sure. You dodged a missile with Nakht. There won't be a powerful necromancer watching your back all the time. We may not be ready for the next thing Nefe is planning to throw at us."

"Fair enough." Tej did not have a counter to that. "But when did you get time to put a bounty on his head, and how?"

"Now we are getting to the best part." Rigasur's chest puffed with pride. "The first part of the plan was to arrange for funds. Famous African billionaire Mosiya Shabani was putting ten million bucks into high-class sex-workers. One fine morning she decided to donate this pleasure-budget of hers to charity. She transferred that money in a trust's bank account."

"You possessed her."

"I did. But just after her donation, she got a sudden tax inquiry into her businesses. A team of International Financial Crimes detained her at Zaire International airport."

"Kshins?"

"Yes, my son. They are on red-alert. They flag smallest of the anomalies. But before she was arrested, the funds got transferred, and I was out of her body."

"Then?"

"Within two minutes, I possessed a local California hacker, Vihujeet Bal, a sixteen-year-old cyber-prodigy. Using his sharp skills, with the keyboard, I set up a bounty on a darknet website, Red Knives Inc. It's a two-sided marketplace where people launch murder and kidnapping bounties. Different hitmen or abductors bid for these. I put Andrele's photographs and details there and waited.

"Meanwhile, I hacked into that trust's bank account and transferred the funds to Red Knives' escrow. I used cryptocurrencies to avoid tracking. Within the next three minutes, I got several bids; all a little less than ten mill. I chose a gang of top-rated professional assassins who call themselves 'Drukza.' I accepted their bid and gave the contract to these gentlemen. Using Vihujeet's skills, I was able to finish all this in about seven minutes."

"Seven minutes? That must be a record." Tej was now enjoying this. Rigasur was at his top game.

"Yes. I knew Kshins were on my tail, so I had to out-pace the speed of their action. I had to possess the best hacker possible, and that's what I did. And in the eighth minute, police arrived at this hacker's apartment and arrested him. My sources later told me that the Kshins also took down the website 'Red Knives' within the next half an hour."

"Oh."

"But by then, the deal got approved, and the website had routed the payment to the Drukza's crypto-wallet."

"You transferred the whole amount to assassins up-front?"

"Drukza is a 5-star rated group on Red Knives. They have more than seventy thousand customer up-votes. Their cust-sat is high, and their hit rate numbers are north of 99.95%. There is no doubting their results."

"Now what?"

"Now a sword hangs on a thin thread, above Mr. Andrele's head. Death itself will be waiting outside his door to reap him." Rigasur took a deep sip from his glass.

"How easy it is to buy and sell death." Tej sighed.

"Aren't you going to praise me?"

"Yes sir, you are the number one schemer this world has ever seen. Your planning is swift and impeccable." Tej spoke in as nonchalant a manner as possible. Rigasur was a necessary evil.

"Okay, coming back to Pete Morales. What do we have?" Rigasur sat down like a kid eager to listen to a tale of a prince and princess.

"Yes, Pete. He was a soul in pain …"

"Get to the meaty part, please."

"Right. There is only one way to wipe out all the Kshins. Every one of them. Not going to be easy, but there is."

"And that is?"

"Z-bombs."

"Thanks, captain obvious. But z-bombs are very tiny, aren't they?"

"The ones we know of are tiny. But there are bigger versions too. A normal z-bomb is a small metal sphere with a five-centimeter radius. Its vortex span area is around five meters. Enough for a human. But as you increase the radius of the metal sphere, its reach increases in proportion. A z-bomb with a radius of five meters will have a blast radius of five kilometers!"

"And that's enough to dematerialize a whole fucking facility." Rigasur was overjoyed.

Tej nodded.

"And Pete must have given you some location."

"He couldn't. I can scour through Histor's brain dump again, and you can get in touch with your sources."

Rigasur paused. "Tej, the truth is that my sources are now very resistant to helping me out. My usual go-to folks are humans and rare Kuleens who are now in hiding. Kshins can target both with impunity. Locating Nefe's time-vision facility was one of the last favors some of my sources did for me. We are on our own, going forward."

"All right, I will dig in Histor's memories."

Tej was lying. He knew exactly what he needed to do. Pete had given him a lot of facts. But he was not ready to share them with Rigasur. Not yet.

Nefe was sitting in her office with her eyes closed when she received a call on her phone. She answered. "You sure no more such bounties are out? Do a full network sweep … Okay. No … no, don't tell him. The fool will panic, and all our efforts will go down the drain. Increase his security cover. And nail-down this Drukza before they try any ideas. Keeping Andrele safe is priority number one."

20
ANDRELE

ndrele stepped out of his house with his brief-case. His security guards accosted him to his armored car. His security cover had been thickened on Nefe's orders, but being given extra security actually put more pressure on him. At the core, he was a simpleton who had devoted his life to building smart algorithms. Now he was stuck in a trap with no way out.

Being a computer scientist, he knew that even if he ran away, Nefe would track him down within a few hours, if not minutes. His only way out was to live a life of a hermit, without any gadgets, any travel to the cities, or their comforts. For him, that was the toughest option. He was addicted to the luxury of technology.

As soon as his vehicle started moving, a car at a distance started following him. The man following him also sent a couple of quick audio messages on his wrist-o-phone. After thirty minutes of zig-zagging through busy streets of the city, Andrele's car was now on the deserted highway. This road led to the time-vision facility located outside the city. The car following Andrele's was at a fair distance.

Andrele's car entered the facility. After going through the customary but quick frisking, he was let in. Members of his team were already present inside and waiting. Once inside, he commenced a fresh search for Tej's current location. His team put in multiple combinations of possible questions for the time-readers.

After putting them to work, Andrele went to the pantry and grabbed a chocolate donut and a black coffee. This was his comfort meal. He relaxed in his chair, listening to old country music when he heard a series of muffled explosions.

He stopped chewing, with food still in his mouth, and sat still. He heard more noises, which he was sure were gunfire sounds. He felt weak in his gut. *This is it.* His time was up.

A firefight had broken out right outside the facility. Two huge trucks installed with explosives rammed into the factory's periphery, blasting through the iron-fence and gates. Several of Nefe's security men were killed on the spot, and many others were injured. Seven large trucks full of armed men tore through the smoke of explosives and entered the area with heavy artillery fire. Despite a clear warning, Nefe's security was not ready for this intense onslaught by Drukza.

The attackers mowed through anything that stood in front of them. After dealing with the men outside, they cut a hole in the door of the warehouse building and swarmed in. They faced much less resistance inside.

Bombean, the leader of the Drukza, entered the building. She was a six-and-a-half-foot tall woman with a muscular build. She wore rugged grey denim trousers and a heavy, sleeveless black biker jacket with nothing underneath. A lot of skull and bone tattoos were visible on her arms, neck, and torso. She wore big eyeglasses, and her hair was tied at the back with a thick black band.

She pointed her Fonata X-33 semi-automatic machine gun to the front, dropping one body after another. Out of hundreds of murder weapons available, she loved her Fonata the most. It gave her a pleasure of the kill no other gun could. As her eyes surveyed the facility, she saw thousands of cages lined up in front of her.

She screamed at the top of her voice as she ordered her men, "You five, find out where that rat is hiding. Rest of you, start putting some good ol' C4 around in here. This whole place is gonna come down."

Her men spread through the facility and started searching for Andrele. Bombean's number two, Dean, entered the facility behind her. He was a lean man, but a thick bulletproof jacket and several knee pads hid his frail structure. He was not a gun-slinging fighter like Bombean and her men. He was the brains behind the missions.

"Boss, are we going to kill all these people?"

"Yeah, mate, looks like we are. Since when do you have an issue with killing people?" Bombean lit a cigar and took a deep puff. She blew thick smoke at Dean's face, who coughed. Bombean laughed and patted his back.

"No, I have no problems, Bombean, but we were paid to kill only one man. All these men should come with an extra cost."

"Oh my, you're right, aren't you? But our contract clearly said we need to do two things: kill this man and demolish this building. So I ain't gonna kill nobody. I'm gonna bring down this whole place. Who lives, who dies, I don't care."

Dean gulped and wiped off the sweat from his forehead. "Okay, I'll be outside in my car, then. Let's leave as soon as we finish. Folks shouldn't stay on celebrating, like the last time."

"Yeah mate, no worries. You sip some cold beers out there. We'll be done in no time." Bombean didn't quite like Dean as a person—she classified him a coward. But she was a huge fan of his strategic planning. She employed a lot of men with muscle who would fight to the death for her. But none of them had the brains to plan and coordinate assassinations, which was where Dean came in. And Dean had a point—there were too many cages with too many men and women inside.

Two of her men brought—rather, dragged—Andrele to her. She puffed the last bit from her cigar and popped the remaining chunk into her mouth. She gave it exactly two chews, then gulped it. This was her favorite thing to do after smoking, something which her gang members found disgusting, though they'd gotten used to it.

"So, you're Mr. Andrele." Bombean tapped her wrist, and a 3D hologram of Andrele's face was projected.

"Face matches."

Bombean adjusted her machine gun to her back and took out a shotgun from her jacket. She pointed it at Andrele's forehead. He was now trembling in fear.

"Before I kill ya, I want you to do a good deed. Free all these people before this place comes crashing down. My men aren't gonna go open all these cages one by one."

"If I free all these people, will you let me go?"

"May think 'bout it." Bombean winked to one of her man clasping Andrele's arm.

Andrele co-operated. A few lever-pulls and button presses later, the cages were open, and time-readers were fleeing as they woke up.

Andrele was again brought down to his knees before Bombean, the tip of her shotgun kissing his forehead.

"You … you promised …" Andrele mumbled in dread.

"I said, I'll think 'bout it. And nah, I'm still gonna blow your brains."

Andrele closed his eyes. His pants got wet. She was about to shoot him when a green light beeped in her wrist-o-phone—she was getting a call.

"What the hell? This is my personal number." Bombean was surprised. She had reserved this number only for her mother for personal emergencies. No one else knew about it. She picked up the call.

"Mom, is it you? All okay?"

"All is not okay." Instead of Bombean's mom, Nefe's menacing voice echoed on the other side of the call. "But if you drop what you are doing right now, all will be okay."

"Who are you, biatch? How do you have this number?"

"Doesn't matter. What matters is that you do exactly what I say."

"You seem like a government type. I can sense that authority in your tone."

"I am even beyond the government. Way above. You won't want to mess with me, Bombean."

Bombean's face went red with fury. "Are you threatening me?"

Nefe laughed. "I am not threatening you. In fact, I am making you an offer. I will give you fifty million dollars. Five times your bounty rate. Name the bank account or crypto wallet of your choice. The transfer will be done in five minutes, tops. Let Andrele go, abandon the facility. That's it … and I will also let slide the fact that you killed several of my men."

"Oh, *you* will let it go? *You'll* forgive me?" Bombean let out a sarcastic chuckle.

"Yes."

"And if I don't take this offer of yours?"

"Then you face the whirlwind. You won't know what hit you."

Bombean froze. She did not respond well to threats. She was the one who issued several of them daily. But the voice on the other end was not joking, either. There was a serious deadpan warning in that tone.

Bombean took a deep breath and spoke. "My answer is still no. Once I take a bounty, I complete it without fail. That's my unwavering ethic. I have a reputation to keep."

"What good is a reputation if you aren't there to keep it?"

Bombean clenched her teeth. She was about to say something when she heard an airplane flying overhead. "What the hell was that?" she murmured.

"That, my dear, is the whirlwind." Nefe's voice crackled on her device. "F-536 Blitzkrieg-Hawk fighter planes. They can shoot moving targets from fifty thousand feet, even beyond dense cloud cover on the darkest of the nights. GPS enabled neutronic thermo-cat missiles. They annihilate the target completely, leaving only ashes. Took some time to scramble these toys, but they are right above your head."

"If this is the way I go, let it be."

"You are making a mis…"

Bombean twisted her wrist and cut the call before Nefe could finish. She pointed her shotgun back at Andrele's forehead. "Any last wishes, Mr. Andrele?"

"Well … I … please …" Andrele could utter only three words before Bombean blew his brains out.

"Sorry, no time for last wishes. All right, girls. Main target down. Let's get outta here." She took a picture of his dead body using her camera and swiped the picture to send it to her wrist-phone. They heard a few more fight plane flybys. Time-readers were still running out of the facility.

Within a few minutes, Bombean's men had laced the whole place with timer-enabled C4 bombs. They packed their weapons, boarded their trucks, and hit the road. When they were five minutes away, the whole warehouse building was mired in multiple explosions, and it shattered to the foundation. One of Bombean's men made a video of the explosion, to be later uploaded to the bounty website Red-Knives.

Up in the air, around two thousand feet above them, an air-force fighter pilot was talking to his superiors.

"Bird leader to the mothership. I see seven trucks in close formation. Two of us birds can take 'em out. Waiting for further command."

"Mothership to bird leader. You are green to fire at will."

"Bird leader to the mothership. This is a civilian zone. There may be civilians involved?"

"Negative, bird leader. We have clear information. These are hostile targets. Terrorists on US soil. Take 'em out. It's a final order."

"I don't like these insects flyin' over our head." Charles, Bombean's second-in-command handed over a 50x zoom binoculars to her. She took them and observed the sky. There were at least five planes in the air circling above them, two of them flying real low.

"Let's get the fuck outta here. Speed up. And what happened to bounty completion proof? Did we upload 'em on Red Knives?"

"Red Knives is down, Bombean." Charles' tone was grim.

"You got to be kidding me, Charlie. They are never fuckin' down. Some of the best motha-fuckin' brains built this portal." Bombean was now realizing the gravity of Nefe's threat. She was sure Nefe was behind the take-down of Red Knives.

Two of the F-536s took a sharp dive and released missiles, which zapped towards the trucks.

"Motherfu …" before Bombean could finish, all seven trucks were blasted into ashes.

A few miles away, Nefe sat in her office, watching the explosions. She wore business attire, ready for the day's meetings. Jarna sat next to her with a sullen look on her face.

"Whole warehouse building is gone. No survivors. This is a big setback, Nefe."

"No, it isn't." Nefe got up and smiled. "It was an experiment. It failed. Though it gave us some small gifts before it vanquished into nothingness."

"Do we build another such facility?"

"No, Jarna. You were right—the time and effort put into this were much higher than the fruits it bore. Out intelligence network built over decades is far superior. We learned of the bounty, the assassins, and everything through that. Let's focus back our energies completely

on Concordia VX. When do we review the adoption statistics with marketing?"

"At 3."

Nefe paused, chewing her lower lip. "This bounty,
this online hiring of assassins. Tej can't do this alone.
He's working with someone."

"Do you suspect any one person in particular?"

"Nah—the list of suspects is long."

21
THE Z-BOMBS

The year was 2070. Tej walked down an empty street in an NYC suburb. He was working the next part of his plan, following Pete's guidance to the last word.

Though the camera density in suburbs was much lower than in cities, he took every precaution. He was inside the body of a clone, but to avoid algorithmic detection by TV cameras, had changed his appearance by modifying his face. To make his look more authentic, he was carrying a bag, cap and other paraphernalia of an oxygen mask salesman.

He strode over to a small house, which had a broken fence and discolored green walls. After a quick glance at his wristwatch, he pressed the doorbell. It was an old-style bell and not the cloud-synced tv-screen one, common in the households of that age. After three rings, a man in his early thirties opened the door slightly and peeped through the space.

"What do you want?" His tone was terse.

Tej could make out that the man had a wheatish complexion, thick eyebrows, and a mustache.

"Sir, I am James, and I work with Mitchell and Cor-love Oxy-Buddy solutions." Tej smiled. "We are doing a free campaign for our new series of oxygen masks." He showed his business card.

"Okay, why don't you come in?" the man whispered. He opened the door only wide enough for Tej to enter, and banged the door shut after he entered.

"Who the hell are you?" The man had now pointed a pistol at Tej's forehead. Tej raised his hands. He could also feel the tip of a sharp knife almost digging into his back; another man was behind him.

"Alejandro, Javier," Tej addressed them, "Your father Pete Morales sent me. I knew your uncle Jake, too." Tej knew the man in front of him was Alejandro, and behind him was most likely Javier. They were Pete's twin sons, who were now living in a distant suburb in disguise.

Alejandro hesitated for a moment, then tightened his grip on his pistol. "Our family is all dead, you fool. What do you know about us? Why are you here?"

"My name is Tej. I fought alongside your father and your uncle against the Kshins. I met your father recent-ly." Tej could have bolted out of that body at any time, but he needed them—and he needed to win their trust.

"You must be some sick pawn sent by the Kshins. Our father died long ago."

"I know—2058. But I met him recently. *Te amo, mis hijos*, he said." Tej repeated the exact Spanish phrase Pete had asked him to say to his sons.

Alejandro relaxed and brought down his pistol. Javier loosened up, too. But then Alejandro smacked the butt of his pistol over Tej's head, knocking him unconscious.

When Tej opened his eyes he was tied to a chair with

metal chains, and his mouth was duct-taped. Alejandro and Javier were sitting in front of him, each of them holding a pistol. Although they were twins, they didn't look quite the same.

Alejandro got up and removed the tape from Tej's mouth with force.

"Arghhh" Tej cringed in pain. "That was unnecessary."

"You see this dial here?" Alejandro pointed to a black band tied to his left wrist, where a blue light was flickering inside a black dial. "This blue light tells us who you are."

"Yes, I am a time-demon. You could have asked me that." Tej was still a bit hazy. The twins looked at each other. They didn't expect him to admit, who he was, so quick.

Tej narrated them specific relevant parts of his story, and also his recent meeting with the "summoned soul" of Pete Morales.

Alejandro and Javier both refused to believe him—but he told them some very specific Kuleen facts that only Pete knew. Several times during their discussion, both the brothers got up, went into a corner, argued, and came back.

"Kshins could have tortured our father and got these facts. Nothing you have said proves that you were on the side of Kuleens."

"I was the one who had to leave your father Pete when Kshins attacked their underground office. I was the one who attacked Nefe during the solar eclipse of 2057 as your uncle Jake distracted the guards."

"Proves nothing, Tej or whomever you are." Alejandro was still unconvinced.

"What do you want, anyhow?" Javier was more sympathetic.

"I want to end the Kshins once and for all, for what they did to you Kuleens, to time-readers, to my fellow villagers. They can't live on this planet without consequences." A deep pain echoed in Tej's words. He paused. "Your father told me that there is a bigger version of the Z-bombs. These mega-Z-bombs can take out anything within an entire five-kilometer radius. I know the target, I know the date. But I do not have the bombs."

"Even if you are right, and even if we believe you, we don't have these bombs," Alejandro scoffed.

"But Pete told me you two were on the team that made first batches of mega-Z-bombs."

"Yes, we did. But those bombs were all confiscated. We can build another one from scratch, but it needs so many raw materials." Javier was frustrated.

Alejandro was furious at his brother for breaking too easily. "We are opening up to him now?"

"He's tied to a chair. We can fry his brains anytime we want and bail ourselves out from this godforsaken house," Javier snapped at his brother. He addressed Tej, "We are staying here in deep cover, away from the eyes of the world. We can't even buy a nail and a hammer without risking tipping off the Kshins. Even if we could, we won't be able to build these bombs without risking our lives at least ten times in the process."

Tej nodded, "What if I told you, you have more than three years to build this? I am planning an attack in 2073. Does that give you time?"

"Impossible." Alejandro shook his head.

"If we buy in small quantities and keep changing identities ..." Javier was brooding as if calculating something inside his head.

"Are you mad, Javi?" Alejandro was surprised that his brother was even thinking about building a bomb, not to mention paying heed to a time-demon they barely knew. "Do you even know if this time-demon is legit?"

"There is one way to find out." Javier got up. He went inside and brought back a small laptop. The equipment was full of dust. Javier cleaned it with a cloth and powered it up.

"What are you doing?"

Javier didn't pay attention to his brother's question and powered the laptop. "All time-demons who worked with Kuleens and their TD-signature were recorded in a Kuleen database. At the beginning of 2058, when the Kshins started their crusade against us, that database was encrypted. It was stored in an anonymous deep darknet location. If we can run this time-demon's ..."

"Tej," Tej re-asserted his name.

"Tej's signature against this database, we will know he is legit." Javier was now typing on the laptop at a fast pace.

"Javi, the moment you connect to darknet through this laptop, somewhere in the Kshins' systems, an alarm will go off."

"Javier, your brother is right," Tej supported Alejandro. "There are other ways to find out. Don't risk yourself now."

"I am scrambling our location signal. The Kshins will take at least two minutes to find out. If I can match this label before that ..."

"Are you mad!" Alejandro pushed Javier aside and closed the laptop with a bang, fuming with anger.

"What do you want me to do, Ale?" Javier got up

and pushed Alejandro back. "Spend our whole wretched lives remaining in this shithole? Staying like a tortoise does in its shell, always under fear of capture and death? No, I can't do it anymore. If you're so afraid to die, you can take off right now.

"Those monsters brutally murdered our whole family, our community, our entire race. They did ethnic cleansing of us Kuleens. What did we do? We ran. Like cowards. I have had just enough of it. Yes, wiping them out is impossible, a far-fetched thought. But even if there's a one in a million chance to do so, hell yeah, I will take it. Do you understand? I'll take it!" Javier screamed.

There was an uncomfortable silence in the room. Javier sat down and opened the laptop. "Now, before I connect to my darknet browser, you have a chance to leave. Go as far away from this place as possible. Tell me, how much time do you need? One hour, two hours, a day? Tell me."

Alejandro kept quiet and didn't move. He was not looking at either Tej or Javier.

"Thought so." Javier started typing on the keyboard.

"Javier ..." Tej started to speak.

Javier shot back, "You keep quiet, sir."

"I was saying if you can untie me ..." Tej requested.

"Not until I match your TD-signature." Javier kept working. He asked Alejandro for his wrist-gadget, which was still bleeping with a blue light. Alejandro untied it and reluctantly handed it over to him. Javier removed its strap and plugged the dial into the laptop like a USB. He was copying Tej's TD-signature to the laptop, and at the same time, readying the dark-net browser for connection.

"You have already spent a minute on this computer.

How much more time we have until we die?" Alejandro taunted.

"I have not even connected to the darknet yet, so our two minutes haven't begun. I will connect to the remote server, submit this TD-signature to that database, and get the result back. The whole process will take less than a minute." Javier kept pressing keys swiftly. "Connecting to the server in 3 … 2 … 1. And we're in." Javier opened a reverse-timer clock on the computer. 59, 58, 57 … both Tej and Alejandro looked at the laptop in anxiety as Javier sent Tej's TD-signature to the server.

The timer clock reached 37 when Javier struck the enter key on the laptop with full force and raised his both hands in a victory sign.

"What happened?"

"I disconnected from the server. Twenty-two seconds tops." Javier was smiling. "No way the Kshins will detect our location."

"What's the result?" Tej was curious.

"Result was a match. You were in the trusted Kuleen circle." Javier got up and started unlocking Tej.

Alejandro had a guilty expression on his face, and he gave Tej a look of apology. Tej got up and started rotating his wrists. He had been tied for almost an hour.

Javier hugged him. Tej felt awkward but hugged him back. Javier let go after a few seconds.

A few minutes later, they were having a cup of coffee.

"The 2073 deadline good for you?" Tej sipped.

"It should be ready earlier. But we need to be smart about our procurement. And how do you plan to deliver the mega-zee? Hurling two small Z-bombs at someone and running away is one thing. But two five-kilometer-radius metallic bombs are a different ballgame altogether. Even if we use lighter materials, both of them will be too heavy for a human being to carry."

"I will figure that out. I work with someone who's a top-class strategist." Tej kept his cup down and got up. "I should leave. You two shouldn't stay here for long."

"One question before you go. Why 2073?" Javier asked as he and Alejandro both got up. "Why not earlier? There is one total-solar-eclipse every year. There will be one in 2071, and 2072 too."

"I got some golden nuggets of knowledge from a time-reader who is no more." Tej mentally recalled Histor's smiling face for a moment. He continued. "Nefe is one of the most powerful Khins, and she's at the top for a reason. She's always been two steps ahead of us, and she rarely makes a mistake, especially not on a solar eclipse day. All around her are humans who are inoculated with Concordia VX. We time-demons can't possess them."

"So? What changes in 2073?"

"On August 1st, 2073, she *will* make a mistake. That is when we hit her and her whole race."

Alejandro and Javier looked at each other. They didn't exactly know what Tej was talking about, but they trusted the conviction in his voice as he said those words. Tej shook hands with both of them, reached the door and opened it.

"How will you find us, Tej?"

"We time-demons are like blind swimmers in dark ocean. We need time-readers to guide us at all times. I'm working with a trusted one. I'll find you." He stepped out and closed the door behind him.

22
THE RED-ZONE

23rd September 2071

World population: **10.58 Billion**, Concordia
VX activation: **8.99 Billion**, Adoption: **85%**

Three commercial choppers landed deep in the desert of Nevada. There were no establishments or structures visible for miles—not even the usual desert plants. The place where the choppers landed was rather cleaned up.

Inside one of the choppers sat Oril, another powerful Kshin commander. He was inside the body of an eighty-year-old Japanese CEO, Hachiro Tanaka. Oril preferred older bodies. He liked their brains full of wisdom and life-long experiences. Above all, their stable demeanor impressed him.

This was another reason he hated Nefe—she was just the opposite. She always took young nubile bodies, and as he saw it, engaged in frivolous mirth. But his primary reason for hating her was fairly simple: she was ruthless, even with her fellow Kshins. She was his prime nemesis in the silent, not-spoken-of struggle for supremacy in the Kshin world.

Today, he and his subordinate Kshins were visiting Nefe at the secret facility code-named Red Zone. This is where the artificial sun, SuryaX, was housed. He got down from the chopper and looked around.

"Brilliant, Nefe. I'll give you that," he murmured to himself. "No one would even imagine there's a gigantic world hidden beneath this wilderness."

He screamed to his pilot over the chopper blade noise. "Send them our incoming signal, Morris!"

"Already did, sir!" Morris shouted back.

The floor beneath them shook a little. A round steel pedestal fifty meters in diameter started to emerge from beneath the sand. This was their elevator to the hidden world below.

Oril looked at the sky. The sunlight was dim—the eclipse was about to start in a few minutes. Oril was already feeling week in his veins. Kshins hated eclipses, as their telekinetic powers were gone. They were left vulnerable to attack by enemies. Oril was no different. He avoided all major activity on eclipse days, especially the total solar eclipses. But today's meeting with Nefe could change his life—that's why he'd taken the trip.

At the same moment, Nefe was sixty floors underground, observing the tiny flares on SuryaX. The huge kilometer-sized ball of fire in front of her was blazing with all its might. The Kshins had named this artificial sun SuryaX, their attempt to recreate a miniaturized version of Suryaksh. Nefe was in an observation room, looking at the sun from a large LCD display.

SuryaX was a star-prototype one kilometer in diameter. It floated inside a bigger metal spherical shell 1.2 km in diameter. This shell was made of tungsten carbide, one of the hardest metals available. This inner shell was further surrounded by two hundred meters of super-coolant liquid. This layer prevented any heat signatures from SuryaX passing through. The radioactive signature was much harder to suppress, but Nefe was not too worried about it.

She stood in this observation room with Breelia, the chief science manager, in charge of keeping SuryaX stable and operating at all times. The low-ranking Kshin, Breelia, had always possessed the bodies of astronomers and quantum physicists and had acquired immense scientific knowledge over the years. If Nefe was the strategic enforcer behind the SuryaX program, Breelia was the brains of it.

"These flares. I see more of them often. Are they normal?" Nefe asked Breelia.

"Yes, ma'am. When the central star of this solar system, i.e. the Sun undergoes eclipse, the whole event has an impact on SuryaX, too."

"But will these flares impact the cavity?"

"No. The cavity is being maintained at 10,533 degrees Celsius, the same as we had at Suryaksh—even though the core of the SuryaX is at seventeen million."

"Good stuff, Bree. I am glad you are taking point on this one. Our whole race will thank you." Nefe smiled and patted Breelia on the back. She smiled.

Jarna's message popped up on Nefe's wrist-o-phone. "Oril is here."

"Send him in," Nefe responded, then turned over to Breelia. "You can go. I'll talk to you later."

A few seconds later, Oril walked into the monitoring

room with two of his subordinates. Jarna also walked in.

Nefe was still looking at SuryaX. She turned back and smiled at Oril.

"How do they say it in Japanese? *Kon'nichiwa?*" She performed the bowing gesture.

"You got it right," Oril responded back in kind. He looked back at the screen showing the footage of SuryaX. "The ball of gas keeping our brethren safe?"

"Yup. All thirty thousand of them. Sleeping peacefully in that cold cavity, while we toil hard outside. Fighting these aliens, so-called humans, and those pathetic time-crawlers."

"Yes, our fellow Kshins will never know what we went through. One flick of a switch and they may be gone forever," Oril sympathized.

Nefe looked at Oril and smiled. "One flick of a switch? I like it. I, too, am tempted to kill them all, and be the lone Kshin to rule this world."

Everybody in the room froze: Oril, his subordinates, and Jarna. *What did Nefe just say? Were those her real intentions?*

Nefe sensed the uneasiness in the room and laughed. "Come on, guys. I was just kidding. I love them all. I am not going to kill them."

Everyone eased up.

"I am only going to kill those who don't bow to me." Nefe moved towards the door. "Come, Oril, we will sit in the coffee shop and talk more. It's been a long time since we met in person."

Being at equivalent rank, Nefe and Oril sat at the same table in a spacious cafeteria. Their subordinates sat on another table at a distance. That was the Kshin protocol.

"What brings you here?" Nefe sipped her scotch and relaxed as she reclined on her chair. "That, too, on an eclipse day."

Oril sat straight on his seat in a formal pose. He hadn't touched his green tea yet. "I wanted to show you these." Oril inserted his hand inside his pants and fumbled with his groin area.

"That's weird. What are you doing there, playing with your balls?" Nefe chuckled.

"Wait for it." Oril struggled with his hand inside his pants and took out two spherical steel objects riddled with circuitry.

"Z-bombs!" Nefe whispered and smiled. "Where did you find them? We destroyed them all."

"I kept a few, for a rainy day." Oril raised an eyebrow.

"How did you smuggle them in here? I am sure my security would have frisked you. Didn't they, Jarna?" Nefe loudly asked Jarna, who was sitting on the next table.

"They did detect them through their metal detectors. I said they were artificial testicles." Oril answered.

Nefe and Oril looked at each other, paused for two seconds, then laughed.

"You old dog, Oril." Nefe took another sip of her drink.

"Your time is up, Nefe. I'm going to kill you today."

Nefe stood up. She was no longer smiling. At the next table, Jarna stood as well. Oril pushed two switches on the two Z-bombs and hurled them towards Nefe. But instead of traveling towards her, the Z-bombs stood floating in the air. Nefe was controlling them with her telekinetic force.

"How ... is this possible? Your t-force ..." Oril stammered.

"My t-force is intact, Oril."

"But today is …"

"Eclipse day? Yes, we usually lose our t-force. But you don't know the science behind it, do you? The star of this solar system, the sun, gives us the t-force. And when the star goes into eclipse, we get weak." Nefe circled around the table and walked towards Oril. The floating z-bombs also floated towards Oril. "But you forgot—there is one more star here, the SuryaX. It's small, yes. But so close. It invigorates my nerves and re-fills them with the t-force."

Nefe looked at her arms and clenched her fists. "So today's not the day you'll kill me, but that I kill you." Nefe opened her fists, and the two Z-bombs went back and hit Oril. Oril was immediately trapped in the Zason-vortex and started screaming. He tried to escape the vortex, but couldn't. Within a few seconds, he disappeared in thin air, as if he never existed.

Nefe walked towards Oril's subordinates and stood in front of them. "Your daddy is gone. What are your plans?"

Both of them got on their knees and bowed their heads.

Back at his safe-house, Rigasur was pouring himself a drink when he saw Tej's clone twitch. He was back.

"Where were you? Want a drink?"

Tej got up from the bed, grabbed Rigasur by the collar, and banged him against a wall. Rigasur's glass fell down and broke.

"You murderer. You almost killed all those time-readers?" Tej was fuming.

"Let me go, Tej!"

"You lied to me. You said you were only going to kill Andrele. But all those innocent souls, you planned to kill them too." He pushed Rigasur against the wall again.

This time, Rigasur pushed back too. "I told you half the truth because I knew exactly how you would react. I did not want to kill them, but I had no choice. That's why I gave out the contract to destroy the facility, too. I did what was necessary, kid."

"Necessary? Putting the lives of seventeen thousand innocent people in danger was necessary?" Tej's throat was heavy. He let Rigasur go.

"But they didn't die, did they?" Rigasur rubbed his neck.

"That was because the assailants were kind enough!" Tej shot back.

"You went to Manika, didn't you? That's how you know all this."

"Yes I did, Rig. Unlike you, she doesn't lie, deceive, or murder. She is my true ally."

"Really?" Rigasur smirked and took a new glass. "I was the one who killed Mozeek. I got you in contact with Histor. I cleaned up the time-vision setup Nefe created to nail us. I have been helping you at every fucking step. And she is your true ally."

"You know what, Rig? I don't need you anymore. I will send you a big thank-you bouquet when this battle is over."

"Without me in this battle, there would be no *you*." Rigasur pointed his finger at Tej.

Tej was about to respond when there was a loud noise. Both of them looked at the direction of the sound.

"Basement," Rigasur whispered. Each of them picked

up a gun and descended into the spacious basement. They moved with caution, expecting the worst.

Five hundred clone bodies were housed in the basement. Rigasur switched on the light, and whole basement area was lit up by the enormous LED tubes on the ceiling. All the clones stood straight, looking in the direction where Tej and Rigasur stood. They were powered ON and were active.

"This is impossible." Rigasur was appalled. "I haven't connected them to a charging point in years. They all should have been lying down on the ground."

"I charged them the moment I possessed them." All the clones spoke at once.

Tej and Rigasur immediately pointed their guns at the clones.

"Who … who are you?" Rigasur stammered. He could sense the presence of something or someone very powerful.

"I am Trikaal."

Rigasur immediately threw his gun away and got down on his knees with his hands clasped, as if in prayer. He also gestured for Tej to do the same, but Tej didn't flinch.

Rigasur whispered. "What are you doing, you dolt. She is Trikaal Devi. Get on your knees!"

"I don't think so." Tej addressed the clones. "So, you are real. Not an ancient fable."

"Of course she is."

All clones spoke together. "We've met already."

"Yes, we did. Though that I thought was a mere dream. It was from your advice that I was ready to work with this snake." Tej was still clasping onto his gun.

The clones spoke again. "Right now is not the time for you two to fight among yourselves. You have a common enemy in front of you."

"Don't you know what he did?" Tej couldn't believe himself. Larem was still rooting for Rigasur.

"As individual entities of the universe, we all are in charge of our own deeds. We sow our own trees and we reap our own fruits. Rigasur, too, will get what he deserves." Emanating from the throats of the clones, Larem's voice held a nonchalant tone. But the ominous doom in those words was not subtle. Rigasur wiped the sweat off his forehead. He didn't even think about leaving his body. He knew there was no running from Larem.

Tej bought his gun down and stuffed it at the back of his pants. "You want us to fight this evil together, Larem. Why don't you join forces with us? In fact, why don't you lead from the front?"

"This fool is gonna get us both killed," Rigasur murmured to himself.

"I can't take part in this battle," Larem responded in the same nonchalant tone.

"Why?"

"Because I am an ocean. Oceans don't take voyages. Sailors do."

"And we are supposed to be sailors?" Tej smirked. "I am sorry, the philosophy is not helping us here."

"Don't push it, Tej," Rigasur almost pleaded.

"No, I have to speak, Rig. I have the Z-bombs now. The bigger ones. But that is not enough."

"I didn't know that you had them." Rigasur was more impressed than offended.

"Yes, the Morales brothers were able to build those for me. But we can't even go within ten kilometers of Nefe's so-called red zone. She has several military organizations defending that area twenty-four by seven. Thousands of men are guarding her and her fellow Kshins and their interests. Two Hundred F-536 fighter planes are ready at four different bases around the Red-Zone. They can be scrambled within minutes."

Rigasur kept quiet. He knew Tej was dead right. They'd made some small wins together. But the path forward was ridden with impossibilities.

Tej continued, "Even if we somehow enter the red zone, all humans in that facility are fitted with Concordia VXes, which won't allow us to possess them. Her personal security is looked after by a hundred super-trained Muay-Thai fighters called Tharr. And why does she even need that security? She is a powerful telekinetic. The moment we step in front of her, she has the ability to tear apart the human hosts we possess before we can even touch her hair. And on eclipse days, when she is weak, her security layers are enhanced multifold."

Larem spoke. "What do you propose?"

Tej shot back. "No, what do you propose? You wanted me and Rig to work together, and we did. We have had a few victories, but to be honest, we are done now. You are the omniscient. You know that Nefe is going to switch on Infernex and plunge the whole world into a living hell. And there is nothing we can do. Mankind is doomed to suffer for eternity."

There was an uncomfortable silence in the basement. Rigasur's lips were sealed. Tej had laid it out as bare and truthfully as possible.

Larem spoke. "This device inside the human body stops you from possessing it. But it can't stop me from doing so. I can crush all these devices."

"So you are going to help us?" Tej was elated. Rigasur was relieved, too. Having Larem fighting alongside them could be a game-changer.

"I'll be there when you need me."

"Great. Let's make a plan, and ..." before Tej could complete his statement, all the clones powered off and collapsed on the ground. "She's gone."

"You continue to surprise me, Tej. We now have Larem on our side—the Larem!" Rigasur tried to hug Tej but he motioned against it.

"Please stay away. We are not friends. We are only working together on this. I don't like you, and I don't need you to like me." Tej was loud and clear.

"All right, Grinch." Rigasur's face bore mild indignation, but inside, he was delighted. They now had a fighting chance.

Tej started to walk back to the upper floor, and Rigasur followed him. "We need to make a plan. How do you know so much about Nefe's red zone and its security detail?"

"Manika can see a lot of things. Whatever doesn't directly involve Kshins is visible to her. I asked her to do a recon of the area around the red zone."

"And you do have some of Histor's memories still in there?"

"Yes, I do."

"All right. If that's the case, then I have a plan. I need to think of the specifics of it. And I need you to dig up Histor's memories for a specific vision. Can you do that, son?"

"Don't call me that."

"What?"

"Son."

Their voices faded as they climbed up the stairs.

23
THE COUNCIL
OF ELEVEN

August 3rd, 2072

World population: **10.61 Billion**, Concordia
VX activation: **9.23 Billion**, Adoption: **87%**

The 83rd floor of the Audiotron building in Brooklyn was emptied and was under heavy guard. Eleven Kshin commanders, who formed the upper core of Kshin leadership brass, had accumulated in a large conference room. They were known in Kshin circles as "The Council of Eleven." Nefe was one of them.

Each of the Kshin in the room had been given a dose of a rare chemical compound called *Qula*. This temporarily dampened their telekinetic powers—a common protocol for Kshin meetings so that they could all harmoniously talk to each other without using their t-force.

All the Kshin leaders were sitting around a large, stylish oval wooden table. Each one had a subordinate sitting behind them on a chair, but at a distance.

Jarna was presenting the workings of Nefe's grand plan to them. Nefe sat quietly on the first chair on the right and observed the reactions of everyone in the audience.

Jarna switched on to the next slide. "August 3rd, 2073 is the day of the total solar eclipse. By then, we will have more than 9.5 billion people with the Concordia VX installed in their bodies. That is 90% of the human population on this planet. This is the critical mass we needed for kick-starting the Magilax Protocol. This protocol will stay in place until the eventuality."

"The Magilax protocol? Care to throw more light on it?" Miag, one of the Kshin leaders spoke as he toyed with a pen in his hand.

"Sure, Mr. Miag," Jarna continued. "At 00:01 hours on August 3rd, 2073 we will begin plugging the world's population into Infernex 3.0. We will do this in batches, so this whole process will take forty-eight hours. Within thirty minutes of being plugged into Infernex, a subject will start generating negative emotions—*negemos*. Since they are connected to Concordia, we will be able to capture 99.99% of their negemos and filter them to XM-Net."

"What?" Miag stood up. "You will push 9.5 billion people into Infernex? Can you imagine the chaos that will cause on this planet? Nefe, are you fine with this?"

Jarna continued, "We will only push them to Infernex when they are asleep, so …"

"I was not talking to you." Miag shut Jarna off. "Nefe? What is this insanity? This is your Magilax protocol?"

"What's the problem, Miag?" Nefe got up with a smile. She walked and stood near Jarna.

"9.5 billion in a span of what, forty-eight hours? Do

we want to rule a fertile planet, or do we want to rule a post-apocalyptic world?" Miag thundered.

Miag had been one of the staunchest opponents of Nefe for the past two decades. She half expected this objection.

Jarna wanted to speak, but Nefe signaled her to stay quiet. "We intend to keep them in there for only three days. After three days, we will pull them out of Infernex. So no, this world will not fall to dystopian ruin. But all the negemos accumulated in these three days will invigorate our thirty thousand Kshin brothers and sisters. This negemos mass will be enough to bring them to life."

"But why these drastic measures, Nefe?" Miag was furious. "We can allow the negemos to accumulate the normal way. There is so much pain and strife in the world already. Those negemos would be enough to bring back all the Kshins inside SuryaX."

"Yeah, enough in a hundred years." Nefe banged her palms on the table. She then calmed herself down. "You have the math in front of you. With your way, we have two problems. Only 0.01% of negative emotions produced by humans on this planet make it to SuryaX. That is not enough to power the weakened souls of our hibernating species.

"And that is not even the main problem. This world is not producing enough negemos anymore. We are no longer in the 16th century. There are no lethal epidemics, no great wars, no tyrants committing genocide. The human species now has excellent healthcare and peaceful democracies. Our biggest headache is the painkiller medicines, which prevent pain from generating before we can feed on it. Infernex solves both the problems we have. First, it deliberately induces negemos, and second, it collects 99.99% of them. It's exceedingly efficient."

There was an uncomfortable pause as Nefe glanced at Miag, who stood near his seat, furious. "Three days without food or water, being tortured inside Infernex. Millions of children and elders will perish. For invigorating thirty thousand of our species, you will murder millions of humans? Is this acceptable to all of you?" Miag now addressed other Kshin commanders in the room.

There were murmurs and discussions all around. The council of eleven were arguing among each other and with their subs.

"Enough!" Nefe banged the table again. Her eyes were burning with anger. The room came to a standstill. "We either do this now or never. We all agreed that I would be in charge of the Concordia and Infernex programs. Over the decades, as you ruled over your companies, countries and respective dominions, I hustled tech companies and resources to build these software with my blood and sweat. And now, when we have a chance to bring back our species to life with a quick bang, are we going to indulge into these stupid humanitarian arguments? And to answer you, Miag, yes. I would murder millions of humans to invigorate even one single Kshin. I don't care for these insects and their worthless lives."

"But what's the hurry, Nefe?" spoke Koll, one of the other Kshin leaders. He made sure his tone was as soft as possible. "Why do this in a mere three days by plugging all the people in at once."

Nefe, too, calmed down. She signaled Jarna to speak.

Jarna addressed Koll and others. "We have run hundreds of computer simulations. This is the best way forward. Plus, time-crawlers have pushed our timeline. In the mid of 2073, we will get the critical adoption number of 90%, and August 3rd is when we have a solar eclipse. It all fits together."

Nefe looked at Koll. He gave a soft nod. Most of the Kshin leaders in the room wanted amicable relations with Nefe. They knew her power and ruthlessness. Besides they didn't care about humans either.

But Miag was not the one to cower down. He'd come here with an agenda to oppose Nefe with his full force. "Time-crawlers have pushed your timeline indeed. But enmity with time-crawlers is your doing, too. You riled up Kumbh; you killed that boy Tej's family. Every decision you have taken has been a bad decision which has hurt us, again and again."

"Why don't we have a vote?" Nefe looked at Miag.

"Yes, why not?" Miag chuckled. This was exactly what he wanted. For the previous two weeks, he had been back-channeling with the other nine Kshin commanders present in the room so that he could get a majority. "Who thinks that Nefe's plan is bound to fail and is not appropriate?" he declared, and then he raised his hand.

No one else raised his hand. Miag kept looking around in anticipation. Kshins who had assured him their full support earlier now sat quietly, as if they were wax mannequins. He slowly brought his hand down and wiped the sweat off his brow.

"You thought you would go behind my back and I wouldn't even know?" Nefe's tone was ominous. "I want security inside!" She ordered on her wrist-o-phone.

Miag was petrified but kept his composure. "What are you planning to do?"

Nefe kept quiet. The conference room opened and around ten armed men walked in. "Take him away!" Nefe pointed to Miag.

The men came and stood near him. When he did not budge, they grabbed his arms and pulled him. Miag started shouting, "Nefe, if you want to kill me with Z-bombs, do it right now."

"That would be an easy death for you. I'm thinking I'll plug you into Infernex. We will all relish your negemos." Nefe laughed.

"I will rip you all apart as soon as I get my t-force back. You sons of bitches, leave me alone!" Miag's voice faded as he was dragged outside the room and the door was closed.

"Anyone else has any hidden love for the safety and well-being of humankind?" Nefe placed her palms on the table and eyed the other Kshins. Everyone in the room stayed quiet, not moving even a muscle.

Tej was back in 3057 BC. He wanted some breathing time away from the future, away from Rigasur's suffocating safe bunk. He wanted to connect with himself before the impending last stand against Nefe.

As soon as he was back in his own body, he left his house. He did not even inform Manika that he was back. He walked up to a small mountain and stood at the edge of the cliff. The sun was deep red, waiting to set beyond the horizon. He stood there for a few minutes, thinking of nothing.

He heard a sound behind him and looked back. Manika was walking towards him. She had time-read his arrival. He gazed at the sunset again.

She walked up and stood beside him. "I know something is bothering you. What is it, Tej?"

"We are all set for our final battle."

"Rigasur has set up everything, hasn't he?" Manika had already seen the visions of what Rigasur and Tej were planning.

"Yes, the black schemer has thousands of ideas boiling in his conniving mind. Son of a bitch is damn good at that. A plan is already set into motion. I only have to walk the track."

"What then? Are you having second thoughts?"

Tej kept quiet. Manika placed her hand on his shoulder and pressed it a little.

"Trikaal Devi asked me to team up with Rigasur, and she again reinforced that I should work together with him. Despite the brutal deeds he has committed. Can you believe that?"

Manika didn't flinch. "Rigasur is a habitual offender. His past, present, and future all are tainted with the blood of innocents. You knew that very well when you teamed up with him earlier. Expecting a scorpion to live like a snail is foolish anticipation."

"Yeah." Tej let out a sardonic snicker.

"That is not what is bothering you. Face it, whatever it is."

"You are right. That's not what's bugging me. After the incident with Kumbh, I had taken an inner vow that I will never possess a living soul unless I really have to. Even while training with Monothiaz, I was kind of hesitant."

"Despite her little pep talk?"

"Yeah, despite that. But now, to defeat Nefe, I not only will have to break that vow but will also have to endanger a few human lives."

"Whose life? Jessica, her current host?"

"Yes, she is one, among others."

"Jessica is already dead. Kshins corrode a body from within. Their consciousness drains the human body of every bit of energy and immunity."

"Still …" Tej rubbed his face.

"Tell me something. Why are you doing this? Nefe is going to do whatever she has planned. I don't believe she is coming back here to this time-slice. You can spend the rest of your life here, in peace. Are you doing this because she plans to throw billions of humans in her software and you wish to save them? Are you trying to be a hero of humanity?"

"No. I don't want to be their unsolicited savior."

"Then it's about revenge. Isn't it?" Manika looked into his eyes.

He averted his gaze.

She continued, "I don't want you to answer this question for me. I want you to answer this question for you."

Tej kept gazing into the setting sun. "I can't forget her laughter. Nefe's laughter. I … can't. She murdered everyone I love and care for. She went on to destroy lives, one after the other. And yet she goes unscathed. She wins every time and she laughs. That is no longer acceptable to me. Her actions can't have zero consequences. I want to remove her existence from this planet, forever. It's not revenge, it's justice."

"Then you have to go where you have never gone and do what you have never done. There is no holding back now. Forget all those inner vows. Unleash yourself."

Tej looked into Manika's eyes. He met her gaze this time. She saw only one emotion in his eyes: rage.

24
COVER FIRE

August 1ˢᵗ, 2073

World population: **10.64 Billion**, Concordia
VX activation: **9.58 Billion**, Adoption: **90%**

08:15 Hrs, Red zone, Nevada, T - 50 hours

There was a major activity around the red-zone. A lot of choppers were landing around that area and several senior Kshin commanders were lining up to get inside. Every person being let in was thoroughly checked. Security looked for Time-demon signatures, explosives, and radioactive material before a person could step inside the facility's main entrance.

The solar eclipse was predicted to start at 10:15 AM on August 3ʳᵈ, 2073, and last for approximately three minutes. Nefe had planned to throw the final switch at 10:15 AM, invoking the Magilax protocol. The switch would plunge around 9.5 billion people into Infernex. This was bound to cause unprecedented chaos around the globe. For safety, all the Kshins were being brought in.

The plan was that Kshins would leave their human bodies and enter SuryaX any time before 10:12 AM on August 3rd. Only Nefe would stay out till 10:15 and flip the Infernex switch at the exact moment when the eclipse began. After that, she would herself leave her mortal body and enter SuryaX. She expected a time-demon attack and didn't want to leave this crucial activity to timer-based switches.

Security was raised to an alarmingly high level. All the choppers and private jets coming in were being directed to specific helipads and parking bays. The two-kilometer radius around the red-zone entrance was a strict no-fly, no vehicle zone. There were security checkpoints and watchtowers every few meters. Any disruptions were to be dealt with the utmost severity. The security teams were given a free hand to blow choppers out of the air or shoot humans at sight.

It was almost impossible to keep the media outlets in dark around such a simultaneous mass movement of top politicians, business tycoons, and members of royal families. As a cover-up, Nefe's PR agencies had been planting false news articles and snippets around the web. The story was that a few select world leaders were gathering together for a major environmental summit called "The last attempt—2073."

Many genuine news channels and news websites had picked up on these snippets and had helped spread the news. Nefe knew this called for undue attention, but she didn't care. She knew that once the Infernex switch was flicked, a major chunk of the global population would be thrown into a pit of darkness. Kshins had prepared for this for decades.

12:45 Hrs., Jensen's Air-base,
Mojave desert, 200 KMs away

US Air-force Lieutenant Colonel Dru Jackson stood in front of a squadron of one thousand fighter pilots and addressed them. Under a public-private joint venture between US military and Vedvance Inc., all the US military soldiers were provided with Concordia VX units at subsidized prices. More than ninety-nine percent of men and women in all segments of the US military had already been inoculated with Concordia. This particular group was one of the last group of a few thousand soldiers who had not been injected yet.

"Soldiers, at ease," Jackson commanded.

All the soldiers stood at ease.

Jackson continued, "Tomorrow at o seven hundred hours, we will have a team of scientists from Vedvance visit this base to inoculate you all. Let's make sure we are present. Concordia is a wide-spread tech adopted by billions across the world, so this should not be new to you. But if you have any questions, I will take them now."

"Sir, we have heard that Concordia causes blackouts," one of the pilots in the third row spoke.

"Son, there always are teething problems with new tech. Cell phones were known to cause cancer once. Now we have those very phones inside our bodies." Jackson laughed. A few other pilots smirked, too.

"But sir, my brother-in-law got one two months back. He's been missing some time every now and then."

"I've got a Concordia back here for a year, son." Jackson tapped the back of his own neck. "I didn't have any issues. It's just tech which will make you a fast thinker, a quick actor, and a smart soldier. Imagine our enemies having this tech inside them while we don't. Would you want that kind of a disadvantage?"

"No, sir," The pilot responded.

"Would you want to lose a battle even before you started the fighting?" Jackson screamed.

"NO SIR!" all the pilots responded.

"Good. I hear your F-536s are fueled and ready for the flight exercises. You're dismissed!"

The pilots walked out and began preparing for the up-coming flight exercise. They donned their suits, checked the fuselage, wings, tail, landing gear, and other machinery. Soon, the planes started taking to the skies in batches of fifty each. Within a few minutes, all thousand fighters were airborne.

13:05 Hrs, The Dragon Bean Café, Montgomery City, Alabama

Two middle-aged bikers sat in their comfortable chairs, eating pancakes and drinking coffee when their eyes had the momentary pink glow and they both froze for a moment. They were now possessed by Rigasur and Tej.

Tej called the waitress, Stella. He asked her to switch the TV to a news channel which was covering the Nevada Air-force exercise live.

"It's started. Are you ready, kid?" Rig eyed Tej with a mischievous smile.

"I don't know. It's been a long time since I multi-possessed." Tej took a big gulp of coffee. "This coffee tastes like crap."

"I know you can do it. You have been trained by Monothiaz. She's the best."

"How do you know that? Were you keeping tabs on

me during your so-called retirement?"

"I know things." Rigasur winked.

"While I am up there, where will you be?"

"I'll possess someone in a control tower. Nefe's forces will take at least five minutes to get ready for retaliation. Don't give them that. So as soon as you align the planes, you hit Mach 6. At that speed, you will take barely a few seconds from the air-base to the red zone."

Tej nodded.

"Let's go now." Rigasur tapped the table.

Both the bikers froze again. Tej and Rigasur were gone. One of the bikers yelled at the waitress, "What is this fighter plane shit-show, Stella? Why don't you put on the DPNN? It's the game day today."

"What the hell, Steve? You just asked me to change the fucking channel," Stella shot back. "What the fuck is wrong with you?" They both started arguing.

A CCTV installed in the café began transmitting images to the Kshin central server.

13:07 Hrs, Jensens Air-base

As the F-536 performed clever maneuvers and created various formations, a small crowd on the ground cheered and clapped. At exactly 13:07 hours, all the thousand pilots switched off their comms. Tej was slowly gaining control, and he did not want any distractions.

He was assimilating all the brains, exactly as Monothiaz taught him. He was not controlling each of them but was establishing a hive-mind, under which they all would do exactly what he wanted. All the planes had stopped maneuvering but were flying in different directions. The crowd and the on-ground air-force staff was clueless.

Any attempts to contact any of the pilots was proving futile.

At 13:09, Tej switched on the comms on all planes and set a pre-decided frequency. He was now in full control.

Rigasur possessed the body of an on-ground air-traffic control operator, Mortee Heinman. He and Tej were communicating on a pre-decided frequency which no one else could hear. "Kid, are you in?" Rigasur's voice echoed inside all cockpits.

Tej chose one of the hosts to communicate with Rigasur. "I am."

"All right, I can see you. You are all misaligned. Quickly align all the birds and hit Mach six."

Tej relayed the instructions to his hive-mind. All the planes started aligning. Within two minutes they were flowing in one direction at the same pace.

"But none of these planes have any weapons, Rig. I checked."

"This was a military exercise. What did you expect?" Rigasur took a deep sip from a cola can next to him.

"What do we do then? Should we abort?" Tej was freaking out. Possessing a thousand bodies was the easier part—maintaining that possession was far more difficult.

"No question. We are on track. Think about it, buddy. You are flying fifteen thousand kilograms of cold-rolled steel. This carriage is filled with five thousand liters of highly inflammable Naptha-kerosene blend jet fuel. Go to Mach six and hit your target. Each of these planes is in itself a missile. And you have a thousand of them. Got my drift?"

"Got it."

"I am sending you the coordinates. Go burn the target."

There was a series of mega sonic booms as all the fighter jets started breaking the sound barrier.

13:13 Hrs, Red-zone, Nevada, T - 45 hours

Thirty minutes earlier at 12:43 Hrs, an enormous cargo plane had landed at a parking bay five kilometers from the red-zone. It was an AI-piloted cargo plane completely manned by computer and supervised by a remote operator.

Out of the plane emerged five mega-trucks, each containing the delivery of a hundred robot soldiers each. These A.I. enabled robots had been ordered from a company called Cybersentient Systems for additional protection of the red zone. Each humanoid robot was seven feet tall, with a full metal body made of tungsten carbide and muscles made of flexible carbon fiber. The trucks had now docked at the entrance door of the red zone and had started unloading their goods.

In the past few hours, all the Kshin commanders and their subordinate low-ranked Kshins had checked into the facility. The number of Nefe's personnel outside the entrance were minimal.

All throughout the arrival of other Kshins Nefe was elsewhere, but she was present in person to oversee this specific delivery of robots. She was dressed in a tight, shining black zipped leather jacket, tight matching trousers, and larger gumboots. It was unlike her usual business attire. Thick black glasses protected her eyes from the sharp sunlight. She watched as the robots were being scanned for time-demon signature at the entrance.

Jarna came and stood behind her. "Why the robots?"

Nefe took a deep breath. "Two days later, once we are

all inside the SuryaX, we need an army which will keep us secure for the next three days—or until we devour enough negemos and all the Kshins inside SuryaX are powerful enough to come out and rule this world. Human guards have served us well, I don't deny that. But I needed something which is incorruptible by influences such as lust, greed, hunger, and anger."

"Then what happens to the Tharr?"

"The Tharr fighters will stand guard around me till 10:15 AM. Once I flick the switch, our algorithms will throw them into Infernex too, like others. At 10:16, after I go inside SuryaX, these Cybersentient robots will take over the security of the red zone completely. They are capable of fire-fighting using semi-automatics and flying heli-convertible cars. They can even operate choppers and use missiles if required."

"You have planned everything to the last detail, Nefe." Jarna was once again feeling proud of her boss.

"I have. But we still need to make all the last-minute checks. Let's get to it. And let's house these robots inside the armory for now. We won't need them till a minute before I invoke the Magilax."

Nefe turned around to head inside when she heard multiple sonic booms at a distance. She immediately clicked her wrist-o-phone and addressed her head of zone security, "Nathan, what's happening?"

A heavy voice screeched over the radio, "Hundreds of F-536 fighter jets are moving towards the red zone from the southwest, ma'am!"

"Radioactive signature?"

"There is some, ma'am."

"Z-bombs?"

"We don't know that yet, ma'am."

"Listen to me carefully. Get the birds in the air. Demolish these fighter jets at any cost. I don't want them within ten kilometers of the red zone."

"Negative, ma'am! They're Mach 4 right now. They'll hit Mach 6 within fifteen seconds, and will be here under two minutes. We don't have time to get our jets in the air."

Jarna panicked. "There was a scheduled flight exercise at Jenson's air-base today. Did we not cancel it? We could have asked the Lieutenant-General ..."

"No, I didn't want to draw unnecessary attention." Nefe turned to Jarna. "Suspend all these security checks and get these robots inside quickly. Have an immediate facility shut-down. I am sure time-crawlers are behind this."

Jarna nodded and rushed away, issuing orders on her wrist-o-phone. Nefe quickly walked towards the facility entrance and spoke on her wrist-o-phone. "Nathan, ask all the critical units to go into emergency bunkers. I am putting a kinetic-field over the red zone. But you are just on the periphery—it may not cover you."

"Sure, ma'am. Orders noted."

A kinetic-field was a formidable defense technology, which Kshins rarely used on earth. As Nefe reached the entrance of the red zone, she could hear the F-536s' noise.

"Fuck, there's no time," she murmured, taking a small blue cube out of her belt and pressing it a little. It vibrated with energy and started to pulsate. She could now see hundreds of F-536 flying right towards the red zone.

"Hey you, come here, quick!" She summoned a muscular armed guard, and he came running. "Throw this as high as possible. Got it?" She handed him the kinetic-shield cube.

The guard took an aim and threw the cube in the air with his full force. The cube was launched around two hundred feet in the air.

Nefe drew her gun, took aim, and fired a few shots at the cube. One of them was a direct hit. The blue cube was split into multiple pieces, which again exploded into even smaller pieces. Each of the exploding pieces built linkages with other pieces at a lightning-fast pace. Within ten seconds, there was a two-kilometer-wide blue net floating over the red-zone.

Inside the Jets, Tej was talking to Rigasur. "I'm going in hot, but I see a faint blue net over the red zone."

"Some defensive tech? I don't know." Rigasur was equally puzzled.

"What should we do?"

"Hit her with your full force? There is no other way."

"What about these pilots? They will all die, too."

"Guess so."

"No, I'm turning back."

"What the fuck? That will screw up everything." Rigasur paused for a moment, but he knew of Tej's iron resolve and his love for humans. "All right, you're ten seconds out. Eject now. The planes will still hit the target, and the pilots will survive."

One after the other, the pilots hit eject on their planes. The F-536s started hitting the kinetic-shield blue-veil but were turned into balls of fire and gas on impact. None of them was able to pierce the field.

Inside, Nefe stood smiling as she saw one plane after another crashing into the field and exploding. Those muffled explosions were music to her ears. "You had your best shot, Tej, and you missed. Now it's my turn."

Thousands of mini-parachutes were landing at a distance. Tej had left those pilots' bodies.

After the blackout they had experienced, the pilots were all clueless. A few minutes earlier, they were in control of their selves and their planes. But now, they were floating in the air, slowly descending to the ground like so many dandelion seeds blown on a summer day.

Nefe scoffed on her wrist-o-phone, "Nathan, arrest these men who trespassed on our private property and attacked us. We'll question them."

"Ma'am, from the looks of their attire, these are all US Air Force pilots. Our private security cannot arrest them."

"All right. Let's hold them in protective custody for their own good. Let me take care of the legal part."

"Very well, ma'am."

The blue kinetic field was slowly disappearing into thin air. Nefe ordered them to re-open the red zone for normal operations but at heightened monitoring.

Half an hour later, Jarna again came back and showed a picture to Nefe. "Our algorithms detected an anomaly at a Café in Alabama just two minutes before this attack. Sudden changes in human behavior perceived."

Nefe looked at the picture. "Can't be a coincidence. One of them is definitely Tej. But who is his plus-one?"

"No clue. They just come and go. They avoid major cities, famous places. Very difficult to even detect their presence. I will keep looking further."

"No need. We are too close to the eventuality. It's time for you to get into SuryaX."

Jarna wanted to counter Nefe but kept quiet. It was time for her to relax and take a long sleep while Nefe wrapped up everything outside.

"Did Nathan report anything from his interrogation of the pilots?"

"No, the pilots are all clueless. Not sure why they don't have Concordia installed in them."

"Adoption within militaries across the world is higher than in general populace, but still not a hundred percent. I'll take care of that within the next two days, too." Nefe walked inside, and Jarna followed.

Back at the safe house, Rigasur was sipping coffee. Tej was applying an ice-pack to his head. "This headache is terrible. I will never ever fly even one fighter-jet again, leave alone a thousand. My head is spinning."

"You don't know what you just pulled off, kid. You have done the Kshins more damage in two minutes then the entire race of time-demons could not do in two thousand years." Rigasur raised his coffee mug.

Tej paused, "The robots are inside?"

"Yes, they are." Rigasur had a victorious smile on his face.

25
EVENTUALITY

**August 3ʳᵈ, 2073 | Red-zone,
Armory area | 05:15 AM, T - 5 Hours**

Around five hours before the eventuality, some noises were heard inside the armory. Two armed guards entered the armory and saw the robots standing toward the center of the armory. They stood in a circular formation, akin to a crowd looking at a street performance. A few of the robots had been dismantled, and metal parts and circuitry from their bodies were strewn across the floor.

"What the fuck is happening here?" one of the guards questioned the robots. "Are you robo-numbnuts running some secret fight club in here?" He chuckled. "Who broke this poor fella?"

All the robots kept quiet, but the guards could hear a shrill drilling noise. Both of them walked further and reached the middle of the gathering. They were appalled to see what was happening at the center. Ten robots were cutting, splicing and welding several metal objects and circuity together. They were building what looked like a partial sphere: the bigger version of Z-bombs.

One of the guards picked his radio and was about to speak, but a large robotic hand clasped his mouth and jerked his neck. He collapsed on the ground, lifeless. The robot picked up the radio with aplomb and switched it off. The other guard drew his pistol but met the same fate at the hand of the robot standing behind him. One of the robots walked to the armory door and closed it. It then removed the circuitry from the wall to jam the entrance. Now it couldn't be opened from outside.

Main Conference Hall | 09:25 AM, T - 50 Minutes

The main conference hall was a huge room: thirty feet high, eighty feet wide, and a hundred and eighty feet long, almost a quarter the size of a football field. The walls, the floor, and the ceiling were made of millions of thin threads of tungsten carbide.

The room had been cleaned out and had only one entrance: a door ten feet high and fifteen feet along one of the smaller sides. There was no one except Nefe inside the hall, and she stood as far away from the door as possible on the opposite side.

The door of the hall led into a narrow but long gallery. A hundred warriors of Nefe's personal security, Tharr, stood guard in this gallery. Each of these muscular men was naked from the waist up and wore black trousers and spiked shoes. Their faces and chests were blackened with traditional Thai symbols of death and destruction. Each of them also carried two short-range pistols, one semi-automatic machine gun, and a bucket-load of bullets. A traditional Thai sword, a Krabi, hung across each of their torsos.

10:00 AM, T - 15 Minutes

Nefe was pressing buttons on a gadget on her left arm, which projected 3D visuals from all throughout the red zone for her. All the Kshins had left their physical bodies and had entered SuryaX. Miran and Jarna were the last ones to enter.

Nefe was doing last-minute courtesy-checks all across the red-zone, but everything was quiet. Helipads and parking bays above the ground, food-storage units deep inside, the armory within the red zone. All were un-eventful exactly as Nefe wanted. Security-patrol movements through the rooms were also as per orders.

Nefe checked the SuryaX chamber and started re-viewing the feed from multiple cameras, which showed her a 3D view of the entire chamber at once. The huge sphere was floating at the center of the room. Five hundred Cybersentient robots were standing guard around it with weapons in their hands. She smiled. She had dis-patched the robots to the SuryaX chamber three hours back. Now they would stand guard for Kshins for the next three days as they rejoiced inside SuryaX and fed on human pain and suffering.

After checking a few more feeds, Nefe did not see any red signs. She had anticipated that Tej would definitely try another angle of attack, but he hadn't. She was so close to realizing the Kshin dream.

What she didn't know was that the robots were not five hundred, but only four hundred and ninety. Ten of them carried within them the materials to build two five-meter diameter z-bombs. Each of those bombs had now been placed to one side of the sphere with a timer counting down to 10:15 AM. By possessing the top executives at

Cybersentient Systems, Rigasur and Tej had pulled off a stealth attack right under Nefe's nose. They had the robots pre-programmed to execute this Z-bombing.

Nefe's zone monitoring system showed her three minor warnings. She usually let her subordinates or other humans deal with these warnings, but right now, she was the only one outside. The First warning text said there was a small gas leak in the kitchen. She pressed a key and saw the camera feed from the kitchen. A few mechanics were trying to fix a pipe leakage.

"Stupid humans," she muttered under her breath. "Why do I even get these warnings?"

The second warning was excessive liquid retention on one of the floors of a food unit which carried preserved juices and other such products. She skipped that warning.

The third warning was that armory door-system has not been working for five hours. She clicked a button, and her gadget showed her a feed from a camera in front of the armory door. The door was wide open. She swiped that warning away, too. Now was the time to relax.

T - 12 Minutes

Outside her door, each of the Tharr warriors experienced a sudden momentary, sharp pain at the back of their necks, emanating from the place where Concordia VX was installed. One specific circuit in each of their Concordia devices was burnt. This circuit had been placed to keep sending a small electric current to the host brain and prevent time-demon possession.

As they rubbed the back of their necks, all of them jolted simultaneously, as if they were all hit with a slight electric shock. Their eyes glowed blue for a moment, and their bodies stiffened. They all were possessed now. All of them removed their sword, their guns, and bullet belts, and placed them on the ground. All their movements were coordinated with each other as if they were a part of a dance ritual. They took a sharp turn and were now facing the door of the main conference hall.

The lead of Tharr team, Chatri switched on his radio and spoke. "Nefe, there has been a development. I need to come inside. Please open the door."

"What is it, Chatri?" Nefe's voice sputtered on the radio.

"I need to inform you in person."

"All right."

T - 9 Minutes

The door of the Main conference hall opened, and all hundred Tharr warriors marched inside in coordination. Nefe closed the door behind them.

"Stop right there!" Nefe screamed. "What is this, Chatri? And where are all your weapons?" She immediately looked at the dial on her wrist which indicated time-demon presence. It was glowing dark blue. She had never seen a TD-signature so intense. It was as if hundreds of time-demons were present in the vicinity.

"I am here to end what you started," all of them spoke together.

"End?" Nefe smirked. "Are you Tej? If you are, you have pulled off the impossible. How did you even cross Concordia?"

"I am not Tej. I am Trikaal. Tej will be here soon."

Nefe gulped. For the first time in a very long time, she felt weak in her gut. She had only read about Trikaal Devi in ancient texts or in scientific studies as Larem. She had made several attempts to track her or contact her over the years, but she never could.

"Are you the Last Reminder?"

"Yes." All of them paused and spoke again, "Tej, it's time."

T-8 Minutes

Back at Rigasur's safe-house, Tej and Rigasur were just sitting together, eagerly waiting for a message from Larem. The plan agreed upon with Larem was that she would bypass Concordia, possess any human near Nefe, and then call in Tej. That was the only role she was willing to play.

Rigasur was about to get up when he crashed back in his chair. His eyes glowed blue, and he spoke as if he was hypnotized, "Tej, it's time."

Tej's heartbeat rose. He responded, "I am coming."

He touched Rigasur's hand—his clone body was lifeless. He was being thrown towards where Larem was.

T-7 Minutes

He was now inside a hundred Tharr bodies and was establishing the hive mind. Larem had done her job and had left those bodies.

Taking all of them with him, Tej charged towards Nefe.

Nefe stretched her arms forward, her palms facing them. She pushed all of them with her telekinetic force, but couldn't apply that equally to each of the bodies. Several Tharrs were thrown across the room, colliding with walls and the floor, but the rest of them kept sprinting forward.

"What are you trying to do, Tej?" Nefe screamed. She swiftly moved her arms and jerked her hands in the air, throwing the Tharr warriors around. Three of them almost reached her, but she pushed them back at the last moment, breaking each of their rib-cages with her T-force.

"Kill you," several Tharrs spoke at once. Many of the warriors were hurt from being thrown around sharply, or because Nefe's t-force crushed them. But others only had bruises.

Nefe pointed her fingers towards the walls and pulled hundreds of sharp carbon fiber threads out of them. She directed those fibers towards the Tharrs, tying the threads around their necks torsos, arms, wherever she could. Tej skillfully tried to avert them, but his numbers were dwindling.

He realized that more uniform his movements were, the easier it was for Nefe to attack the hosts, so he decided to introduce some randomness. He chose fifteen Tharrs who were not hurt, and all of them ran together towards Nefe. He coordinated their movements in a zig-zag line motion so that it was difficult for Nefe to direct her t-force.

Nefe shouted, "I am not going to be killed, Tej! If you kill this body of mine, you will just be killing Jessica. I will flow inside SuryaX."

As the fifteen Tharrs ran towards Nefe, she kept flicking them to the side, crushing their chest bones and rib-cages one by one. But two Tharrs managed to reach her unscathed. One clasped her legs, and the other grabbed her neck, strangling her with the full force.

That did the trick. The grasp on the neck immediately weakened her powers. The time now was 10:13 PM— only two minutes to the eventuality. Tej now removed himself from all the other Tharrs and totally concentrated his consciousness in the one strangling Nefe. Nefe's eyes were flickering, and she was gasping for air.

"We have placed two Z-bombs in the SuryaX room. Once you are inside, you and your race will be gone forever." Tej had a smirk on his face.

Nefe's eyes widened.

Three of the Tharrs who fell down regained consciousness and saw one of the Tharrs strangling Nefe. Their first instinct was to stop Tej. One of them jumped onto Tej and started pulling him back. Two of them ran outside. One of them picked up his sword, and others picked up an iron chain, and they ran back in.

One of them stabbed the sword through Tej's torso. Blood oozed out of his internal organs and his mouth. Other wrapped the chain around his neck and started tightening it.

Tej was now stabbed, being strangled, and being pulled back by three Tharrs. His grasp lightened for one second.

Nefe utilized this momentary lapse and yanked out a handcuff from underneath her dress. She snapped it on Tej's wrist and hers. It was the consciousness synchronizer. Tej regained back his grip, but he could see a feeble smile on Nefe's lips. Their consciousnesses were now tied together. If he killed Nefe's host, he too would be pulled along with her into the SuryaX.

The clock hit 10:15, and in the SuryaX chamber, the Z-bombs activated.

"Behead him," one Tharr said to the other in Thai.

Tej listened to that, too. He knew time had run out. He pushed with his full force and began crushing Nefe's throat with his muscular hands. "That's how you killed my disciple-brothers. This is how you murdered Kuntala. And this is how you die." He could hear the sound of cracking bones as he crushed her hyoid bone and the thyroid cartilage.

Both bodies crashed to the ground. They were both inside SuryaX now.

The Z-bombs fitted with small rockets were now floating in the air. Within five seconds, they started revolving around the spherical structure at full speed, creating a gargantuan Zason-vortex.

After a few seconds, the whole sphere dematerialized instantly, as if it never existed. Chamber's walls buckled out and cracked as the pressure maintained inside was disrupted. The robots standing around the sphere were flung away like rag dolls. A shockwave emanated from the chamber and ran outwards, cracking the metal and cement walls of several surrounding rooms. A mini-quake jolted the whole red-zone for a few seconds before everything came to a standstill.

SuryaX was gone, and so were Nefe and other Kshins. But Tej was gone, too.

EPILOGUE

August 20th, 2073

More than two weeks had passed since the eventuality event. The Kshins were gone, and the power structures they had cultivated for decades were gone too. Hundreds of world leaders, politicians, celebrities, and mafia heads were free of Kshin influence at once.

The world's top 1% soon got engaged in a fresh conflict of power. The last two weeks had seen seven military coups and three assassination attempts against heads of states. Hundreds of small and large gang wars erupted in major cities across the world. However, the common man remained largely uninfluenced.

Rigasur was aware of this and laid low. At the time when upper echelons of power were engaged in a brutal tussle for supremacy, he wanted to pass by as a common man. He planned to wait this period out before making his next major power move.

He sat at Concourse 42 of Heathrow Airport, waiting to board his flight to New Delhi, inside the body of one of the clones. Now that the Kshins were gone, he felt like a free man, not in constant fear of detection by their cyber armies. Sitting on a comfortable chair in a coffee shop, he read a tabloid and sipped his hazelnut beetroot latte.

He noticed that one of the letters in the headline of the newspaper article was missing. The paper at that place was burnt out. The word 'rover had an "r" missing. That was strange—he had not noticed it earlier when he skimmed through the page.

Then he noticed another such letter. This time, a "u" was missing. Again, the paper was burnt out in that location. He started putting together the missing words in the orders they were disappearing. The letters combined to form "Rudrakshini."

Looking around in fear, he gulped. But everything seemed normal. People moved around with their luggage, boxes, briefcases, and kids. Some ran for their gates; some sauntered. He wiped the sweat off his forehead and started packing his stuff into his bag pack when a pat on his shoulder startled him.

A girl in her late teens was standing behind him, smiling. She wore a white top, blue jeans, and a golden-brown jacket, and her neck was adorned with several imitation jewelry necklaces. Her hair was neatly tied at the back with a white ornamental clip. Pulling a chair, she sat near him, placing her arms on the table.

"Sweetie, whomever you are, I was just leaving." Rigasur zipped his bag and got up.

"Calm down, Rig. I am a time-demon myself."

Rigasur sat back again, still eyeing the girl with distrust. "Are you here to kill me?"

"No, sir. I am here on Rudrakshini's orders. She is

looking for Tej. He promised to end his quest and report back to her. But he seems to have forgotten that. Thought you could help."

"Tej is gone. Sucked into the Z-bomb vortex. Wiped out of the face of this planet. He is non-existent."

"I work with a lady who reaches out to entities in other realms. For her, nothing is ever non-existent."

"Then why don't you find him yourself, kiddo?" Rigasur taunted.

The girl got up, held Rigasur by the collar, and with all her strength, pulled him up. She was too strong for a sleek girl.

Her breathing was fast, and her tone was sharp. "You listen to me, you piece of shit. You don't want to be saying no to the Queen of Necromancers. When she says you find Tej, you go and fucking find Tej. And you certainly don't want to start a beef with me by calling me stupid names like 'kiddo.' If it was up to me, I would have iced you right here for repeatedly deceiving my father."

Rigasur shrugged her aside and sat back on his chair, adjusting his shirt. His heart was beating faster than usual. The girl was right. Rudrakshini was not someone he wanted in his list of enemies.

The girl got up. "Find Tej, and you already know how to find Rudrakshini Devi." She started to walk away.

"Wait. What did I do to your father? Who the hell are you?"

She turned back, "I am Pri, Tej's daughter."

TO BE CONTINUED

ABOUT
THE AUTHOR

arun Sayal is a science fiction author who has built considerable repute in the writing world within a short span of time. His science fiction works such as 'Time Crawlers' and 'Demons of Time' have been phenomenal hits on Amazon. Testimony to that fact are over five hundred positive reviews on, Amazon and other platforms, within just months of publishing these books.

9 789353 827458